PRINCESS

'Unless there are strong feelings one way or another, shall we choose a girl by chance?'

He looked around the table. No one objected. Cianna shrugged, then Iriel. Yi merely sighed. Nodding, the Captain delved into a pocket, drawing out dice. Turning to a grey-haired seaman with skin like leather he raised his eyebrows.

'Your choice, Builes?'

'The little slut, Captain,' the man answered, with a grin for Yi, 'the one who the troll fucked across the barrel of shit. Low.'

'Seven or fewer and she is with you and your riggers,' Baltrank answered, and rolled the dice.

They came to rest showing a three and a two. Builes' grin grew abruptly broader and he rose from the table, extending a callused hand to Yi. She rose, her face downcast, and allowed herself to be led from the cabin, his hand fixing firmly to the roundness of her bottom as she was steered through the door. Others followed, jostling eagerly for a good place in the inevitable queue.

PRINCESS

Aishling Morgan

To Rhonda

This book is a work of fiction.
In real life, make sure you practise safe, sane and
consensual sex.

First published in 2004 by
Nexus
Thames Wharf Studios
Rainville Road
London W6 9HA

www.nexus-books.co.uk

Typeset by TW Typesetting, Plymouth, Devon

Printed and bound by Clays Ltd, St Ives PLC

ISBN 0 352 33871 7

Contents

You'll notice that we have introduced a set of symbols onto our book jackets, so that you can tell at a glance what fetishes each of our brand new novels contains. Here's the key – enjoy!

cp (traditional)

cp (modern)

spanking

restraint/bondage

rope bondage/hojojutsu

latex/rubber/leather/enclosure

fem dom

willing captivity

medical

period setting

uniforms

sex rituals

1

Aegerion

'Do you think she will fight?'

'She is a Lady, disgraced or not. She will attempt to take it in stoic pride.'

'Do you think they will display her burst maidenhead?'

'Without doubt. It is part of the ritual. Now concentrate on your work.'

Iriel returned to her sewing, concentrating on making the stitches as tiny as possible. Across the room from her, beyond a long table piled with cloth at one end and neatly spread with partly finished garments at the other, Mistress Loida stooped low over a pattern, cutting-shears in hand. After less than a handbreadth of stitches Iriel spoke again.

'Should we not attend the shaming, Mistress? Would it not do good for my own sense of decency?'

'What sense of decency is that?' Mistress Loida demanded. 'You have none, save what I impose on you with the flat of my hand. Now work.'

Again Iriel returned to her work, trying hard to apply herself to the delicate task of following the precise curve needed in fixing together the two cuts of silk in her hands. Again she failed, a sudden surge of noise drawing her attention to the window and the street beyond. She looked up, to see the backs and heads of the crowd outside, red hair and tawny, rough cut or plaited and tied in the male and female fashions, and beyond, the high wheels of a tumbril. Unable to push her excitement under any longer, she dashed for the window, to stare out at the scene, mouth open, her head filled with scorn and pity, amusement and shock.

In the tumbril, high above the heads of even the tallest among the crowd, stood the Lady Kaissia, a girl no older than Iriel and of similar build; tall, slim, full at the chest, but blonde where Iriel's own hair was red. She was still dressed, in a long blue gown, soiled and torn at the hem, but she was fixed to the central post of the tumbril, her hands tied tight together behind it. Her face was a mask, mouth set hard, eyes staring out, seemingly focused on some point in the far distance.

'Iriel!' Mistress Loida snapped.

'Sorry, Mistress,' Iriel answered quickly, turning back towards her work only to discover Mistress Loida already on her feet and in the act of rolling a sleeve purposefully up one brawny arm.

'Time for a spanking,' the Mistress stated.

Iriel's emotions changed sharply, to self-pity and consternation. She gave one horrified glance to the window, outside which were maybe a dozen people who would only have to turn to see the inevitable exposure of her bottom, and the spanking that would follow. Cursing herself for her own stubbornness, she made a dart to one side, more than happy to earn the extra slaps she would get for resisting if it allowed her to avoid the humiliation of being punished in front of the window.

Mistress Loida was ready, and snatched out as Iriel skipped past her, but still she was not fast enough. Free for at least an instant, Iriel dashed for the storeroom. Mistress Loida followed. Her back to a pile of cloth bales, with no means of escape, Iriel waited, determined to fight despite knowing the utter futility of her struggles. She would be spanked, bare-bottomed, prob-

2

ably until her tears came, something in which Mistress Loida took great pride. The big woman appeared in the doorway, grinning as she saw the look of determination on Iriel's face.

'That's right, make a fight of it,' Mistress Loida sneered. 'It will improve the sport.'

Iriel set her jaw and crouched low, wondering if a sudden break might let her reach the door and so the freedom of the street. It was foolish, meaning postponement of her punishment at best and more probably a full public spanking, bare in the street, with the crowds gathered to watch the Lady Kaissia's shaming there to enjoy the spectacle. Afterwards maybe she would face the consequences of having her naked tuppenny on show in the street.

Still she tried, feinting, then darting low as Mistress Loida swept a great arm in. One fat foot extended from beneath the Mistress' skirts, perfectly timed, to trip Iriel and send her sprawling on the floor. The next instant a heavy hand had locked in her hair. She was pulled up, squealing and attempting to kick out with one leg, then forced forwards, towards the door.

'No! Not by the window!' she wailed, immediately realising Mistress Loida's intention. 'People will see!'

'All the better,' the Mistress answered, 'for them, for you, and for me. And besides, it might just be your time today.'

Iriel's response was a broken sob. She fought harder still, scratching with her hands and kicking with her feet as she was dragged, crawling, into the main room and to Mistress Loida's workbench. Seeing the crowd beyond the window she shut up abruptly, but too late, a huge, red-haired peasant turning in curiosity at her squeals, then reacting with amusement as he saw what was about to happen. Tapping a friend on the shoulder, he drew attention to the coming spanking, the second man's delighted, lust-filled face the last thing Iriel saw

3

before she was upended unceremoniously across her Mistress's knee and her long dress thrown up to cover her head.

Bitter, burning consternation rose up in her throat as she was locked into place, one huge arm tight around the narrowness of her waist. Her bottom was to the window, the bulging seat of her petticoat already on show. Up it came, her drawers were showing and the agony of her emotions grew stronger still. Then her drawers had been split and it was all showing, the tight roundness of her bottom, the red-furred purse of her tuppenny with the folds of inner lips pouting from between the outer, and worst, the little brown pucker of her bottom ring. A long squeal of despair broke from her lips as her most intimate secrets came on view, and Mistress Loida spoke.

'The fuss you make, little Iriel, anybody would think you were highborn. Now hold still, and if you kick or pinch it'll only last the longer.'

Iriel barely heard, her overwhelming shame and fear too strong to think of anything but the position she was in and what was about to happen to her bottom, and maybe her tuppenny. There were watchers, too, their voices loud with mirth and crude observations from the open window behind her, and even as the spanking began and pain exploded across her rear cheeks their every word seemed to cut into her head.

'Now there's a fine sight, and a ready cunt if I'm not mistaken.'

'Ready and ripe! She how she wriggles and kicks!'

'Plump too, her bottom as well. Ho, Mistress, will she be for the taking once you've done your duty?'

All the while Iriel's bottom bounced to the slaps. Mistress Loida did not answer, either to rebuke the man or offer the use of Iriel's mouth. It was something Iriel had occasionally been made to do when it amused the big woman to see her apprentice sucking on a man's

4

cock, tear-stained cheeks bulging first with effort, then with jism. A moment of relief broke through Iriel's pain, only to die under a flood of new and hotter shame as Mistress Loida spoke.

'Be sure of it, big fellow. Just as soon as her bottom is rosy she'll be in the back room, ready for cock. It's time we broke you in, my girl.'

Iriel let out a high-pitched squeal of despair as her worst fears were realised. She would be put out for fucking once she'd been spanked. It was a moment she'd known was coming, and again and again she had sworn to allow one boy or another to burst her maidenhead, but always she had resisted at the last moment. None had succeeded in ravishing her, but now, with her bottom on fire and her tuppenny already growing warm, she knew there would be no real resistance. The precious little piece of skin that guarded her tuppenny would be burst around the cockhead of some hulking soldier or evil-smelling peasant, whoever was biggest or strongest among the onlookers. He would not be the only one. Up would go the cocks, men she had never met, bluff artisans, burly peasants smelling of dogs and dung, coarse-mannered men-at-arms, fucking her in her virgin blood.

At the thought, and the sudden need that came with it, her fighting redoubled. It could not happen. It was impossibly shameful, and her need for exactly that more shameful still. Her screams grew louder and angrier. Her legs began to kick up, both together, a sight that drew a gust of laughter from her audience. Her arms were flailing too, in every direction, at one moment back in a futile effort to protect her bouncing bottom, then hammering on Mistress Loida's tree-trunk legs, then spread wide on the floor as her whole body jammed forward to the impact of a spank.

Her fingers touched something as they found the floor, something hard. Even as she realised that it was

5

Mistress Loida's shears she was snatching for them, and an instant later had driven the point through her tormentor's skirts and into the heavy leg beneath. The spanking stopped, the seamstress screamed and Iriel tumbled to the floor. Immediately she was up, running for the door even as Mistress Loida's screams of pain broke to rage, and to words.

'Viper! She-toad! Bitch goblin! Stop her! Her maiden cunt to the man who –'

She broke off in a curse. The door had been open, a heavy set peasant blocking it, dirty smock lifted to expose a thick red cock, half stiff. He had snatched out as Iriel ran at him, but she had feinted, ducked low and rolled past, to scramble up between the legs of another man. Mistress Loida with her curses and angry demands were left behind, the sound of her voice fading as Iriel pounded down the street, her skirts still high where they had been tucked up, her red bottom cheeks wobbling behind her drawing coarse laughter and crude jokes.

Only when she was two streets away did she slow enough to adjust her dress, covering her bottom, then smoothing out her skirt as she came to a halt in the gloomy mouth of an alley. A moment later a knot of laughing men ran past the end, jostling each other and calling out obscene suggestions for what to do with her when she was caught. She stayed still, well back in the shadows, her chest heaving, her face tingling with the same prickly heat as Mistress Loida had inflicted on her buttocks.

She was free, for the moment. Yet the escape had been pointless, an ill-judged reaction to her pain and fear. She knew that the time for her maidenhead to be broken was due, in fact overdue, and that any sensible girl would have surrendered, allowing the reaction to her spanking to ready her tuppenny and thus lessen the pain. Yet she had found it impossible to surrender gracefully, or even to hold back on her resistance just enough to ensure that she was thoroughly ravished yet could retain her pride.

In her imagination it always happened after a group of men had fought among themselves to be the first with her, something that she longed for. The thought alone could be guaranteed to leave her tuppenny wet and her stomach fluttering. Yet on the few times she had risked fucking among groups of men they had been far too courteous, suggesting the use of dice or the toss of a coin to decide her fate, which she found humiliating.

Now it was going to be different, and yet more humiliating. Mistress Loida would make sure of that. Instead of being fought over, or even a typical spanking and fucking, a way in which many of her friends had lost their maidenheads, she would probably be put in the town pillory, soundly birched, dunged, and left out for public fucking. The man who burst her maidenhead would probably be whoever was set to guard her. Worse, after the populace had been aroused by the Lady Kaissia's shaming. She was sure to be thoroughly used, and not necessarily just up her tuppenny.

She left the shelter of the alley, her head hung, full of trepidation and self-pity, knowing that the only sensible course was to return to the shop and try to make amends, yet quite unable to do so. Mistress Loida had only done what was expected of her, keeping discipline and ensuring normal behaviour on the part of her apprentice, yet Iriel found it impossible to feel remorse for her response, or to accept that the seamstress's actions had really been for her own good. So, rather than turn back the way she had come, she followed the narrow street to its destination, the dockside.

It was a broad space, paved with flagstones of grey granite between the edge of the quay and the tall grey storehouses and shops that faced the sea. There were stalls scattered about, each with its trade; food or drink, making nets or pots, painting or tarring, peg-turners or rope-sellers. There was also the great wooden scaffold on which the Lady Kaissia was to be shamed, a platform raised over a manheight above the flags and large enough to accommodate a dozen people.

Now feeling guilty for her earlier delight at the prospect of the young highborn woman's ordeal, Iriel turned away, telling herself she would not watch, but instead buy a plate of fried fish and take it to the tumble of rocks beyond the sea wall. There she would be safe, alone, able to sit and think in the pale sunshine, to sulk, maybe even to do something about the relentless tingling in her tuppenny.

Pushing through the crowds, she began to walk along the quay, trying hard not to look back. A dozen ships were in: eight low, black-hulled craft, both fishing vessels and raiders; a larger vessel of the same sleek design; and three traders, each flying the black and gold pennons indicative of the High-Prince's guarantee of safe passage. Two of the traders were Dwarven, broad, heavy vessels bound with iron and with no obvious means of motive power. The third was strange, a big carrack, brilliantly painted in emerald green and gold, the sterncastle high and set with numerous diamond-paned windows, her name, the *Gull of Cintes*, painted in tall curling script. From one of the windows a small man peered out, his skin yellow-brown, an elaborate beard extending stiffly from his chin. He was watching the scaffold.

His face was set in a particularly horrid blend of lust and amusement, without the slightest sympathy. Behind her, in the direction of his gaze, Iriel could hear the slaps of flesh on flesh and the cries of pain above the murmur of the crowd and the everyday sounds of the harbour. Kaissia was being given her initial spanking. As Iriel knew, Kaissia would have been stripped naked, a hideous shame for a highborn lady, and the spanking would be on the bare bottom and by hand, an indignity usually only given to lowborn girls.

Suddenly it was impossible not to look. Iriel turned, to find the scaffold in plain view across the crowd. Kaissia was there, stark naked, her beautiful clothes scattered on the wooden boards of the scaffold, held tight down across the knee of a big, red-haired woman, just as Iriel had been held across Mistress Loida's knee. Only it was worse, far worse. Kaissia's naked white body stood out like a flame, long legs waving to the smacks, arms tied hard behind her back. Her golden hair was tossing high, her red bottom cheeks bouncing, her well-furred tuppenny blatantly exposed, the little pink star of her bottom ring too, all of it in full view of perhaps half the population of Aegerion.

Iriel could only stare, mesmerised by the sight of a highborn girl naked and punished. Her sense of pity grew stronger, realising that her own emotions under punishment would be weak compared to what Kaissia was suffering, and that even what was to be done to her when she went back was nothing to the ordeal about to be inflicted on the young highborn woman. The naked spanking was just the start.

Others stood in the area cleared by High-Prince Nerangarian's guards, those artisans whose trades were needed to complete Kaissia's shaming. Nearest the scaffold was a burly woman Iriel knew only by sight, her wands, inks and the stained skin of her brawny forearms and powerful hands revealing her as the tattooist who would cover Kaissia's breasts in patterns to ensure that the shaming was permanent.

A little to one side was the town dung-gatherer, Fo, a huge, hideously ugly man with both hair and skin brown as if stained by the substances of his trade. A girl stood beside him, his daughter Yi, also dressed in little more than rags and with the same deep brown hair, yet lithe and pretty despite the streaks and smears on her flesh. Both had the marks of run sweat on their dirty skin, the result of having trundled a huge and steaming barrel of mixed dungs from their compound at the edge of the city.

Beyond Fo were two men Iriel did not know, but who had the look of the country about their clothes. They were manhandling a covered cage which shook to the motion of something within. As an angered bellow reached her, Iriel realised that what was in the cage was some great man-beast, and she knew the implications of its presence. Kaissia, once stripped, spanked, tattooed and smeared with dung, would be put in to be ravished by whatever man-beast they had caught. Still the spanking continued, slap after merciless slap delivered to Kaissia's writhing buttocks.

Iriel's feelings had grown abruptly sharper, deep sympathy, yet once more a touch of anticipation, which she struggled to hold down. It did not stop her watching, her eyes riveted to the scene even as her stomach twitched in response to the thoughts in her head. It was just, she knew, correct, a fair and usual punishment for Kaissia's crime, which was to have given herself to a bull-nymph, not once, but several times. Only the fucking was not normal, yet she knew that the High-Prince was generally considered merciful, weak even, in not adding further details to Kaissia's ordeal.

On the scaffold the spanking stopped, the sound of the last slap reverberating among the tall dockside houses of Aegerion, providing the only human noise alongside the cry of sea birds, the gentle slap of waves and the creak of wood and cord. Iriel saw that Kaissia had reacted shamefully, proving the accusation of wantonness levelled against her. White juice was smeared between her thighs, and the lips of her tuppenny were red and swollen. Then, as the spanking woman took a firm hold on the chubby red peach of her victim's bottom, Iriel's mouth went slack.

Kaissia's bottom cheeks had been hauled apart, big fingers digging into soft female flesh, to stretch the little pink and brown ring wide, also her tuppenny, a gaping hole, running white juice and with the ragged edge of the torn hymen clearly visible. A mutter ran through the crowd, a sound rich with passion, and Iriel found herself praying that if she had to be put out for public ravishment it would not be until the next day. Yet she knew that Mistress Loida would not miss the opportunity to have her fucked by so many eager men and a knot of apprehension tightened in her stomach.

On the scaffold Kaissia stood, pulled up by her hair, unsteady as the fingers of her bound hands pushed down in a vain effort to soothe the purple ball of her smacked bottom. She was sweating, her ivory pale skin glistening, her beautiful blonde hair a bedraggled mess, yet she was not crying. The large blue eyes were clear of tears, but glazed, as if she was unable to take in what was happening to her.

With Kaissia spanked, the tattoo began to prepare, climbing to the dais with a heavy chair, then returning for her equipment. Two guards took hold of Kaissia, to pull her down onto the chair, unresisting, her face still set in bewilderment. Iriel stared, watching as the girl was bound further, her ankles fastened to the chair legs, her upper body locked into a cradle of rope to force her chest out and keep her big breasts high and wide.

Unhurried, the tattooist woman set up her things, placing a stool beside Kaissia, positioned to make sure the crowd still had a good view and placing her wands and inks neatly on the boards of the scaffold. Still Kaissia stared vacantly out over the heads of the crowd, making Iriel wonder whether some witch had not managed to drug or bewitch the girl to numb the pain.

Briefly Iriel glanced around, wary of Mistress Loida or the men who had pursued her. None were visible, every face fixed on the scaffold, some serious, some lustful, a few, female, showing sympathy. Two, close by,

11

caught Iriel's attention. Both were women, both had the typical flame-red hair of the Aeg. One was tall even among the men and, though dressed in a rich and stylish gown, she held a long axe of curious design, a most unusual sight. The other was more plainly dressed, perhaps a maid, and viewed the world with a wary, aggressive stare.

Iriel's attention turned back to the scaffold as the tattoo woman took one of Kaissia's breasts in hand. Kaissia was full chested, bigger even than most Aeg girls, and firm, her breast making a fat ball of girl-flesh in the woman's hand, the rigidly erect nipple poking from the top. With her face set in concentration, the tattoo woman leaned close, her wand poised, then drove it sharply against Kaissia's flesh. Iriel winced but the tormented girl made no sound, merely hanging her head in what seemed the final admission of defeat.

The big woman worked deftly and fast, indifferent to everything but the soft flesh she was called on to paint, puncturing it over and over with quick, precise motions. Each left a new stain on Kaissia's flesh, blue against pale cream, expanding slowly into a swirling pattern, the ritual marks of shaming, which the girl would bear all her life, and show, bare-breasted and set to drudge work, performing tasks even the lowest peasant girl would think beneath her.

Slowly the pattern grew, the girl motionless in her bonds, seemingly unaware as her proud breasts were painted for her shame, first in blue, then in red, the pattern intricate, precise and unmistakable. Only when her nipples were pricked did she look up, her eyes still blank, her mouth wide with a runnel of drool escaping from one corner. The tattooist worked on, pricking into the stiff bud with exact little motions, tainting the delicate nipple flesh a brilliant red, first one, then the other, to impart to Kaissia's breasts a look of indecent arousal.

12

As the woman stood away a murmur of approval went through the crowd, appreciation for her speed and art. A guard stepped forward to dash water into Kaissia's face and over her chest. For a moment the highborn woman showed no reaction, then she shook her head, clearing her wet hair from her face to look out, still dazed, yet proud. Iriel immediately felt a touch of the same emotion, and the need to thump her hand on the hull of the ship beside her, the Aeg gesture of approval for a valiant act. It was wholly inappropriate, she knew, for Kaissia's punishment was entirely just, yet it was hard to resist. The wild-looking girl nearby had no such qualms, striking the wood, then grinning to show the sharpened teeth typical of the barbarians from the heart of Aegmund as her tall companion spoke to her.

Iriel's brief moment of elation faded as the guards began to untie Kaissia. Next came the dunging, a process that surely must break the girl's spirit, and even if she held back then there was the man-beast. It would fuck her, beyond doubt, its strength far beyond her means to resist, although to judge by the rumours of what had happened with the bull-nymph, and by the amount of thick white juice running down Kaissia's inner thighs, there might be no resistance.

Both envy and disgust filled Iriel's head. Kaissia was said to have been caught on a lonely part of her father's estates, naked, in ecstasy, on all fours, with her bottom stuck up to meet the thrusts of the bull-nymph, a creature half her own size and of intelligence barely beyond that of a dog. It was true that bull-nymphs exuded a heady scent said to be sometimes used by witches to arouse women, yet the creatures were shy and reclusive, seldom seen and hard to tempt from the forests. For Kaissia to have egged the creature on, stripped, somehow disposed of her chastity girdle and offered herself for fucking, let alone to have her maidenhead broached, was an act so blatantly wanton, so offensive to propriety, that for a moment Iriel's sympathy died. Yet it rose again as she watched the huge dung-gatherer and his daughter work the barrel up on to the scaffold.

Kaissia was standing, loose, but still with her hands tied behind her back. Two guards held her arms, and her pretty face wrinkled briefly in disgust before setting once more into an expression of haughty pride. Fo wrestled the barrel into position, his daughter standing back, well out of the way. One spadelike hand thrust into the barrel, coming up holding a steaming handful of dung. Kaissia quickly shut her eyes, only for the filthy mess to be slapped onto her belly, hard. Fo was grinning as he smeared dung over Kaissia's stomach and into the thick gold growth of her mound, then lower, to make her eyes pop in shock and disgust as her tuppenny was penetrated. Her body twitched, her resolve weakening, but still she held out, allowing herself to be turned around, her bottom to the crowd, the cheeks still red from spanking, a smudge of white and a smudge of brown showing between her thighs where they met her cheeks.

Again Fo stuck his hand in the dung, to pull out a still larger handful, which he smacked to Kaissia's bottom, making the fleshy cheeks wobble once more as they were fouled. Still she resisted, even when the dung-gatherer pushed two thick fingers between her meaty cheeks, rubbing the filth well in, only to break with a sob as her bottom ring was penetrated. Fo laughed, spent a moment easing his finger in and out of Kaissia's bottom, then withdrew.

Iriel was shaking, overwhelmed by pity and disgust and sheer shock, yet all the time thinking of what she herself had coming and wondering if the men would want to inflict similar indignities on her. In the pillory she would have little choice in what happened, and even

14

if a guard was set over her he would not stop anything he felt was merely done in a spirit of jest. From the ripple of low laughter that passed through the crowd, that all too obviously included the soiling and penetration of girls' bottom rings.

Kaissia stood, still held, bits of dung falling from her buttocks and belly as she was turned about once more. She now looked sullen and her lower lip was trembling, yet still her face was dry. Fo gave a grunt, scooped up another big handful, paused a moment to let what was about to happen sink in, then pushed the full, steaming load into Kaissia's face. Iriel heard her own gasp and her stomach tightened hard as the filth was rubbed into the shamed girl's face, not fast, but plastered slowly over her features and into her hair, Fo taking his time to ensure a job well done.

When the big dung-gatherer did remove his hand, it was to reveal Kaissia's face as a filthy brown mask, so thickly coated that her features were barely recognisable, while thick clots covered both her tightly closed eyes. Fo chuckled, wiped his hand in Kaissia's hair, then suddenly ducked down, scooped her up and dropped her, bottom first, into the barrel. Iriel caught the squashy noise as bottom cheeks met dung, then a thick bubbling sound as Kaissia sank in, to wedge in the mouth of the barrel, her body submerged in filth from ribcage to the backs of her knees. Immediately she began to struggle, wriggling in the filth to send wet dung slopping over the rim of the barrel.

There was a moment of silence, the crowd shocked at the sudden and inappropriate act, which was no part of the ritual. Then came laughter, loud and unabashed, from a single man. Iriel turned, looking up to where the harbour keep loomed over the quay, to see High-Prince Nerangarian leaning on the parapet, the white and gold of his beard split by an open grin. Others joined in the laughter. Fo made a deep bow and in response High-

15

Prince Nerangarian threw something down, a gold Thalar piece, which the dung-gatherer's daughter caught and quickly slipped into the recesses of her ragged gown.

Bowing once more, Fo moved to his barrel, to haul Kaissia out, brown and dripping. Below the scaffold the two rough-looking men Iriel had noticed bent to lift their cage, eliciting a new bellow from within. There was an immediate stir from the crowd. The tall girl to Iriel's side muttered a question, to which her companion replied with a shrug. Iriel found herself biting her lip and trying to tell herself first that Kaissia deserved what was about to be done to her, and second that she did not want the same treatment herself. Neither effort worked.

Iriel blew her breath out, disturbed by her own emotions. Her stomach was fluttering, her tuppenny warm and tingling, her nipples stiff. For all her sympathy for Kaissia and difficulty in accepting the justice of the coming fucking, she knew she would watch, and that her own need, already as strong as at any time she had taken men's cocks into her mouth, would grow stronger still.

The dung barrel was off the stage, Yi mopping up what had spilled or dropped from Kaissia's soiled body as the cage-handlers moved it to the very centre of the scaffold. One man made to remove the cover, but High-Prince Nerangarian stopped him with a gesture. Guards moved Kaissia forward, reluctant to touch the filthy girl, but with swords drawn to deny her escape. She stayed still, her body dripping filth, her eyes closed, her emotions showing only as a slight trembling and the tightening of the muscles in her neck.

High-Prince Nerangarian called down an order. A guard hefted a bucket, once more dashing water over Kaissia's head, and again, then using a cloth to clear the muck from around her eyes, which came open. She

16

looked at the cage, no longer able to hold her poise but biting her lip in apprehension. Iriel caught a whiff as a gust of wind blew towards her, the reek of dung, but with something else, a pungent musk. Then the covering was pulled from the cage and the man-beast within was revealed, a young troll, no taller than a large man, but heavier, massive muscles rolling under coarse grey skin the texture of stone.

At the sight the tall girl beside Iriel gasped and immediately began to push forwards through the crowd. Soon only the top of her head was visible, and Iriel turned her attention back to the cage. Kaissia had lost every trace of poise, her face now set in raw fear, her whole body shaking. She tried to move back as the hideous man-beast turned slowly, his nose wrinkling to her scent, his hand already on a monstrous grey cock a good three handbreadths in length.

Kaissia tried to move back, her control slipping, only for her skin to meet the prick of swords. She glanced up, right at the High-Prince, who met her gaze with an icy stare. Again the guards prodded, forcing her forwards as the two troll-handlers pulled on the heavy chain attached to the man-beast's foot. It bellowed in rage, let go of its cock and snatched a grey arm out, to catch the chain and jerk, spilling both men onto their backs. Both guards went forwards, one to jab at the troll, the other to haul on the chain. The crowd roared in laughter, only to fall abruptly silent.

The tall girl who had been next to Iriel was on the scaffold, axe in hand. One sudden motion and Kaissia's hands were free, another and the troll cage was open, the bolt sheared through. High-Prince Nerangarian yelled out in fury, a guard turned, to meet the swing of the girl's axe and stagger back, his life saved but his balance lost as he toppled over the edge of the scaffold.

Shouts rang out, commands, then screams as the massive troll lumbered forwards to the door of the cage.

Guards moved in, but the tall girl was already on the scaffold steps, dragging Kaissia by the hand, her wild-eyed companion also close. Iriel thumped her fist on the planking of the ship, an instinctive gesture being taken up by many. Others called out in anger, those close to the scaffold in fear as the great man-beast lurched towards them, dragging the heavy cage behind him.

Iriel stood up on her toes, eager to see what was happening as the crowd around the scaffold dissolved into chaos, with shouts, curses and bellows mingling with the steady thumping of fists on wood or stone. All she could see was a jumble of heads, and then the troll had reached the edge of the scaffold, to slip and fall, bringing the iron cage down behind him amid fresh screams and curses.

The crowd began to press back, panic setting in. Iriel was forced hard against the ship, the breath knocked from her body. Briefly a gap opened, closing almost immediately, but not before she had caught the rail of the ship and swung herself high. A group of little yellow-brown seamen scattered in surprise as she landed on the deck. Several had their cocks out, masturbating beneath the shelter of the ship's side as they watched the shaming, but instantly the situation had changed.

Not one reached the level of her chin, yet from the lust in their eyes their intentions were obvious, or at least their hopes. She circled her fingers in an insulting gesture, hoping they would back off. None did, instead they began to edge forwards, long-fingered hands extended, faces set in lust, yet cautious. Iriel kicked out, catching one in the stomach, only to have others immediately grapple her skirts. She went down, hard, the men closing in immediately, pulling at her clothes, groping at her breasts, hard cocks prodding her through her clothing.

At the realisation she was to be ravished she went wild, fighting by instinct as she always did, with no

18

thought for holding back, kicking and clawing, the full strength of her body in every motion. The men persisted, one climbing between her legs in an effort to force her to spread her thighs, only to catch a fist driven into his crotch. Then she was free again, lying panting on the deck, her skirt torn, one breast sticking out from the ruins of her bodice, with the men stood back, now doubtful.

Hastily she covered her chest, and even as her immediate sense of triumph began to fade it was replaced by disappointment. She had done it again, fought off the fair attentions of suitors, for all that they were foreign seamen. For a moment she considered some gesture of submission in the hope that they would make a proper job of her ravishment, only for instant rebellion to rise up in her mind. Cautiously, still eyeing the men, she got to her feet. She was shaking, her stomach a hard knot, the muscles around her tuppenny and bottom ring twitching. Part of her desperately wanted to surrender, to simply walk through the open door to the ship's sterncastle and let them have her. Another part rebelled, yet they sensed her indecision and began to come forwards once more, only to give back suddenly in fear at an angry shout from towards the quay.

Iriel turned and ducked at the same time, even as Kaissia and the barbarian girl staggered onto the deck, backwards. The tall girl was on the gangplank, swinging her axe in short, vicious strokes towards a ring of guards, yelling defiance and demands for parley. She was ignored, the guards pressing forwards, slow and cautious, but with a precision and skill that could have only one end. Iriel bit her lip hard, expecting the girl to be cut down at any instant, only to realise that it was the last thing the men intended as High-Prince Nerangarian yelled an order. The girl was to be troll-fucked herself, caught and ravished and troll-fucked, a thought

19

that set the muscles of Iriel's tuppenny into urgent contraction.

Then, as her eyes lifted, the pulsing of her sex grew stronger still. Beyond the knot of fighters, the quay was near empty, save for another ring of men by the scaffold. Among them was the dung-gatherer's daughter, Yi. The troll had caught her, and held her by the hair, bent across her father's dung barrel, her face set in horror and disgust, her breasts spilled from her torn bodice, her little round bottom bare as she was fucked from the rear. A good length of rigid grey cock protruded from the mouth of her tuppenny, even as the huge man-beast pushed in, and each time her quivering breasts dipped into the muck in the barrel. The men waited, swords drawn, ready for a lapse in the troll's concentration.

Iriel stared, her whole body tingling, imagining how the girl would feel, stripped and ravished by a troll, breasts bare, bottom bare, her tuppenny full of fat grey cock. Unable to stop herself, she put a hand to the front of her skirts, to squeeze the soft bulge of flesh beneath as she struggled to tell herself that what she was watching was an awful thing, not something she needed herself.

A great gout of jism exploded from Yi's sex as the troll came up her. The men moved in, fast, but not so fast as the troll. He whirled, come still spurting from his cock as he lashed out, his other hand still locked hard in Yi's hair. The men gave back, cursing. The troll advanced, the cage behind him, Yi now screaming in pain and fear as she was dragged by her hair. High on the tower, High-Prince Nerangarian bellowed an order. Three guards detached themselves from the ring around the tall girl, turning to face the troll as he came forwards, his face set in rage and fear and confusion now that his cock was spent. He dropped Yi, who scrambled away between two guards, knocking into a

20

third as she ran for the ship, dung-tipped breasts bouncing wildly on her chest.

Abruptly the tall girl darted to one side, swinging her axe even as she moved, to slice through the hawser holding the ship to the quay. The men reacted, moving in, only to be met with vicious cuts as the girl jumped sideways, whirled as if in dance and sliced the second hawser. Immediately Iriel felt the ship move beneath her feet. She ran for the rail, only to be struck aside as the tall girl barrelled up the gangplank an instant before it slipped free of the quay.

The little yellow-brown seamen had vanished, and no surprise. The tall girl stood on the deck, legs braced, face set in wild, triumphant glee, the bloody axe clutched in her hands. Iriel backed away, sure the girl was mad and determined to jump from the ship. Yet as she pulled herself up, she saw they were already moving away from the quay, with at least two man-heights of open water between hull and dry land. Her resolve faltered at the thought of her heavy dress, then broke as the troll waded into the guards, flailing and snatching at them, to force them back despite High-Prince Nerangarian's screamed demands that they fight. The High-Prince was also pointing at the ship, his voice hoarse with anger. The tall girl answered him with an insulting gesture and a flourish of her axe.

Iriel backed quickly away, sure that at any instant the seamen would rush the deck, or the tall girl strike her down in blind rage, or the High-Prince summon up archers to the harbour wall. To jump was madness, to remain on deck madness, to hide in the sterncastle madness.

Her heel clicked on something hard, metallic. Looking down she saw the inset ring of a hatch. She snatched it up, desperate for a haven, any haven. Inside was darkness, a mere hole, no steps, no ladder. Hesitant, she glanced around, only for an arrow to slam into the woodwork of the sterncastle. No longer hesitant, she

21

dropped, kicking her feet out for support, finding none, hanging by her hands, one toe touching wood. She dropped, onto bare planking. Above her the hatch fell shut with a click.

Silence enveloped her, warmth and darkness, rich with a sweet, musky perfume. Even as she recognised it as the scent of bull-nymph the urge to spread her legs for fucking rose up. She fought it down, telling herself it would not happen, it could not happen, yet horribly aware of the wet sensation between her thighs, the stiffness of her nipples, the gentle pulsing of her tuppenny and bottom ring. She wanted fucking, she needed fucking. Her spanking, Kaissia's shaming, Yi's fucking, the sights and sounds of the fighting were all coming together to bring her to a heat she had never experienced before, and now there was the tang of nymph musk. She groaned aloud, struggling to think clearly, of how she would escape the ship, return to shore, to be caught, spanked, pilloried and ravished.

It was going to happen, anyway, and as her will began to weaken she caught a faint noise; a scraping, a faint excited chittering, then a wet slapping sound. Abruptly the scent grew stronger. Iriel let out a sob, now fighting to keep her thighs tight. Again the chittering sounded, closer. She jumped to one side, to touch against something soft, alive, which moved quickly away. Once more there was silence.

Iriel threw her head back, her eyes closed, mumbling prayers to her mother, her grandmothers, her father, as her resistance slipped away. The softest of voices came back, whispering into her brain, telling her to abandon herself. Then another came, screaming thinly for resistance, and a third, and more, until her head was filled with the clamour of voices. She was clutching her temples in an agony of emotion as she slumped down, her back to the bulkhead, her thighs up and wide, her tuppenny spread.

Again the soft chittering began, and again the meaty slapping noise she now recognised as cocks being brought to erection. She realised that there was not one bull-nymph, but many, crouched around her in the darkness, cocks in hand, waiting for her resistance to snap; maybe eight ... maybe ten ... maybe twelve ... maybe enough to ravish her by sheer force for all their small size.

With that thought a last flicker of pride rose and died in her head. With one hard tug she pulled her bodice open. Another and her breasts were free of her chemise, ll and round and sensitive in her hands. She gripped her skirt, hauling it high, the petticoat too, and split her drawers, pulling them wide to show off the wet, eager mouth of her tuppenny.

Even as she caught her own sex-scent, so did the nymphs. The chittering rose in a gleeful crescendo. Iriel moaned, taking her breasts in her hands as she slid to the planking, thighs spread wide, her hole already in contraction, running juice, open and eager for fucking. Hands touched her, uncertain at first, then more eagerly as she responded with a low, helpless moan. They gripped her legs and her lifted clothes. Hands took her breasts, pulling her own from the soft flesh, to caress and knead. A mouth found one of her nipples, sucking eagerly on the taut bud. Her head was taken, gripped by her hair, twisted, and a firm, fleshy cock was fed into her gaping mouth. Immediately she begun to suck, eagerly swallowing down the musky cock taste, too far gone, even to feel shame.

They came between her thighs, no longer fearful. Small, lithe bodies jostled for position, for her tuppenny, none able to enter her for the others. She reached down, still sucking wantonly on the cock in her mouth. Taking one small body, she pulled him close. His cock bumped her tuppenny, rubbing in the fleshy folds above her maiden hole to send a sharp jolt of pure pleasure the

23

length of her spine. She arched her back, pushing out her tuppenny for penetration, now an eager participant in her own ravishing.

The one in her mouth came, tugging his cock free at the last instant to ejaculate in her face, thick, musky jism splashing across her cheek and into one eye. She caught at his cock, to take it back in her mouth and suck down the rich, salty juice, now wanton, desperate to have her tuppenny filled. Sure enough, as the one in her mouth slid away the bulbous cockhead between her legs pushed at her tight little hole. Her mouth came wide in rapture, her whole being focusing on the pressure against her hole as it rose to pain, revelling in the glorious moment her maidenhead was torn wide, only for the cock to slip in her juice, downwards, to be thrust solidly up into her bottom ring. She was slimy, and her anus gave, bringing a gasp of shock from her lips at the sudden pain. It was in though, her bottom penetrated, and the cock inside jamming deeper. Struggling, determined to have her tuppenny filled, she tried to reach down. Immediately her hands were taken, pulled onto erect cocks, her fingers folded around the thick shafts. Eager hands snatched her hair, another cock was forced into her mouth. Still she wriggled, squirming her bottom on the intruding penis even though it was too late, the nymph pushing his cock deeper and deeper up into her sloppy hole, inch by inch, filling her rectum. She felt herself bloat, but as the bruising pain began to die, so an overwhelming, dirty pleasure rose up in her. There was a last flicker of self-disgust and she found herself bucking on the erection in her bottom.

All thoughts of decency gone, Iriel squirmed in wanton delight on the rough wooden boards as she was buggered, sucking one cock, two others in her hands. Another nymph mounted her chest, to rub his erection in the soft, meaty valley between her breasts. Jism splashed over her hand, then more, across her face from

24

some unseen nymph, even as the one in her mouth exploded down her throat.

Still the one in her bottom kept going, pulling her ring slowly in and out on his cock, a feeling utterly dirty yet so delicious she never wanted it to stop, save that when it did it would be the signal for her other, more precious hole to be used. Another nymph stuck his cock in her mouth, the one between her breasts came, over her neck and face and into her cleavage, leaving a slippery mess for his replacement to fuck in. Still she was buggered, deep and hard, the cock in her rectum seeming to reach right up to join the one being jammed into her throat.

Hot jism bubbled over her second hand and one more had come. Again her mouth filled, briefly making her gag, to cough up a mixture of jism and spit onto her chest, adding to the lubrication for the one fucking her breasts. Then, abruptly, her bottom was full, the cock up her hole jammed deep one last time before she felt her rectum swell to the sudden explosion of jism. She gasped in ecstasy, more come drooling from her lips. The one between her breasts came, full in her open mouth, into which he plunged his cock, balls and all, to set her cheeks bulging even as more jism was pumped up her straining bottom hole.

Then it was over, suddenly, the cock in her mouth withdrawn, the one in her bottom pulled slowly free to leave her ring bubbling dirty juice down her crease. She moaned, burning frustration rising in her head at the thought of her maidenhead being left intact, only for the sound to change to a sigh as she felt one more of the creatures come between her legs.

She reached down, to hold the lovely cock being pushed at her virgin tuppenny, guiding it home, tugging on the shaft as she put the full, rounded head to her wet flesh. The creature chittered in delight, pushed, tight against her maidenhead, then slipped, once more almost penetrating her bottom ring. This time she was ready,

25

she still had hold of his cock, and with a satisfied purr she put the head back to the proper hole, holding it in place as her fingers went to the little sensitive bump at the top of her tuppenny. She began to rub, masturbating shamelessly in a welter of jism and juice, her pleasure rising steeply even as dull pain came to her hole, then a sharp stab, but she was coming, in blinding ecstasy even as her hymen burst to a cock already pumping sperm into the cavity beyond.

2

Staive Cintes

Iriel had lost all track of time. The nymphs had finished with her long before, and she had been lying in a jism-sodden dream, masturbating lazily to make herself come over and over again to the thought of her ravishment and the smell of the bull-nymphs' musk. Only the tang of sea air brought her out of her daze, and the sharp jolt of shame as light flooded down on her soiled body brought her fully around.

The hatch above her head had opened, to reveal a square of rich golden light and the head of the tall girl. Abruptly Iriel closed her thighs and slapped her hands to her breasts, blood rushing to her face at the realisation of just what she had done before fear hit her at the undoubted consequences.

'I . . . I could not help myself!' she stammered. 'It was not my choice! I was ravished! Please!'

'Be calm,' the tall girl laughed, 'and when you have quite finished playing with your tuppenny, come on deck. You will want a voice in the council we are taking.'

Iriel didn't answer, the girl's calm, amused tone just too greatly at odds with the hysterical reaction she had expected. The scene on the quay came back, her memory returning only slowly through the disabling haze of nymph musk. She managed a smile, remembering Kaissia and wondering if the tall girl was not herself shamed.

'Come,' the girl said, reaching down, 'let us have you out of there, or I'll ravish you myself, the way that musk stinks.'

Iriel climbed unsteadily to her feet, her skirts falling to cover her legs as she pulled her breasts back inside her well-soiled bodice. Thoroughly embarrassed, also confused, she allowed herself to be pulled up onto the deck. The other girls stood about, Yi by the rail, Kaissia and the barbarian near the mast. Looking up, Iriel saw the little yellow-brown seamen, working in the rigging with frantic energy; another, richly dressed and elaborately coiffed, was calling urgent orders from the sterncastle deck. Glancing out across the sea she saw the loom of Aegmund, with five black-hulled raiders lit bright by the falling sun. Sudden fear welled up, all the concerns pushed down by her musk-induced lust returning, and worse. The tall girl laughed.

'We have the length on them, do not fear. Captain Baltrank states that Aeg sail design is clumsy and obsolete. From the way we have been drawing ahead from the very start of the chase, I believe him.'

'Captain Baltrank?' Iriel queried.

The tall girl jerked her thumb towards the man on the deck above them.

'While you have been amusing yourself with the cargo, we up here have been about the business of departing Aegerion without first being dipped in pig dung and put to troll cock.'

New blushes rose to Iriel's face at the crude words, but the tall girl merely laughed, then spoke again.

'I am Aeisla, born an artisan in the barony of Korismund on the northern borders of Aegmund but now a Reeveling. Here is Cianna, from the backlands, there Kaissia who you evidently know. Beyond is Yi, the daughter of a dung-gatherer and presumably also known to you?'

28

'Yes,' Iriel answered, awe flooding over her as she realised who she was talking to. 'You are Aeisla, truly, of the three sagas?'

'I am,' the tall girl answered, 'and Cianna was with me in Makea. She is now my maid.'

Iriel could only manage a dumb nod, then looked to the other girls. Kaissia had been washed, and was dressed in a petticoat and chemise considerably too large for her, presumably Aeisla's. Yi was also clean, but retained her ragged dress, now more soiled and torn than before. Cianna was as before, and entirely calm, while the other two looked nervous and forlorn. Aeisla went on.

'Captain Baltrank, needless to say, is not overly pleased at this turn of events. Yet he is pragmatic and preferred the possibility of swords and arrows later to my axe immediately. He intends to outrun the Aeg raiders before considering further action. Meanwhile, there is little he can do about our presence save put us ashore at a place of our choosing. The question is, where?'

All four girls were paying attention, Cianna casual, Kaissia sulky, Yi frightened. Iriel considered the question, indecisive, thinking of what lay in store for her if she returned. Public humiliation, beating and ravishment would be the least of it. She might be accused of collusion with Aeisla, maybe ducked or put in a dung barrel to test her truthfulness. To remain on the ship was little better, in the company of lecherous seamen, an axe-wielding giantess who was reputedly mad, a file-toothed barbarian, a shamed lady and a girl who had been ravished by a troll.

'What of Mund?' she suggested. 'In Thieron or some other fine city we might employ our trades or find our station. The High-Prince's anger would mean nothing, even allow us to build an escutcheon.'

'It is possible,' Aeisla stated. 'However –'

'Mund!' Kaissia interrupted, glancing down at where her chemise bodice hid her tattooed breasts. 'I would be put in a celibentuary! Where then your honour and pride, Aeisla?'

Aeisla shrugged. 'True, and to make for Mund also means turning our track back, dodging High-Prince Nerangarian's raiders and navigating the Grey Deans. I am against it, and Captain Baltrank is sure to be also. The same is true for the Glass Coast, which would be difficult for me in any case.'

'It was there she slew the great warrior Kroth,' Cianna put in proudly.

'More by luck than skill,' Aeisla added, 'but in fair combat. By their tradition I thus take on his honours, which in turn go to whoever slays me. There are other matters also, but doubtless you have heard the saga.'

'Ateron?' Cianna suggested. 'Or any point along the north coast of Aegmund. 'We could make our way to Korismund.'

'I am still shamed!' Kaissia pointed out.

'The interior then,' Cianna replied, 'where few would care.'

'I care!' Kaissia snapped. 'Who would marry me, with the marks on my breasts and doubtless rumours circulating of how I was shamed so publicly? Any highborn man would be ashamed to ravish me.'

'Where then?' Aeisla asked. 'The Aeg are hardly popular across the Roads, and I know how they treat the girls. In Aponan or Poran they would chain us in a house where men would pay for the use of our bodies, or pump beer into the cavities of our bottoms and take bets as to which of us could spray the furthest. Doubtless there are other games, equally degraded. They take slaves, too, so we would very likely be sold, split up and traded elsewhere.'

'Slaves?' Kaissia broke in. 'As with your sagas in Vendjome and Makea? To be the property of another, like a dog or a horse? Never!'

Cianna responded with a shudder of horror, as did Iriel. Yi merely cast a sulky look towards the distant land.

'Utan?' Cianna suggested.

'To live with dwarfs?' Kaissia demanded in disgust.

'There are worse fates,' Aeisla replied. 'They are strange, but do not take slaves.'

'A fine life that,' Cianna put in, 'with folk whose heads barely reach our chests? Who would I fuck with?'

'Not Utan then,' Aeisla sighed. 'Yet we must choose. If we remain on the ship we will eventually arrive in Oretea.'

'Is Oretea a bad choice?' Kaissia questioned. 'These seamen seem docile enough, and Captain Baltrank is not wholly repulsive, while I see his arms are marked with tattoos. Perhaps I might yet find a worthy life.'

'Perhaps,' Aeisla answered, 'but I doubt it. The Oreteans take slaves, and girls with blonde or copper hair are highly valued, all natives having the black locks you will note on the crew. On ship we are safe enough, but in port I suspect we would be taken and sold.'

'Not so,' Captain Baltrank interjected as he descended the companionway to their deck. 'We are not Vendjomois, who enslave all but their own race. In Oretea slavery comes only to those who have earned it, the criminal, those taken in debt or in war. So long as you could support yourselves there would be no danger, and besides, many opt for slavery by choice. A slave must be provided for, by law. You would be protected, fed, subjected to no harsher punishment than the statutes permit –'

'It is unthinkable!' Kaissia broke in, the other girls quickly nodding in agreement.

'Then you would have to work,' he went on. 'Do you have trades?'

'I am a dung-gatherer,' Yi said quietly.

'I am a seamstress,' Iriel put in, 'an apprentice only, but –'

'Worthy trades both!' Baltrank put in heartily. 'And you others?'

'I am a maid by training,' Cianna admitted.

'Kaissia is highborn,' Aeisla stated, 'and I am elevated. Common work is beneath us, but might we not be desirable as wives among those of suitable rank?'

'Frankly, no,' Baltrank answered. 'As I suspect is the case with your own upper echelons, marriage is only permitted between those of appropriate house. To marry a barbarian girl, if you will excuse the term for the way we view your people, would be unthinkable. You could enslave yourselves, certainly, to any family of your choice so long as the man rules.'

'No,' Aeisla answered.

Baltrank shrugged, then went on.

'Why be obstinate? You have no trade, yet you are beautiful. As a slave little more would be expected of you than to disport yourself to advantage, make love to order, perhaps offer the occasional lewd entertainment –'

'I have heard it before,' Aeisla cut him off, 'the phrase has stuck in my mind – "nothing to do but powder your cunts". It is not acceptable. Is there nothing else a woman of high status might do in Oretea? Some diplomatic or military role, even scriptural?'

'I can write,' Kaissia put in. 'I have been commended for the beauty of my capitals.'

'It is possible, I suppose,' Baltrank admitted, 'although in my view foolish. Why labour when you can rest? As to your other suggestions, I hesitate to dispute your ability after viewing your axe work, Aeisla, and yet the idea of a woman in the Oretean army would be laughed to scorn, even a giantess.'

Aeisla gave a sigh.

'If four of us can hope to thrive, or at least live with honour, then I am for Oretea.'

'A wise choice,' Baltrank agreed, 'and doubtless once

in Staive Cintes, our home port, matters will resolve themselves.'

He paused to stroke the elaborate curls of the heavily oiled beard that hung down to the slight swell of his belly. His eyes, small and black beneath heavy lids, flicked quickly across the girls, then back to Aeisla.

'Thus and so, it is a long voyage to Staive Cintes, the better part of a month at the least, even allowing for favourable winds. We may travel in two manners, in friendship or in enmity. I suggest the former.'

'By all means,' Aeisla answered.

'I also,' he went on, 'wish no bickering jealousy among my crew. There must be order, and none favoured above another, myself included. Thus I must either respectfully suggest that all five of you remain celibate for the duration of the voyage, or that each pick those she wishes to keep satisfied.'

'Those?' Cianna queried.

'Naturally,' Baltrank answered. 'There are five of you and twenty-four of us. Should you be allotted to myself, the two mates, the navigator and perhaps the supervisor of cargo, I can guarantee unrest. Alternatively, should each of you choose the man most favourable to you, nineteen will remain unsatisfied, again risking difficulties. This is why there are no women on Oretean ships when on the long hauls, and the reason for my offer: celibacy or plurality. Naturally I would prefer the latter once more, and will go so far as to take advantage of my rank to claim exclusivity. What of it?'

Aeisla glanced to the other girls. Cianna gave a happy shrug. Kaissia heaved a sigh. Yi continued to look at the deck. Iriel grimaced, thinking of the bull-nymphs.

'At present it is hard to make a decision,' Aeisla stated. 'I for one would gladly couple. Otherwise, allow us two, no, three days of celibacy to decide. More and I suspect jealousies will begin to grow in any event.'

'You are wise beyond your age,' Baltrank responded, bowing a trifle. 'Three days then.'

Iriel threw Aeisla a thankful glance, then looked to a pair of seamen who were drawing a bucket up from the sea a few paces along the rail.

'Might I wash?'

For the next two days the *Gull of Cintes* sailed west and south, turning the point of the Grey Cape on the third. Pursuit had been abandoned, yet a group of Aeg horsemen were looking down from the cliff top, black against grey sky, sat perfectly still on their mounts until lost from vision. The sight filled Iriel with a sense of melancholy, and she continued to watch until at last the rough grey cliffs of her homeland had faded to a line of hazy violet low across the horizon.

Only with the evening meal did her mood restore itself. The cruelty and ill humour of Mistress Loida was behind her, and with it the threat of public humiliation, pain, soiling and ducking. In their place she had a distant and strange city to look forward to, in which, if what Baltrank said was true, she would easily be able to find a place to exercise her trade, and for pay rather than mere food and lodging.

Meanwhile, once the meal was done, she and the others would be choosing their companions for the remainder of the voyage. Debate had been brief, Aeisla and Cianna more than content for sex, Yi reluctant but soon giving in, Kaissia alone refusing to make a decision. The shock of the way Iriel had been taken by the nymphs had died more quickly than she had expected, to be replaced by a desire to try out the new found pleasures of her body. Never had she suspected that the introduction of a cock to her tuppenny could feel so wonderful, for all her friends' assurances. While still deeply shameful, her buggery had also been a pleasure, at least once the nymph's cock had been firmly installed up her bottom.

What would have been an unbearable disgrace was also made easier by the fact that the Oretean seamen thought no differently of her for surrendering herself to the nymphs. Nor did the other girls, Kaissia and Yi not surprisingly after their own experiences, and Aeisla and Cianna apparently indifferent. Only Captain Baltrank had remarked on the matter, and then only to joke that she should not exhaust his valuable cargo before they reached Staive Cintes.

Something inside her had changed, her fear of the penetration of her body replaced by a need for exactly that. Looking back, the thought of her grudging or miserable acceptance of the cocks she had taken into her mouth seemed foolish, and if there was still an underlying sense of shame and embarrassment, it faded as her need grew stronger.

The meal was taken communally as always, the Captain heading a broad oval table in the main cabin of the sterncastle. The usual dish of lentils and spice-preserved meat was served, something Iriel was still struggling to get used to, but on this occasion along with mugs of the heavy red Oretean wine, which made her head spin. It also left her facing the prospect of satisfying several men with more excitement than trepidation.

With the platters scraped clean and the mugs refilled, Baltrank got to his feet, to rest his broad fists on the table top. Grinning, he glanced around the table, then drew a slim roll of charta from within his clothes. Unrolling it, he began to speak.

'Our Aeg companions,' he stated gravely, 'have agreed to indulge us in the pleasures of their bodies, as we have theirs. All will be satisfied, yet by my rank I claim sole access to the leader among them. Aeisla, I would be honoured to entertain you in my cabin.'

'Kaissia is senior among us,' Aeisla suggested. 'You should make your offer to her.'

'I am highborn, you are a merchant!' Kaissia objected immediately, only for her outrage to vanish, replaced by a look of sulky dejection. 'I am shamed. Do with me as you like.'

'Shame is a concept, nothing more,' Baltrank stated, grinning. 'You are beautiful, if inconveniently tall, and your tattoos hold no meaning for me beyond enhancing the beauty of your breasts.'

'Do you think so?' Kaissia asked, doubtfully.

'Accept his word on it,' Aeisla put in. 'Why question only to discover flattery?'

Kaissia nodded and bit her lip, then extended her hand. Baltrank took it, gave a polite bow to her and went on.

'Aeisla then, must make do with Ziles, Oltran, Teigel and Navigator Steithes, all men of rank.'

The four senior men named sat to either side of the Captain. All turned bearded grins to Aeisla, who responded with a small, cool smile as Baltrank continued.

'Among the remainder, one girl shall go with the riggers, one with the deckmen and one to the galley and holds, thus taking nine, six and four. Uneven, I realise, but this way we prevent difficulties with accommodation. Unless there are strong feelings one way or another, we shall choose by chance?'

He looked around the table. Not all the men were present, but none objected. Cianna shrugged, then Iriel. Yi merely sighed. Nodding, the Captain delved into a pocket, drawing out dice. Turning to a grey-haired seaman with skin like leather and a pinched face, he raised his eyebrows.

'Your choice, Builes?'

'The little slut, Captain,' the man answered, with a grin for Yi, 'the one who the troll fucked across the barrel of shit. Low.'

'Seven or fewer and she is with you and your riggers,' Baltrank answered, and rolled the dice.

They came to rest showing a three and a two. Builes's grin grew abruptly broader and he rose from the table, extended one callused hand to Yi. She rose, her face downcast, and allowed herself to be led from the cabin, his hand fixing firmly to the roundness of her bottom as she was steered through the door. Others followed, jostling eagerly for a good place in the inevitable queue.

'Armedes?' Baltrank asked, turning his gaze to a solidly built man with a round, pudding face and his chair pushed back to accommodate the bulk of his gut. 'Who for the deckmen?'

Armedes gave an uneasy glance at Cianna's teeth, then looked to Iriel and nodded.

'High.'

Again Baltrank rolled the dice, only for them to show both ones. Armedes shrugged and pulled himself upright, to take Cianna's hand. Two others followed, leaving Iriel looking wistfully after them and thinking of the men she would have to satisfy: Corbold, the monstrously fat cook; his fleshy young assistant Luides; the man who dealt with the nymphs, Huin; and the odd, gangling carpenter whose name she did not know. None were at the table, each either busy or due to join the later sitting.

'Doubtless Luides will collect you presently, Iriel,' Baltrank stated, 'and now, Kaissia, if you would?'

Kaissia allowed him to assist her to rise and she was led up the companionway to his cabin on the upper level of the sterncastle. Aeisla also rose, leaving with the four senior men, hand in hand between First Mate and Navigator. Iriel waited, thinking on the prospect of having to keep four men satisfied for a month or so.

Presently Kaissia's cries of pleasure and a rhythmic thumping could be heard from above. The door swung open, to reveal Luides. He smacked his thick lips together at the sight of her, then began to pile the used utensils from the meal onto a tray. Iriel watched, wondering how his soft, flabby body would feel on top of her, yet feeling somewhat put out that he seemed to put his menial task before his right to enjoy her. At last he spoke.

'Lend a hand, girl, or it will be midnight before you get to sheathe a cock in your cunt.'

He finished with a lewd chuckle. Iriel stood to help, resignedly stacking plates until she had as many as she could carry, then following Luides from the cabin and below decks, to the galley. Corbold was there, stirring a pot of lentils. He looked up as they entered, grunting, then speaking.

'So you are ours, Iriel. I had hoped for little Yi, who displays a pleasing reluctance, but at least we do not have to contend with the wild girl. Stir these lentils while I cut the meat. Luides, see to the table for the next sitting.'

'You wish me to work?' Iriel queried. 'Here in the galley?'

'Why not?' Corbold shrugged. 'So far what have you done but rest yourselves on the deck and distract the seamen from their tasks? You eat, do you not?'

'That is true,' Iriel admitted.

'Then stir the lentils,' he ordered, 'and do not fret, we will see to your cunt soon enough.'

Iriel took the big spoon from him and began to stir, thinking of Kaissia, already fucked, and the others, presumably naked and sucking on cocks even as she worked. Corbold gave her bottom a heavy slap as he went to the meat barrel, but no more, leaving her pouting resentfully over her pot as he began to select strips of cured mutton from the pungent spice. Presently Corbold spoke again.

'You have Huin, also, do you not, and Kantch?'

'Kantch is the carpenter?' Iriel queried.

'Yes,' Corbold told her, 'and a bugger to boot, preferring arsehole to cunt. Still, Luides will be grateful.'

'Luides? Why so?'

'Because in getting your arsehole pierced he will be spared the use of his own,' Corbold explained.

'He . . . he . . . with Luides!?' Iriel asked, horrified.

'We are at sea,' Corbold stated blandly. 'Now, let us get this finished and you'll soon be on my cock. I, for one, prefer cunt.'

He came close, to drop a double handful of cut meat into the lentils. Iriel caught his scent; sweat, spice, and a sweet-sharp reek she guessed came from the substance he used to oil his beard and the bald dome of his head. Again his hand found her bottom, this time kneading, his fat fingers squeezing one cheek, then pushing between to send a shiver through her. She had pulled away a little, by instinct, but he drew her back in, fondling and pushing the material of her drawers up into the crease of her bottom.

'Meaty,' he remarked, 'firm, yet meaty.'

Luides came back in, followed by Huin and Kantch, both grinning. The cooks set to the task of serving, the others to Iriel. She closed her eyes, resigned to her fate and trying to think of handsome young men rather than the strange four she was obliged to deal with. Huin had taken her breasts in hand, and was feeling the plump globes through her bodice, as if in wonder. Kantch was behind her, his hands replacing those of the cook on her bottom.

'Never have I held such large ones,' Huin remarked. 'They are like the round melons. Come, girl, let us have them out, I wish to see.'

'Is this the place?' Iriel queried, her voice already hoarse from the attention to her body.

'As good as the next,' he answered, his fingers already fumbling with the laces of her bodice. Behind her, Kantch had begun to haul up her dress.

'Let me,' she said, pushing Huin's hands away, to slip the knot and wrench her bodice wide, the way it was designed to work, so that girls could be ravished without constantly having to repair their clothes.

Tugging down her chemise, she spilled her breasts out, to lie plump and naked in twin nests of lace and cotton. Huin licked his lips and took them in hand again, shaking his head in wonder as he began to fondle.

'Glorious,' he murmured, 'so full, so fat. All the while we have been in Aegmund I have wondered how you giantesses look naked. Why is it you have no whores in Aegerion?'

'Whores?' Iriel queried, closing her eyes once more as he began to play with her nipples.

'Whores,' he stated, 'those girls who dwell in brothels. Houses of pleasure, where a man may go to ease his cock in cunt.'

'There are no such places,' she sighed. 'If you wish a girl, simply ravish her.'

'I tried this,' he answered. 'She beat me black and blue and spat on me as I lay in the gutter.'

'To win a girl you must be strong, or clever,' Iriel moaned. 'As your Captain is, to make this offer . . .'

She trailed off as he began to suck on one of her nipples, taking the stiff bud firmly between his lips. Kantch had stripped her bottom while they spoke, hauling her skirt and petticoat high and pulling her drawers apart, never speaking once. Now, with her skirts bunched around her waist, her began to rub his crotch on her bottom, moving the hard bulge of his cock up and down in her crease.

'Leave something for us,' Corbold remarked as he left the room, Luides following.

'Plenty for everyone here,' Huin replied and buried his face between Iriel's breasts.

Kantch moved back, but only to free his cock, which pressed between her bare cheeks a moment later, hot and hard. Her passion now too high to hold back, she pushed out her bottom.

'Not, not in my ring,' she managed. 'It hurts . . . and is dirty. Use my tuppenny . . . my cunt.'

He merely grunted, but as her bottom came out his cock had slipped into the slimy crease between her cheeks and the head found her proper hole, to slip up without pain. She moaned as she filled, and took hold of Huin's head, holding him to her chest as he mouthed and sucked at her breasts. Kantch began to fuck her, deep, hard strokes that made her bottom bounce and tremble.

She pushed back more firmly. The motion of the ship was slight, a gentle rolling Iriel found much easier to cope with than the alarming movement of the smaller vessels she was used to, yet with the wine inside her it was spoiling her sense of balance. Kantch took her hard by the hips, Huin around her ribs and she was being held, the cock in her tuppenny moving inside her, her breasts tingling to the attention of lips and tongue.

They began to guide her down, to her knees on the floor, Huin moving back, to introduce an already erect cock into her mouth as she got onto all fours. The fucking grew harder, more purposeful, Huin's grip tighter, using her mouth as a slide. At last she felt properly ravished rather than simply molested, and even as Kantch withdrew from her tuppenny to slide his juice-smeared cock up between her buttocks she managed no more than a muffled mewl of protest at what she was sure he intended, buggery.

Sure enough, holding her tightly by her lifted clothes, he pushed his cock to her bottom ring. For a moment she tried to fight, clenching her anus to make the damp, fleshy ring squirm and pulse against the pressure of his cock. It made no difference, Kantch simply forcing his way in, her ring popping with a sharp stab of pain that broke her resistance, and she was filled with the sensation of having been overcome as the full length of his cock was packed up into her rectum.

41

Kantch began to bugger her, Huin to fuck her mouth with his hands twisted into her hair, rowing her body between them, back and forth on their cocks, her lips and bottom ring pulling in and out to the motion, her breasts swinging in time. Huin came first, deep in her throat, to make her gag and leave her with jism hanging from not just her lower lip but also her nostrils as he pulled back. The next instant Kantch grunted and filled her rectum with come, then pulled slowly out to leave her anus pulsing and dribbling behind her, her tuppenny gaping for more.

She stayed down, her eyes shut, her breathing low and even, feeling the men's jism trickle slowly from her body, wanting more and sure the cooks would return at any moment. Sure enough, the door banged and Huin spoke.

'We have her ready for you, Corbold, greased both ends but in want up her cunt, you dirty son of a baboon, Kantch.'

Kantch merely grunted as he wiped his cock on Iriel's dress, then stood to make way for Corbold. Iriel wiggled her bottom, inviting the fat cook to use her, all decency and regret fled in the urgency of her lust. The boards groaned as he got down behind her, his fat belly pressing to her bottom. A new hand twisted into her hair and she was fed Luides' cock, fat and fleshy, tasting of male sweat, cooking spice and earth. She began to suck as Corbold's own erection slid easily up her sopping tuppenny hole.

They took her in hand and once again she was being rowed, back and forth, spitted on two cocks, her ecstasy rising until at last she reacted in pure lust. Her hands went back, tugging her clothes clear, to find her tuppenny, to rub, to grip the cook's fat, wrinkled scrotum as he pushed in and out of her, to rub again, to stroke the junction of cock and hole, to rub again.

Luides' cock erupted in her mouth as she started to come, thick, salty jism exploding from around her lips to splash his balls and fall to the floor. He groaned in pleasure, more come pumping into her mouth as she eagerly sucked it down and rubbed ever harder at her tuppenny. She began to come, her hole tightening on Corbold's cock, then going into spasm, squeezing over and over on the thick shaft as his belly slapped on her upturned bottom and her breasts swung in the pool of jism and saliva beneath her on the floor.

As Luides' cock slipped from her mouth she cried out in ecstasy, her whole body shaking to her orgasm as she was fucked. Her mind was full of wanton thoughts, of how she'd been taken and used on the floor, in her mouth, in her tuppenny, in her bottom ring, all made receptacles for male cocks and for their jism. Then it was how her maidenhead had gone to a bull-nymph, burst across the cockhead of a man-beast, her bottom entered too, and how good it felt to just be mounted and used by as many males as could possibly accommodate themselves in her body.

A week after Iriel's first fucking by the crew, the *Gull of Cintes* reached a cape that dwarfed the Grey Cape, sheer cliffs lifting maybe two hundred manheights from the sea and higher beyond, towards a colossal peak, the tip of which rose above hazy purple cloud.

By then life had settled to a routine of galley work, meals and regular fuckings. Their place also became established according to their rank, save that Aeisla rather than Kaissia was looked to as their leader. Awed by Aeisla's reputation, Kaissia made no attempt to dispute this, while Iriel quickly found herself developing a sense of loyalty to the strong, confident Reeveling. Kaissia, despite being not only shamed but indebted, had begun to reassert something of the natural haughtiness that went with her rank, principally to Iriel and Yi. Cianna continued as always, Yi slowly coming to terms with her new life and having to keep nine men sexually satisfied.

Despite feeling that she had the least physically appealing men to satisfy, Iriel was at least content that her accommodation was better than Cianna's and Yi's, who had to make do among the hammocks of the riggers and deckmen as best they could. For her there was a choice, if not a perfect one. Corbold had his own tiny cabin beside the galley, which although comfortable enough had the disadvantage that his massive bulk left little or no room in the bunk. Kantch also had a bunk, at one side of the carpenter's shop, but while his lanky body and relative height made both sex and sleeping convenient, he had a nasty habit of greasing his morning erection and intruding it unexpectedly into her bottom. Not that she minded the buggery too much, but the grease stung and it invariably left her desperate to reach the pot before her bottom erupted. Huin and Luides slept in hammocks, but would frequently come for her in the night.

She had quickly come to know each of the four men's cocks by taste alone. Corbold's had an odd, sickly sweet flavour, almost sugary and rather like his breath. It tended to make her gag when she sucked, while his weight was uncomfortable, so that with him she preferred to be taken from the rear. Huin was better, merely salty and masculine, which was fortunate as his favourite trick was to fuck her breasts and mouth together, coming either down her throat or in her face. Luides tended to play with himself while cooking, so was always greasy and tasted of spice, while Kantch was the worst of them for his habit of buggering her at every opportunity. For all the drawbacks she found herself coming to want her orgasms more than ever, and to behave with utter wantonness once she had become aroused, making her wonder just how wonderful fucking would be with more appealing men.

She also came to learn about the ship and of Oretea in general. The green and gold colours represented those of the ruling house of Staive Cintes, the country being ruled by family groups of greater or lesser importance. She also learned the function of the curious black tubes mounted on the castles, bombards, which hurled iron balls great distances by a process akin to magic.

For day after day they sailed south and west, across great low swells rolling in from the western ocean. The land was to the east, where a range of high mountains reared above jagged cliffs and tiny bays of black sand. Occasionally Iriel glimpsed a dwelling on the slopes or a plume of smoke rising from a gully or a grove of stunted trees, but whatever men inhabited the place, if men they were, they were never visible.

After the second week even the lonely cottages were gone, the great mountain sides bare but for coarse grass and scattered trees immediately below the snow. Slowly the mountains became less grand and ever more barren. Trees disappeared completely, as did the snow, until finally the mountains gave way altogether, to be replaced by dunes of featureless sand beyond which nothing was visible. They turned west, standing well out from the shore to avoid sand bars where the great dunes and the sea met.

After three days the dunes ended in a point, white sand washed by surf, a place of utter desolation, yet which fired the seamen with excitement. Their course was adjusted, to due south, and for another day and a half they sailed in long tacks, at last reaching a low, grass-grown coast. Again they turned south and west, and as the dusk gathered lights became visible far down the shore.

Next morning they came into Staive Cintes. Iriel and the other girls watched from the rail, doing their best to keep out of the deckmen's way but too fascinated to go below. For Iriel it was the only city she had seen beside Aegerion, and very different. In place of the tall, high-gabled grey-stone houses of the Aeg, Staive Cintes consisted of squat, block-shaped structures, the raw yellow of sand or washed in glaring white. Here and there, domes or squat towers rose above the other buildings, copper green or a brilliant pale blue, while tall palms sprouted from what were presumably gardens.

The harbour was a wide blue pool behind what at first seemed to be a line of dunes, but as they came around was revealed as a great breakwater against the outside of which the sand had piled. There were other ships, more than Iriel could ever recall seeing in the harbour at Aegerion; trading carracks like the *Gull of Cintes*, green-hulled warships with the black mouths of bombards extending from each side in lines, what seemed to be fishing vessels, and highly decorated craft with no obvious purpose at all.

Iriel watched in fascination as they drew close to the quay. As at Aegerion, a broad area of flagstones ran the length of the waterfront, with warehouses behind, piles of nets and cargo, and the stalls of merchants and the vendors of seafood set here and there. There the resemblance ended. The small stature and yellow-brown skin of the Oreteans she had grown used to, but while the clothing of all but the high-ranking seamen was plain and functional, that of the citizens was not. Even the longshoremen who warped the *Gull of Cintes* ashore wore brilliantly coloured turbans; orange, purple, viridian green. The clothes of the stallholders were more vivid still, loose trousers of silk tied with sashes and ankles knots, split vests that left the belly and chest showing, even on the women. These women, although tiny, with little rounded bottoms and breasts never larger than a fair-sized apple, still looked indecent, and Iriel wondered why they were not simply ravished on the ground. On most, delicate catches of filigree joined the two sides of their vests, but many among the poorer and the younger had no such safeguard, so that, with the movement of their bodies, breasts, slices of rounded flesh and even pert nipples were frequently exposed.

46

All five girls had come to the rail, and descended the gangplank as soon as it was in place, to gather on the quay with the seamen, several of whom bent to kiss the rough yellow stones at their feet. Aeisla and Cianna came together, the others remaining with the men they had serviced, no two among them having any particular attachments. Luides joined Iriel, his round, fleshy face beaming.

'Advise me,' she asked him. 'What should I do to secure a position in trade?'

'Simply visit the appropriate shops and ask,' he said. 'There are clothiers, and if they have no openings, sail-making might prove a choice, or the sewing of sacks, net-making even. Not that you wish to take employment yet, surely? We are newly ashore, full paid!'

'I have no pay, nor anywhere to sleep, unless I am allowed on the ship.'

'No pay? Not so, Captain Baltrank distributes the purses once he has been to the purser at House Eriedes. You have worked the galley, have you not?'

'Yes, but –'

'Then you will be paid. Me, I am for a brief visit to my family, a draught of good black beer, then the House of Cunt.'

He smacked his lips in anticipation, then went on.

'You should go there, were you not so proud. I would introduce you to Madame Hivies, who would be glad to have a girl of your strange beauty working for her, either piecework or in-house.'

'I do not understand, is this what you call a brothel?'

'Yes, and the most popular in Staive Cintes, if not truly the best. Most girls bring their men there for half what is paid, which is piecework, while others live in, thus gaining board and shelter, but less money and the occasional application of Madame Hivies' dog-switch to their backsides. You would earn well, ten times what an apprentice seamstress could hope for.'

'It is impossible, strange too. Why would a man pay for what he can take, and thus honour the girl?'

'Strange to you, perhaps. In Staive Cintes any man who takes a girl – ravishes her as you say – would have the watch after him, and she would not feel honoured, far from it.'

'I do not understand at all, but I will not be going to this House of Cunt. Corbold, or Huin perhaps, will be able to provide advice.'

'Huin will be seeing to the nymphs. As to Corbold, ask him.'

Iriel turned to see the fat cook coming down the gangplank, his round red face split into a grin, only directed not at her, but at a dumpy Oretean woman who came straight to him, followed by a group of a dozen well-fed children.

'Corbold will want to be with his family,' Luides remarked. 'As I will be with mine just so soon as I have my purse. If you wish to meet later, I will be at the House Taepenk, where you may taste black beer, sour bread, olives, honey cake and all the fine things of my land.'

He moved off as Captain Baltrank appeared with a bald old man in a robe of brilliant emerald silk. Iriel looked around, feeling somewhat lost. Aeisla and Cianna were together, with the Navigator Steithes, Yi was with a group of riggers, while Kaissia was nowhere to be seen. At last she went to join the queue, tagging herself on to the very end. After a moment Aeisla called out to her, saying she would be at somewhere called Oxtan's Yard. Iriel responded with a wave but stayed in the queue, waiting patiently until her turn came.

The bag given to her by Captain Baltrank proved to contain a number of coins, six silver pieces roughly the size of a Thalar, five of copper, larger and heavier, and a single piece of gold, thick, yet no larger than her thumbnail. Taking herself to one side, she carefully concealed the silver and gold in an inner pocket, put the copper in an outer and returned to the open quay. None of the other girls were visible, and she crossed the quay to the largest of those streets opening onto it, looking around herself in wonder and drinking in the strange sights, sounds and smells.

Everything was bright, intense, the sunlight so strong it hurt her eyes. The scents were also stronger now that she was in the shelter of the street, spice and baking bread, fruit and meat, dung and decay, all so richer by far than in Aegerion. It was also odd to be so much taller than those around her, only the very largest of the men equalling her height, while no women came up to her chin.

As Captain Baltrank had promised, none accosted her, despite numerous curious glances, some admiring, some questioning, some shocked or even fearful. Several times she passed pairs of armed men in neat green and gold uniforms, but otherwise the citizens seemed to go without protection, even the men, which seemed highly peculiar, yet none seemed to wish to take advantage.

Walking to the top of the low hill, she paused beneath the high white wall of what seemed to be a keep or palace of some sort and looked back. The street led arrow straight to the quayside, with the sea visible over the rooftops, cut by the masts of ships. Her confidence had increased, also her hunger, and she determined to sample some of the exotic delicacies Luides had spoken of, keen for anything so long as it was not lentils and spiced meat.

Her first enquiry produced only a puzzled glance, and she had to repeat her words several times, the woman she had stopped unable to comprehend her accent although there had been little difficulty with the seamen. At last she was shown towards a building, in the dim cellar of which she consumed two large mugs of the thick, potent black beer Luides had recommended before discovering that she was not in the House Taepenk.

The owner gave her instructions, which only resulted in her getting lost, and twice more she stopped at inns, each time ordering a mug of beer before asking directions. Finally she found the place she wanted, a single-storey compound to the north of the dock area. An arch led in to an open yard, in which people sat at tables, eating, drinking from the earthenware mugs and talking. Several curious looks were turned to her as she entered, but once more nobody disputed her right to be there.

She chose a vacant table and sat down, feeling somewhat dizzy. Determined not to look foolish, she put three of her big copper coins out in front of her, as others had done at the surrounding tables. A man in a leather apron approached, giving her a quizzical glance.

'Black beer,' she stated, trying to sound confident, 'with a plate of bread, olives and honey cake.'

'Olives and honey cake together?' the man queried.

'I was advised by Luides, from the *Gull of Cintes*,' she answered. 'I hope to meet him here.'

'Yes,' the man answered, 'I had heard there were barbarians in. I will fetch a platter, at three-tenths, yes?'

Iriel nodded, not at all sure what she was doing but happy so long as she was fed. As the man departed, one of those at a nearby table turned to her.

'You were with Luides then, on the *Gull*? I am his friend Meles, this Nuidan, this Dound, that Bages. And what is your name?'

There was a wolflike quality to his grin, and his eyes had been fixed on her bodice more than her face, but Iriel found herself smiling at the four young men, glad of any friendly attention. Also, the least of them was notably more handsome than Luides, for all their small size.

'I am Iriel,' she said, 'and I was galley maid, yes, beneath Corbold.'

'Join us,' he offered, the others quickly making room for her at the bench. 'Rumour says you are from barbarian Aegmund, and took the ship by force before reaching an agreement with Captain Baltrank?'

'Not by force, no,' she answered. 'The saga belongs to Aeisla, who took the part of the Squireling Kaissia for the embellishment of her escutcheon.'

'I had heard one stepped in to prevent another being given a dose of troll cock?' the man introduced as Nuidan sniggered. 'Is this how you treat malefactors in your land, by having them fucked by man-beasts?'

'What had Kaissia done?' Meles demanded.

'She was punished for taking a bull-nymph as lover,' Iriel said, blushing slightly.

'Taking a bull-nymph as lover?' Dound queried. 'What lady of rank does not have a bull-nymph to hand for her carnal amusement?'

'So,' Bages queried, 'if it is a crime to let one man-beast into her cunt, how so that the punishment is to be forced to take another?'

'There is a difference between a bull-nymph and a troll, Bages!' Nuidan scoffed. 'In bulk, in manner, above all in cock size. You saw the one at last year's fair, his cock had the dimensions of a young marrow!'

'But the barbarian girls are big,' Bages objected. 'You could take a troll cock, I imagine, Iriel?'

Iriel's cheeks had flamed red, but the men merely laughed and Meles gave her a good-natured slap on the back. Grimacing slightly nonetheless, but feeling she ought to explain so as not to make her fellow Aeg look foolish, she went on.

'Kaissia had given in to her urges with the bull-nymph, yes, but that was a private thing. She had also surrendered her maidenhead, by deliberate choice, picking the lock of her purity-girdle.'

'Purity-girdle?'

'A device of chain worn around the hips to prevent

51

the easy attaining of a highborn girl's maidenhead. Kaissia should have waited until some highborn man achieved her.'

'Achieved? Fucked, you mean?'

'Yes. She should have waited to be ravished by one who wished to take her in marriage. By fucking with the bull-nymph she disgraced herself. Thus she was shamed in public, spanked naked, her breasts tattooed with a distinctive pattern, then she was smeared in dung. She was also to be put to the troll's cock, but Aeisla felt it was an unwarranted act and intervened in rage.'

'If this was the case here,' Meles laughed, 'we would have half the female population of the town up for punishment every morning!'

The others laughed, then lifted their mugs as one and took draughts of beer. The man in the leather apron returned, to place a mug in front of Iriel, also a plate, heaped with chunks of delicious-smelling fresh bread, waxy green objects she took to be olives, a long sausage of a deep red colour and two triangular pastries. As she began to eat, Luides appeared in the archway, hailing his friends, then taking a place beside her on the bench, pushing Bages aside with a thrust of his corpulent backside. Immediately Dound whispered something in his ear.

'She does not take money,' Luides laughed. 'If you want her, merely fuck her on the floor, but be cautious, she will fight until her cunt is pricked. She is strong. Either that or you must use cunning.'

Iriel looked up, the blood rushing to her cheeks, stung by the sudden prospect of ravishment and hoping they would at least give her time to let her tuppenny juice up before putting her to their cocks. Quickly she swallowed her mouthful.

'Wait at the least until I have eaten,' she said quickly, 'and yes, I will fight unless there is good reason to surrender, but perhaps not so very hard.'

Meles made a curious clucking noise in his throat. Nuidan lifted his eyebrows and twisted his fingers into what was evidently an obscene gesture. Luides spoke.

'Do not be concerned, Iriel. Here the watch would intervene in moments. Still, perhaps after –'

'What do we care for the watch?' Meles laughed. 'I'll bet we could have her fucked and pregnant before old Taepenk so much as noticed!'

'Besides,' Nuidan added, flourishing the knife he had been using to cut pieces from a sausage, 'we are armed, and five. Four could hold the watchmen off while each took his turn!'

The others laughed. Iriel raised her eyes from her plate, suddenly interested.

'You would fight the watch ... the men who go armed about the streets, knife against sword, for the pleasure of having me?'

'He is boasting, ignore him,' Luides advised.

'Not so!' Nuidan declared, making another flourish. 'I would fight the watch for a fuck of you, Iriel, right here on the flags of Taepenk's!'

Her tongue flicked out to moisten suddenly dry lips.

'Truly? Here and now?'

'Yes,' Nuidan declared. 'I swear it.'

'Liar!' Luides scoffed.

'Not so! I have done it before.'

'When?'

'Just last month, while you were on ship. Did we not, boys? At the caravanserai, when Assanach's train came in with a group of Makean slavegirls. We fucked them two by two, a copper a go, in the camel shed, and as Dound and Meles here were finishing their rides, who should turn up but Twelveman Cound himself. I held him back with a dung shovel while they finished the fucking!'

'That is so much camel shit!' Luides protested.

'No,' Nuidan insisted. 'We did it, ask Assanach, ask Twelveman Cound himself if you dare!'

Luides gave a grunt and shook his head.

'He did this?' Iriel asked Dound.

'I saw it myself,' Dound assured her.

'How about it, then?' Nuidan asked.

'I am not certain I am worthy,' Iriel replied. 'Tell me more as I eat.'

Nuidan went on, explaining what had happened and making flamboyant gestures to illustrate how he had fought. The others gave further details, each to his own credit, Luides adding only the occasional sceptical grunt as he dealt with his own meal. Iriel continued to eat, her arousal growing slowly as she listened. As at Kaissia's shaming, it was impossible to fight down her excitement, or her sense of honour at the risks they were prepared to take for the pleasure of her tuppenny, not far different from those a highborn man might have to take to achieve his lady. Suddenly a thought occurred to her, dashing her hopes.

'I am only an artisan,' she admitted. 'Nothing more.'

'I do not care,' Nuidan answered, 'come into the piss house and I'll show you.'

'The piss house?' she answered. 'Why not here? As you said, you may take turns with me while the remainder hold off the watch, but you are to fuck me kneeling, so that I can see the combat. If we go into the piss house, who will see to call the guard?'

Bages went into a sudden fit of coughing. Luides shook his head. Nuidan put on a crafty expression.

'Here, in the open, the four of us may not be enough to shield the man filling your cunt, and who knows, eight, maybe twelve watchmen may come to Taepenk's call. In the piss house one man could hold the door against a dozen twelves. You will be soundly fucked, while Taepenk is sure to notice, and there are other ways to attract his attention also.'

Iriel nodded and bit her lip. The heavy, strong beer was making her head spin, and they had aroused much

54

the same feelings in her as at the shaming. It was making her want nothing more than to take their cocks, one at a time, especially those who a moment before had been fighting against high odds for the pleasure. She swallowed her last mouthful and washed it down with the remains of her beer, then rose.

'Come then, but take your time with me. No man puts himself in my tuppenny until he has traded blows with a watchman.'

'You are offering yourself, truly?' Luides asked in astonishment.

'I am,' she answered, 'if you too have the courage, join your friends.'

He made to answer, then shut up abruptly.

Nuidan produced a grave nod, then spoke again.

'Go to the piss house, Iriel, I shall join you presently. You four, start a ruckus.'

'I have a better suggestion,' Meles said. 'You are the best fighter among us, no question. It would be much more appropriate if you were to take last place, having held off the watchmen. I am the least strong, and so should go to the piss house first.'

'True,' Iriel agreed.

'Not so!' Nuidan argued. 'I am the instigator here, and in no mood for your slops! Besides, who else but I could hope to hold the watchmen off moments after discharging my shot?'

'I am as good as you,' Dound declared loudly, 'stronger for certain. I should be first.'

'Not so, I!' Barges put in.

'Why?' Nuidan demanded, and not only Barges but Dound and Meles responded, voice on voice, until Iriel had lost the sense of it beneath their accents and slang.

Luides alone remained silent, shaking his head, but with his eyes smiling as he took a draught of the black beer. Flattered, and ready for cock, Iriel waited for the men to reach a decision, speaking only when it became clear that none would give way.

'Men, please,' she interrupted. 'I shall take Luides in with me, naturally, as he has already been with me on the ship. You four must then argue, as you are now, but outside the piss house. This will attract the watch, and you may follow in turn as circumstances permit, but with Nuidan last, to bring me to my peak while the others fight.'

Nuidan opened his mouth to speak but shut it as the grinning Luides stood up, his hand extended to Iriel. She took it, her stomach fluttering, her head spinning with drink, her tuppenny tingling in anticipation of the hopefully large cock about to be put inside her. Luides led her across the court, several of those present turning their heads, but only to look at her with the same curiosity she had encountered since arriving in Staive Cintes.

The piss house was at the rear of the building, a long, low room, open to the evening sky and divided by partition, neck high to Luides, but only reaching Iriel's chest. At once grateful for the concealment and irritated that she would be unable to actually watch the combat, she nevertheless chose a cubicle and squatted down, as if to pee into the long trough beneath her.

Her nose wrinkled at the scent of urine, sharp, yet also hormonal, then at that of Luides' cock as he pushed his loose trousers down to expose himself. She leaned forwards, to take him in her mouth, tasting cooking grease and spice as always. He sighed in pleasure, extending a hand to balance himself and twisting his other hand into Iriel's hair to hold her firmly in place. She sucked harder at the sudden, mild pain of her hair being pulled, feeling him swell in her mouth and listening for sounds of the others.

For a while there was nothing, and she contented herself with the feel of Luides' slowly expanding penis, until her mouth was full of fat, solid cock and the urge to take it inside her tuppenny had grown too strong to resist. She came up, for one moment leaving a string of saliva connecting her lower lip with the bloated head of Luides' erection. Even as the strand snapped she caught the first sounds from outside, Nuidan's voice, then that of Bages, raised in mock anger. Another of the men laughed.

Eager for fucking, Iriel rose and turned, flipping her dress up and splitting her drawers to show off her bare bottom. Luides took her by the hips as she squatted down, supporting herself with difficulty as he pushed her lower to let himself get his cock to her hole. The moment he succeeded he pushed, filling her tuppenny with a wet sound that was repeated as he began to fuck her.

Iriel clung to her knees, struggling to keep her balance and still enjoy the feel of the cock inside her. Outside the four men were arguing, with laughter in their voices, a sound that delighted her for the sheer contempt it showed to the dangers of combat. Bracing her legs wide, she put her hands on the wall, her whole body now shaking to Luides' firm, deep pushes.

The urge to rub her tuppenny was strong, but she held back, determined to come with the sound of male anger, triumph and pain in her ears. Luides fucked faster, grunting as he pumped his cock into her hole, deeper, harder, his podgy gut slapping on her bare bottom until she too was grunting, her control slipping, her hand going back, only for him to gasp in ecstasy and fill her hole with jism.

Slowly he withdrew. Iriel stayed down, panting softly, her bottom high and ready for entry, warm come running down her tuppenny, her muscles already twitching. Outside nothing had changed, shouts and laughter, no more. She shook her head in disappointment.

'Get . . . get a man for me,' she puffed. 'Tell him to be slow!'

Luides answered with a grunt and left. Iriel waited, her head hung, dizzy with sex and beer, desperate for her tuppenny to be filled and not caring who filled it. Quickly she tugged open the laces of her bodice and adjusted her chemise, spilling her breasts out into her hands. As she began to fondle herself she heard steps, an oath, and looked round, to find a complete stranger behind her, a wizened old man, staring at her spread rear view in astonishment. She made to speak, only for Dound to appear, barge the old man aside and push up behind her, his trousers already down. Iriel sighed as his half-stiff cock pressed between her buttocks, and then he was rubbing himself in her crease and chortling in sheer joy.

She stuck her bottom out, to feel the wrinkled flesh of his scrotum up against the lips of her tuppenny, her cheeks spreading to leave his shaft rubbing on her anus. He gave a pleased grunt, took his now hard cock and pushed it rudely up her hole. Once more she hung her head, her body shaking to the motion of her fucking, her breasts swinging beneath her, then starting to bounce as his thrusts got harder.

'No, slow . . . slow,' she gasped. 'Do not –'

It was too late. He had come, flooding her hole with jism, to leave her dripping fluid and panting in frustration as he withdrew, gave her bottom a firm slap and left. She stayed down, biting her lip, desperate for more cock and unsure if she could hold herself back from masturbating. The old man had gone, and she found herself hoping he would complain, even as Bages appeared behind her, erect cock already in hand. She stuck her bottom out obligingly and up he went, the other men's jism squashing out over her tuppenny lips as her hole filled and for the third time in just moments she was being fucked against the piss house wall.

Her teeth gritted, her eyes tight shut, she fought against the urge to rub herself. Outside there was still the raucous sound of male voices, raised in mock argument, and laughter, and suddenly a new voice, genuinely angry. Nuidan responded, his tone derisive, challenging, and Iriel's mouth curved up into a happy smile as she pushed herself firmly back against the cock wedged deep into her body.

Bages had her by the hips, his hard belly slapping on her bottom as he fucked her, his cock squelching in her sopping hole. It felt wonderful, a fighting man, perhaps not ravishing her as his prize, but taking his pleasure up her hole as reward for his courage. She reached back, struggling to keep her balance, braced with her legs and one arm as she was fucked, her hand now on her tuppenny, rubbing in the juicy, jism-sodden folds. He cried out, and he had come, hot semen splashing on Iriel's hand as it squirted from her hole. She snatched at it, slapping the sticky, slimy handful to her tuppenny, rubbing harder, then slowing as he withdrew, teasing herself and listening.

Outside there were angry voices, Taepenk, deep and loud, Meles, mocking, Nuidan, petulant. Bages spoke, then laughed, a braying, arrogant sound. Taepenk responded, threatening to call the watch. Iriel bit back a sob of frustration. She was still rubbing, at the edge of orgasm, wanting cock so badly, yet also the climax she needed.

It was too much. Her senses slipped, the voices outside no longer clear but a jumble of sounds as she started to rub firmly at her tuppenny, smearing the jism up between her lips and over her mound, rubbing at the little tight bump at the very centre of everything. Footsteps sounded once more, directly behind her, hurried, but she was already coming, gasping out her ecstasy, but forcing herself to slow, and to speak.

'Put it in. Fuck me . . . now . . . hard.'

'Enough of that, you dirty whore!' a voice snapped from behind her, Taepenk's, and she was taken, whirled around, to lose her balance and sit down heavily in the puddle of jism and juice beneath her.

She looked up, astonished, but so close to orgasm that she could not stop herself from spreading her thighs to the man above her. His words hadn't penetrated, only the thought that if he had overcome five young men and was now going to ravish her as his prize it would be better still. Her hand went to her tuppenny and she began to rub, expecting to be taken at any moment.

'Get up!' Taepenk snarled. 'If that's how you wish to earn your keep, go to the House of Cunt and pay your half like any other!'

Iriel paused, her hand poised over her tuppenny. Her every instinct told her to rub, to bring herself to her desperately needed climax, but what he was saying had begun to sink in. She stopped and spoke.

'Aren't . . . aren't you going to have me? I am yours, spoils to your victory. Fuck me, come in me, as is your right.'

'Don't think to come the slut with me,' he answered. 'I know every one of your whore's tricks. Out.'

'No, I . . .' Iriel managed, utterly confused and also rejected. 'Don't you want me?'

He merely grunted and jerked his thumb over his shoulder.

'The watch is coming. Now out, or you'll get a taste of Madame Hivies' lash.'

'The watch are coming? My friends will fight them.'

She broke off, wondering where Luides and the others were. Their voices could no longer be heard, and they had all too obviously failed to resist Taepenk, an unarmed, middle-aged tavern keeper. He was looking puzzled, then answered her.

'Fight? Nuidan and his mob? They'd not dare fight with a one-legged washerwoman!'

'But, but, he has shown great prowess. He fought to ravish some girls, with a watchman . . . one Cound.'

'Cound!? Nuidan fight with Twelveman Cound!'

Taepenk broke off in loud laughter. Iriel covered herself, her emotions turning to anger and shame as she rose. She realised she had been tricked from the first, skilfully brought on heat and used for fucking, not a bad way to surrender, but something that left her emotions burning without the prospect of the climax she should have taken in reward for her surrender.

Struggling not to pout, she walked from the piss house. None of the five men she had been with were visible, confirming that they had fled. Two watchmen were, though, small but solidly built men in the green and gold of House Eriedes. One was talking to the old man who had witnessed her fucking. He spoke and they turned towards her, faces set in amusement.

Iriel licked her lips in suddenly renewed excitement. Now it was plain. They would treat her as she deserved, as High-Prince Nerengarian's men did with unruly girls in the streets of Aegerion, overcome, generally spanked, always fucked, the harder they fought the better the ultimate outcome. She would fight as well, hard, but not too hard. They would overcome her, ravish her then and there, holding her down as they took turns to fuck her, not the perfection of being overcome by one powerful adversary, but the best she could expect among pygmies.

She hurled herself forwards, screaming, her teeth gritted. The first man went down as her fist drove into his throat, taken completely by surprise, the second staggering as she kicked out at his legs, to trip and fall backwards across a table, spilling beer and food alike.

For a moment she was free, taken aback by the effectiveness of her attack. The arch to the compound was empty, just paces away, but she hesitated, still wanting to be ravished, her new-found delight in her body overcoming the urge to run. The second watchman rose from among the debris on the ground, then the other, clutching at his neck and coughing. Iriel stood back, ready, but determined not to fight quite so hard.

Neither approached, while the customers had either fled or were flattened against the walls of the compound, Taepenk also. The watchmen drew swords, cautiously. Iriel snatched up two of the meat knives from a table beside her. Neither man came forward, but the one who could still breathe properly blew two shrill notes on a whistle, answered moments later by the sound of running feet.

Iriel's pride swelled as a second pair of watchmen appeared at the gate, then further as more appeared, pushing in. One, senior to judge by the golden rings on his sleeves, pushed forwards as the others formed a ring of steel around her. She braced herself, suddenly alarmed that their intention might go beyond the sexual. At the thought a voice came to her, urging her to die well, and she screamed and hurled herself at the leader, only to run full tilt into his expertly thrown net.

A moment later she was helpless, cords twisted tight around her body, the knives useless in her hands, yet still fighting, and demanding loudly to be fucked as she was pulled from the compound.

3

The House of Cunt

Iriel awoke to brilliant sunlight, dry heat and a sour, spicy reek, all unfamiliar. For one brief instant there was confusion, and then she remembered the fight in the tavern, being dragged through the streets in the net and dumped into a cell somewhere beneath the citadel. Fear rose up with her memory, and a sharp pang of homesickness.

She pulled herself into a sitting position, groaning at the sudden ache of her body, and also at the pain in her head. Briefly, she said a prayer to her father, finding the strength to take stock of her situation. Her clothes were torn and dirty, but still on, her body bruised and stiff, but she had not been ravished. Her hands were tied in front of her, making it impossible to cover her breasts. She felt sticky and dry, also desperately thirsty, while there was a foul taste in her mouth. The cell was high and narrow, completely bare, the single window maybe three manheights above her head, and barred. A low door of iron gridwork opened onto a dusty corridor. The walls were rough yellow stone, carved in many places with the curling Oretean script. A wide-brimmed earthenware pot and a jug stood in one corner.

The jug was full of water, warm and stale, but infinitely welcome. Taking hold with some difficulty, she drank, splashed a little on her face and drank again, then sat back against the wall, trying to think. Quite clearly she had done something wrong, but it was hard to be sure exactly what. The watchmen seemed to have resented her challenge, and rather than simply ravishing her for her insolence, as any normal male would have done, they had treated her with an odd mixture of contempt and respect, more as if she'd been a dangerous animal than a girl. Then there was Taepenk, who not unreasonably objected to disturbance in his tavern, but also seemed to resent her making herself available for sex, despite her offer to him. Possibly he, like Kantch the carpenter, preferred boys, otherwise it made no sense.

On the ship Aeisla had lectured them about the different customs of the Oreteans, as had Captain Baltrank. She had paid little attention, assuming that aside from differences in the laws, people would behave much as they always did. Evidently this was not the case, and her apprehension grew sharper as she realised that she had absolutely no idea what to expect. In Aegerion, any rowdy girl who challenged two guards could expect to be laughed at, roundly fucked and then left. Certainly she would not be thrown in a cell, although persistent offenders had been known to be put in the pillory where their excess wantonness could be taken out of them. In Staive Cintes she had been thrown in a cell, and might await anything – whipping, tattooing, dunging, some other, less familiar punishment.

She was still trying to tell herself that whatever her crimes they could hardly be serious enough to warrant a sentence of death when she heard footsteps and voices. Two watchmen appeared, one carrying a net, the other a trident. Iriel stood, doing her best to hold a dignified pose as the door was unlocked, both men eyeing her warily.

'There will be no need for a net,' she stated.

The answer was a sceptical grunt from the man with the trident as he entered the cell, crouched low, his eyes on her face. Iriel stayed still. The netman entered, scuttling crabwise to one side, his face set in concentration, his tongue protruding from one corner of his mouth. He threw the net, engulfing her, yet keeping a cord in hand, which he pulled tight, trapping her knees. Iriel squealed, nearly losing her balance, then again as the man with the trident prodded her bottom, ordering her out.

She went, led by the cord with the trident man behind her providing an occasional prod of encouragement. The passage was dim, and lined with cells much like her own, some empty, some with occupants, sullen or raucous, one or two pleading with the watchmen, more hurling insults or making obscene suggestions. All were ignored, Iriel being taken past and up one flight of steps, then another, to a wider corridor in which a number of people were gathered, watchmen, some typical Oreteans in their loose trousers and open jackets, others in elaborate robes. A few spared her curious glances, nothing more. She was taken to a bench and sat down between the watchmen, still confined in her net and wishing she had tried to use the pot in her cell.

Time passed, people came and went, often through a pair of tall, elaborately carved doors some way down the passage. Twice she attempted to make conversation, but one watchman would answer only with surly grunts, the other not at all. When her bladder began to hurt she asked to be allowed to pee, but was met with a snort of contempt. Finally a man signalled them and she was led towards the double doors.

Within was a high chamber, unfurnished but for a dais at one end on which rested a high-backed chair painted in green and gold. In it sat an elderly man in an emerald rode, his hands folded in his lap. Another man, also elderly but bald and in a robe edged with green, stood beside the chair, a sheaf of charta in one hand. Four watchmen stood around the dais, big men by

Oretean standards, each with rings on the sleeves of his tunic and armed with a sword. The halls of highborn Aeg families looked similar, and Iriel attempted a curtsey, sure that she was in the presence of the head of the House Eriedes. He gave her a glance of mild curiosity. The bald man spoke.

'This is the girl Iriel, Justice, one of the barbarians newly arrived on the carrack *Gull of Cintes*.'

The seated man frowned, then spoke.

'Why did you not come to Oxtan's Yard, girl?'

'I . . . I meant to,' Iriel answered. 'I wished to eat and drink first.'

'Why not at the yard? No matter. I am Eriedes Ghaidus, Justice here in Staive Cintes. As you are of foreign race, Iriel, and also barbarian, I am inclined to leniency. There was a disturbance of some kind, so I believe?'

His manner was mild and Iriel felt a touch of relief, only for it to die as the bald man spoke.

'The charges are severe, Justice. Both Twelveman Cound and Madame Hivies call for the full penalties of law.'

'What has Madame Hivies to do with this?' the Justice queried. 'There was a brawl, as I understood it?'

'Just so, Justice, but the watch were called as this girl whored in the piss house at Taepenk's. It later proved she had not registered, nor so much as approached Madame Hivies.'

'Indeed? What then are the full charges?'

The bald man cleared his throat and held up a piece of charta.

'The girl Iriel, an Aeg, is charged by Madame Hivies thus: the first, failure to register with the Association of Whores, thus the second, unlicensed whoring. The third, whoring in unlicensed premises, to wit, House Taepenk. The fourth, failure to charge Association rates. The fifth, failure to pay panderage. The sixth, failure to comply with the new panderage rate, the two-thirds take as established for new whores. We then come to those charges made by Twelveman Cound. The first, resistance to lawful arrest. The second, grievous battery to the persons of two watchmen.'

'Serious indeed,' the Justice stated. 'Do you have anything to say for yourself, Iriel?'

For a moment Iriel could only gape, then she found her voice.

'I am not a whore!'

'You deny you took money for the erotic use of your body?' he demanded. 'Be careful what you say, Iriel, there were witnesses, specifically, Yoides, brother to Clerk Loumank here.'

'Just so,' Loumank confirmed.

'No,' Iriel stated, 'I do not deny that ... that I fucked. I deny that I am a whore.'

'You are married, then?' Loumank queried, now with a laugh in his voice. 'Certainly you are not married to five men!'

'You are not a slave?' the Justice queried.

'No!' Iriel responded in outrage.

The Justice laughed. Iriel, blushing furiously and entirely confused, struggled to choose her words.

'No, Lord Justice ... no, I am not married, nor am I a slave. I ... was a little drunk. They teased me into fucking, these five, but I took no money. In Aegmund this is not our custom.'

'You are claiming that you allowed five men the use of your body and took no money?' the Justice demanded in disbelief.

'Yes,' Iriel answered.

'This is a self-evident lie!' Loumank scoffed. 'She is unmarried, yet free and she fucked with five men. Therefore she is a whore.'

'To deny taking the money will avail you nothing, Iriel,' the Justice went on. 'Indeed, the opposite. Loumank?'

'I would need to consult Madame Hivies,' Loumank answered, 'but I would anticipate further charges, an aggravation of her failure to charge Association rates at the least.'

'I did not take any money,' Iriel said weakly.

Her bladder hurt badly, and she felt as if she was about to cry through sheer frustration. Steeling herself, she spoke again.

'Lord Justice. I have broken the laws of your city, this I understand. I challenged the watchmen, yes, but in the expectation of being overcome, unaware that they would be so weak and so slow. I took the five men into me also, but I asked no payment and I am not a whore. I do not even fully understand the term. I submit myself to your judgement, but beg leniency for my circumstances.'

'A brave speech,' the Justice answered, 'and yes, I can see that your ignorance –'

'Neither ignorance nor stupidity are valid pleas, Justice,' Loumank put in.

'Indeed not,' the Justice agreed, 'yet I believe I retain my right to seek a balanced judgement?'

'Just so,' Loumank answered quickly.

'Then I shall do so. What do Madame Hivies and Twelveman Cound demand?'

Again Loumank cleared his throat before he began to read.

'So that the accused may answer for the six charges brought by Madame Hivies, application is made for a fine of ten times the illicit earnings and to serve in the House of Cunt for one week at full take, thereafter at three-quarter take until such time as Madame Hivies judges her crimes to have been absolved. Also to be whipped. For those charges brought by Twelveman Cound, application is made that she be scourged, branded and suspended in a cage over the citadel gates, this last to serve as an example to others who seek to challenge civic authority. He also recommends that she be sold into slavery, thus preventing further nuisance, or else hung.'

Iriel wet herself, her bladder bursting to spray urine into her drawers. She barely noticed the hot fluid running down her legs and into her boots, ignored as she stared, mouth wide, at Loumank. For a long moment there was silence, broken only by the faint pattering of Iriel's piddle on the floor, then the Justice spoke.

'Twelveman Cound must learn to ameliorate his demands, also to fit them to those of his seniors. How is she to serve in the House of Cunt while suspended in a cage, much less hung? No, his demands are excessive. Madame Hivies, by contrast, seems reasonable save in attempting to take the mantle of judgement on her own shoulders. What is the exact sum demanded as fine?'

'Five men at exotic rate and free positioning of whore, thus nine marks of copper, by fivefold and tenfold,' Loumank stated. 'Thus in total, thirty-seven silver Marks, six copper.'

'Do you have this sum, Iriel?' the Justice queried.

Iriel's answer was a weak sob. With the realisation that she was not to be hung or sold the shame of wetting herself had sunk in, creating a lump in her throat too big to allow her to swallow. She had finished, but her puddle had spread beneath her, sending a trickle of yellow fluid out from under her skirts and across the floor.

'Speak up, girl!' Loumank demanded.

'I have my pay,' Iriel managed, miserably.

'Hardly enough,' Loumank sniffed. 'What, on a trader? Six coppers a day at best, for a month, so fifteen silver Marks at most.'

'More, I think,' Iriel sniffed. 'I have one gold piece, six silver.'

'Eighteen silver then,' Loumank said.

Iriel hung her head, defeated, watching downcast and struggling to hold back tears as a long ribbon of golden-coloured pee snaked out towards the dais. The Justice chuckled, then spoke again.

'Thus and so, I judge that Iriel be sent to the House of Cunt, where she is to register as a whore. For one week she will work at full rate to the House but be provided food and shelter, thus settling her debt to Madame Hivies. She is to be treated no more cruelly than her behaviour demands. She is also fined thirty silver Marks to the civic authority, the balance above what she owes to be made up as seems appropriate.'

'I . . . I am to be made a whore?' Iriel asked.

'You are already a whore,' the Justice answered, 'as are all women who take men into themselves outside of sacred union.'

'No,' she managed. 'How can I be punished so cruelly, for falling victim to a lewd trick?'

'Punishment?' the Justice queried. 'That is not your punishment, but merely the means of your recompense to those you have wronged, and so that you may pay for the dispensation of justice to you.'

'Pay?' Iriel asked. 'I must pay to be judged and sentenced?'

'Certainly,' the Justice replied. 'Who else would pay? The civic authority? The House Eriedes? Clerk Loumank, perhaps?'

He finished with a chuckle, then went on.

'As to your punishment, Madame Hivies may have you whipped, but Twelveman Cound's demands are excessive. I judge that you be branded, and in the Watchhouse yard to answer Twelveman Cound's desire for an example, but not until you have served your week in the House of Cunt. It is done.'

'Done?' Iriel demanded, her anger rising abruptly. 'To be made a whore, to have my body marked as shamed? I am lowborn! It is my right to fuck, and if you were men you would fuck me here and now, as you should have last night! Cowards! Weaklings!'

'Silence!' Loumank snapped. 'The Justice has been most lenient. For the same crimes, any woman of Staive Cintes could have expected a week in the cage, branding and slavery at the least. Your humble thanks would be appropriate.'

Iriel didn't answer, struggling in the net. A sharp prod of the trident in the flesh of her bottom made her cry out, but in anger, only for the other watchman to duck down, pick her up and haul her across his shoulder. Still wriggling furiously, she was carried from the chamber, catching Loumank's disgusted demand for a mop to be brought an instant before the doors swung shut.

Slowly her anger gave way to humiliation and fear as she was carried down the wide corridor to another room, this time smaller and with a single wizened man in a green-bordered robe seated behind a desk. He looked up, first in annoyance, then surprise as the watchman dumped Iriel on her bottom.

'They are heavy, these outlander girls,' the watchman stated. 'Thirty silver Marks, this one. She has eighteen, I believe.'

'Then how am I to make up the remaining twelve?' the clerk demanded.

'She is to work for Madame Hivies,' the watchman said. 'Once she has worked off her debt, you may collect the balance. This is not my concern.'

'But it is mine! No, I cannot forever be adjusting my books to cope with vagrants. What of jewellery?'

'I have none,' Iriel admitted sullenly.

'Ha! And that dress will fetch nothing whatever. What is it, sacking?'

'Mundic cloth!' Iriel answered him. 'It cost a half-Thalar!'

'Worthless. What is that you have beneath it?'

'My petticoat.'

'Show me.'

A watchman ducked down to pull up the hem of Iriel's dress, exposing her petticoat.

'Silk,' he stated, 'coarse but heavy.'

'Get it off her.'

Iriel gave a squeak of protest, but the watchman already had a firm grip on her petticoat and simply upended her, only to have the garment stick where the net had been pulled tight immediately above her knees. The other watchman moved close and put the trident to her throat. She held still, trembling with fear and shame as the net was loosened. Her dress fell to expose her underwear, the petticoat was hauled roughly off, revealing her drawers, which followed, leaving her bare from the waist down but for her shoes, her bottom and tuppenny flaunted for all to see. The clerk took the clothes, inspecting them as the net was once more tightened around Iriel's knees.

'Unusual,' he stated, 'and worth maybe five silvers refashioned, less the cost of work. Why are they wet?'

'She peed in them,' a watchman stated.

The clerk gave a single disgusted snort.

'What else?'

'I have nothing!' Iriel protested.

'Her hair?' a watchman suggested. 'It is fine, and the strangest colour, like new copper.'

'Not my hair, please!' Iriel wailed.

'Who would wish a wig the colour of copper?' the clerk demanded. 'Save Madame Hivies perhaps.'

'She is going to Madame Hivies anyway,' the other watchman answered, 'who would not thank you for shearing her new whore.'

'Madame Hivies' opinion is of no consequence,' the clerk answered. 'My seven silvers are. Cut it, and I'll mark it at the price. Perhaps a puppeteer will take it, or a harlequin.'

'No, please!' Iriel begged, trying to squirm away across the floor, but one watchman was already drawing his sword as the other put his trident to her neck again.

'Stay still,' he demanded.

She obeyed, now shaking hard as the swordsman began to tug her hair through the net, and still babbling pleas as her head was pulled up and a long hank cut free, most of her hair, to leave the remainder in a ragged halo around her head. Twisting what he had cut off into a knot, the watchman passed it to the clerk, who made a note in his ledger. Iriel had begun to cry, but forced the tears back.

A hand and a carefully placed boot helped her to her feet and she was led from the room, no longer resisting, following meekly with little awkward steps only as long as the tightly fastened net allowed. Her head hung in misery, her vision blurred with unshed tears, she tried not to think of her ruined hair and how foolish she would look, or of her naked body beneath the tattered dress.

Outside the citadel was brilliant sunlight and stifling heat. Again she had to struggle not to cry openly as she was led down the same long street she had walked free only the evening before, and to a two-storey house within a whitewashed compound halfway down the hill. A fat guard lazed in the sun at the arched entrance. He acknowledged the watchmen with a lazy salute and she was led through, into a garden, shaded by palms and with a fountain at the centre, a fountain in which the water spurted from the open pee-hole of a rolled-up girl. She was cast in bronze, her ankles tied behind her head, her metal face set in an expression of agonised shame.

Iriel thought of how she'd wet herself in the judgement chamber and suddenly it was too much. She burst into tears, great racking sobs that shook her whole body. Her vision dissolved in a haze and she slumped down, only to be pulled sharply up by the cord with which she had been led.

'Your new whore, Madame Hivies,' one of the watchmen stated, his voice respectful. 'Stand straight, girl. Show yourself.'

Iriel paid no attention, her head hung, tears streaming down her face and dripping from the mesh of her net. She caught a low, cruel chuckle, then a voice, rich and female.

'So I see. Justice Ghaidus granted my application, then?'

'Not in full, Madame,' the watchman answered. 'She is yours, for whipping and for discharge of her debt to you, so long as it takes no more than a week. She is then to be taken to the Watchhouse for public branding, after which you are to allow her standard terms.'

Madame Hivies grunted but made no objection, walking slowly around Iriel before speaking again.

'Fair,' she stated. 'Exotic, certainly. Why is her hair like this? The others wear it long or in elaborate braids.'

'Clerk Mendes had it cut and took it as part payment of her civic fine,' the watchman explained.

'Wretched little man,' she responded, 'still, it adds to her wild look. All the others refuse to work for me, but demand for this one will be all the higher for that. Take her out of the net.'

'It is best to keep her in restraint, Madame,' a watchman began, only to be cut off.

'Don't you think I know how to handle girls?' Madame Hivies stated. 'You men, you have no idea, but you will see, when she comes to the Watchhouse for branding she'll be meek enough.'

'Yet still . . .' the watchman cautioned, but began to undo Iriel's net as his companion stood back with his trident ready. Madame Hivies laughed.

'Pitiable! Call yourselves men! She is a girl, for all her size!'

'She felled two good men.'

'Listen, girl,' Madame Hivies said as the net was lifted over Iriel's head. 'Disobey me and I will have you tied and your cunt stuffed with crushed pimento. Now, will you behave?'

74

Iriel didn't answer, not understanding except that the punishment was certain to be painful, but sure that she should fight, no matter the cost. Yet her hands were still tied, and she made no attempt, hanging her head meekly in mock acceptance instead. Madame Hives had come to stand in front of her again, a dumpy woman obviously once beautiful, now soft and lined with age. Her hair was lacquered and pinned, her body hidden beneath a flowing robe of golden silk. In one hand she held a small and supple whip, similar to a dog quirt.

'You see, simple,' Madame Hivies laughed. 'But leave her hands and I shall show you another trick for difficult girls, one you'll have seen played upon the debtors in the slave market maybe. Hundact, show her off.'

The fat guard came away from the arch to duck down and take the hem of Iriel's dress. An instant later it had been hauled high, forcing her arms up, and bunched above her head, leaving her nude below her waist and with only the sorry remains of her chemise to cover her breasts. Then her laces had been twitched open and they too were bare, heavy and blatant on her chest, but no more so than her bottom and tuppenny. Madame Hivies laughed as Iriel began to squirm in the shame of her exposure. A small, soft hand closed on one of Iriel's breasts. She jumped, then squeaked as her nipple was given a firm pinch to bring it erect.

'Firm, responsive too,' Madame Hivies remarked, 'and never have I seen such a large pair on a girl so young. I had expected them to droop more. They will sell, no doubt.'

Iriel tried to wriggle away, just as Madame Hivies let go, making her breasts bounce and quiver. The urge to kick out was strong, but the guard had her dress tight in his grip and she knew she would only end up making herself look foolish as she danced to the dog quirt.

A hand touched her belly and her stomach jumped. Again she tried to back away, realising the woman's intent, only to have the fat guard's knee pushed firmly between her buttocks, forcing her to stick her belly out even as a podgy finger invaded her tuppenny. She gasped, unable to choke the sound back, and again as a thumb settled among the folds of her sex, rubbing on her bump. Unable to help herself, she began to squirm on Madame Hivies' hand, fighting to stop her body reacting as she was casually, methodically, masturbated.

Her orgasm took only moments to come, rising up against every effort of her willpower, to leave her tuppenny tightening against the woman's hand and her bottom cheeks squeezing against the fat guard's knee. All three men laughed to see her reach climax so easily. She heard other laughter, both male and female, evidently girls and their clients watching from the upper storey of the house. Madame Hivies finished and she was left sobbing and shaking, the juice from her tuppenny running liberally down between her thighs.

'Good,' Madame Hivies continued. 'Yes, she will sell. Move your knee, Hundact, I wish to see her bottom. Yes, big certainly, fleshy, but firm and in good proportion.'

She had taken hold of Iriel's bottom, kneading, then pinching, delivering a firm slap, then abruptly pulling the cheeks wide. Iriel squeaked again as her bottom ring was put on show, her shame burning in her head as she was inspected from behind.

'No virgin behind, I think, a pity,' Madame Hivies stated.

She let go of Iriel's cheeks, only to slip a finger between, then push it suddenly up, into the cavity beyond. Again Iriel squealed in shock and humiliation.

'No, definitely no virgin,' Madame Hivies went on, casually fingering Iriel's bottom ring. 'Yet tight enough. Release her, Hundact, but keep her dress up at the rear.'

Iriel's dress was dropped away from her head but remained held up at the back, showing her bottom. She found herself in bright sunlight once more, her cheeks twitching in anticipation of what she was sure was coming, her whipping. As she had guessed, several people were looking down from the windows around the compound, small, yellow-skinned girls mostly, two with skins of a mid-brown, one a peculiar blue-black tone. All were naked, little breasts hanging over the windowsills, and all were heavily made-up, their nipples, lips and cheeks rouged, their eyes heavy with kohl and coloured grease, their hair elaborately coiled and set with gauze and beads, to create an impression of overwhelming lewdness. There were men, too, unremarkable Oreteans save for being stark naked.

Blushing furiously, she looked down at the ground. They had seen her stripped, her breasts fondled, her tuppenny and bottom ring penetrated, by a woman. The shame of it was a physical pain, and her head was full of voices, urging her to fight, to do anything but accept her humiliation in meekness. She tried to fight it, telling herself it was useless with her hands tied and three armed men against her.

'What is your name, girl?' Madame Hivies asked.

'Iriel.'

Immediately the dog quirt lashed out, catching Iriel full across her bottom. She gasped in pain, tensing her cheeks against the second stroke. It never came.

'You name,' Madame Hivies stated, 'is . . . is Coppertop, a little play on words your clients will appreciate and you should know. A coppertop is the crude word for a man's erect cock, when the head pokes up through the foreskin. Now, what is your name?'

'C – Co –,' Iriel managed, voices screaming into her head.

She gave way, one leg lashing out to catch Madame Hivies in the midriff and send her staggering back into the fountain, where she lay dashed, the water from the statue's pee-hole running down her front. Iriel twisted and ducked at the same time, dodging the thrown net, then kicked again, knocking the fat guard's legs from beneath him. The watchman's trident prodded out at her even as he blew a frantic double note on his whistle, but she fell back, grappling the shaft with her legs to jerk it from his grasp. Immediately she was on it, struggling to grip it with her bound hands, only to be forced to roll as the net was cast again, up against the fat guard, who swung his great flabby buttocks over her face even as the others grabbed her kicking legs. An instant later she was pinned helpless.

Iriel hung nude in the whipping frame. Not a stroke had been delivered, yet her body was a mass of pain. Bent double across one of the iron rods that composed her prison, her legs dangled down at one side, her body at the other. Her arms were behind her back, pulled high above her to leave much of the weight of her body on her tightly bound wrists, a chain leading up from the binding to the highest member of the frame. Her head hung low, her inverted position sending the blood to her head to leave her dizzy. Her breasts hung too, moving sluggishly beneath her body to the agonising jumping of her muscles that had begun shortly after she was strapped up. Even her legs hurt, stretched wide and tied to the sides of the frame, to leave her bottom high and flaunted, completely vulnerable, with every detail of her tuppenny and bottom ring on plain show.

Yet the pain of her body was minor to the agonising burning in her tuppenny. She had been stuffed with pimentos as threatened, little red fruit the juice of which burned with a crazy, stinging pain that had brought her onto the most desperate heat of her life, pure pain blended with a need to have her hole fucked that went far beyond pleasure. Her nipples burned too, and the skin of her breasts, where the woman who had pulped the pimentos in front of Iriel's face had wiped her hands. The pimentos had been put up her with a forcing stick, packed up into her hole as if stuffing a chicken.

All of it had been done in front of an audience, the frame constructed on the flat roof of the House of Cunt. Iriel had been led out in the chains she had worn for a day, stripped naked, lifted onto the frame, her legs and arms adjusted to ensure the complete destruction of her modesty. She had been left for a while, to let her pain build and the crowd gather, with the brothel guards ringing bells and calling out for the populace to come and see her punished. Then, with maybe three hundred people gaping at her naked body, she had been stuffed.

The crowd were in festival mood, laughing and jeering, calling out obscene suggestions and observing the mixture of white girl-juice and red pimento dripping from her bulging hole and running down over her sex lips and the little bump between. Others remarked on the slow pulsing of her bottom ring from when a pimento-smeared finger had been briefly pushed up into her rectum, still others on the size of her breasts and nipples, the length of her legs, the size of her bottom.

It hurt so much she could barely think, and her resolve not to cry had broken even as the forcing stick worked in her hole. Now her eyes were blind with tears, yet still she could hear, every crude comment, every intimate remark adding to the shame and misery that burned in her mind with no less force than the physical agonies of her body. Even the cries of the street vendors selling spiced pastries, drinks and fruit seemed personal insults.

Not one person had shown sympathy, only lust, amusement or cruelty, and now, as Madame Hivies herself climbed from the open stair which gave access to the roof, a soft, expectant hush fell over the crowd. Iriel shut her eyes tight; frightened, small and vulnerable as their lewd delight in her pain and degradation seemed to wash over her. Not one voice was raised in protest, the women as eager as the men, and as her persecutor stepped close, Iriel learned what it meant to be utterly alone.

'A pleasure to see such a fine crowd,' Madame Hivies remarked happily. 'Welcome all, especially my customers.'

A ripple of laughter spread through the crowd. A few remarks and jokes were exchanged at the expense of those men known to frequent the House. Madame Hivies reached out to tousle Iriel's hair, then went on.

'For the benefit of those few who do not already know, this red-haired barbarian slut is to be my new whore. Before she is put to work, she needs to learn a little respect, a lesson I now intend to begin, but which you, my friends, must bring to conclusion. For the next week she will be available to all, at half Association rates and in any position your inventive little minds can think up; cunt, mouth and arse.'

A murmur of appreciation ran through the crowd, which began to shift, eager men pushing towards the arch in which one of the senior girls sat with a ledger, taking bookings. Madame Hivies responded with a beneficent smile, then pulled her dog quirt from the broad sash of scarlet silk at her waist.

'Thank you, my friends,' she called, 'and now, while she is nicely warm, I shall begin, both to punish her, and to teach her something of her own nature.'

The crowd responded with laughter and further obscene suggestions, demanding that Iriel be made to come, to suck cock while she was whipped, made to beg for her strokes, take the punishment with a marrow inserted in her anus, and more, many impossible, all both painful and humiliating. Madame Hivies listened for a while, then raised her hands for silence.

'Worthy suggestions all, my friends, and yes, why should we not add a little spice? After all, she must be taught that her sole use is for your amusement. Hundact.'

The fat guard who had helped subdue Iriel and also hung her up on the frame lumbered forwards, to bow to Madame Hivies.

'Put your cock in her mouth,' she ordered, 'that she may suck you while she is whipped. Vea, another pimento, and be sure to break the skin. Put it in her anus.'

The woman who had stuffed Iriel gave a little bow and scampered down from the roof level. Iriel hung still, praying for strength and that the whipping would begin to end the torture of waiting. Hundact came close, to pull a set of huge and dirty genitals over the top of his trousers. Climbing on the frame, he pushed the fleshy mass against Iriel's face, to the delighted cries of the crowd.

'Suck it, slut,' he demanded.

Iriel resisted, pulling back from the rubbery mass of cock and scrotum, only to have it pressed more firmly still against her face. Hundact reached down, to hold her nose tight between forefinger and thumb. Still Iriel resisted, fighting to keep her pride until it seemed that her lungs would burst, but breaking at last, to gasp in air, and Hundact's cock as it was forced roughly into her mouth. The crowd cheered and clapped as her mouth filled with the taste of sweat and stale jism.

She struggled not to suck, but the natural urge was there, and as once more his fingers closed on her nose she gave in, mouthing on the thick penis that had already begun to swell. The crowd saw, and biting shame hit her as new and louder laughter rose up from around her. Hundact gave a pleased grunt and began to fuck her mouth, even as something slim and smooth was fed into her already smarting anus, the pimento. It began to burn immediately, the same hot pain she had felt in her tuppenny when first stuffed, and in moments she was gasping on Hundact's cock.

'She is learning,' Madame Hivies commented. 'Not fast, but she is learning.'

81

Hundact grunted and took Iriel firmly by the hair to control the motion of her mouth on his cock.

'Come when I say, not before,' Madame Hivies instructed, and lashed the quirt in.

Instantly a line of raw fire sprang up across Iriel's flaunted bottom cheeks. Her eyes popped wide, her legs kicked against her restraints and she tried to scream, only to gag on Hundact's penis. Clapping and laughter rose up from the crowd, calls for harder strokes and shouts of 'One!'

Again Madame Hivies struck, and again Iriel jerked to the sudden pain, and again, and again. The crowd were yelling out the count in pure glee as Iriel's entire world dissolved in miserable agony. Her whole body was in spasm, her muscles jumping to each stroke to spread the pain of the cuts from her blazing buttocks along her every nerve, stroke after stroke, with Hundact driving his now erect cock into her throat at each one.

In moments she was blubbering, tears spurting from her eyes and running free down her cheeks, spittle dribbling out around the big cock pumping between her lips, mucus bubbling from her nose, only to be fed back into her mouth with Hundact's pushes. Her breasts were bouncing, agonisingly heavy under her chest, her bottom cheeks twitching, closing and spreading, her anus and cunt pulsing on the burning pimentos.

Still the crowd counted, yelling out in unison to each whip stroke and cock thrust – ten, eleven, twelve – as Iriel writhed and jerked in an unbearable agony she could do nothing to escape. Then her bladder burst, urine spraying out behind her in a high arc from her tormented cunt, to patter down on the roof and draw delighted laughter from the crowd.

Madame Hivies didn't even break her rhythm, laying the strokes in hard across Iriel's buttocks even as the thick, golden urine stream sprayed and splashed – thirteen, fourteen, fifteen, sixteen. Still the piddle came, breaking on the whip lash to spatter Iriel's bottom and legs, stinging in her welts to bring her fresh agony, spreading the pain of the pimentos down her inner thighs and up into the crease of her bottom.

Still the horrible dog quirt lashed in – seventeen, eighteen, nineteen – as Iriel's pee stream died to spurts, one to each cut of the whip and contraction of her burning cunt. Hundact took her breasts, squeezing them hard as he fucked her head, now grunting in passion, braced hard against the frame and her tormented body. Vaguely Iriel heard Madame Hivies bark an order, but the whipping never stopped – twenty, twenty-one, twenty-two – the crowd chanting loud in her ears as Vea clambered onto the frame.

The whore's fingers found Iriel's tuppenny folds and a roar of laughter rose from the crowd. Even through her all-embracing pain Iriel realised what was to be done to her – she was to be masturbated as she was whipped, made to come during beating. Her shame and self-pity hit a new level, yet even as Vea's fingers began to rub she knew she was lost.

Still the whip strokes came in, delivered with all Madame Hivies' strength, only now Iriel's pain was blended with a helpless ecstasy as the contractions of her cunt grew stronger, faster, more rhythmic. Again Madame Hivies called out an order and immediately Hundact began to push harder and deeper still, jamming the head of his penis deep into Iriel's windpipe. She started to gag, and to come, the muscles of her body straining against each other, in agony, and still the whip strokes came in.

The orgasm hit her, the muscles of her belly and bottom contracting hard at the exact moment Hundact filled her throat with hot jism. An instant later it was spurting from her nose, gush after gush, mixed with mucus and spittle, then sick as her stomach revolted. Still Hundact fucked her mouth and still she came, unable to stop herself under the agile fiddling of Vea's fingers.

Hoots of derisive laughter rose from the crowd as Iriel's body jerked in helpless spasms, climax after climax tearing through her, even as her buttocks jumped to the whip strokes and her sick bubbled out over Hundact's cock and balls. Helpless, her body reacting by instinct alone, images of herself tied and whipped and sucking cock burned in her mind, unbearable shame and unbearable ecstasy.

A final peak hit her as Hundact pulled his cock from her mouth. She screamed, all her sensations coming together in one final crescendo and it was done, her senses swimming, the last few strokes cutting into her bottom before her cunt closed, squashing out the mass of pimento pulp within, to fall to the roof with a squashy sound. Iriel hung limp.

The brilliant Oretean sunlight struck in through the window of Iriel's room in the House of Cunt. She lay on the bed, exhausted, indifferent to her nudity, the slim silver collar by which she was chained to the wall, even the jism bubbling slowly from her gaping tuppenny.

In the course of the morning she had been visited by 47 men. Nearly all had fucked her. Most had also used her mouth. Several had penetrated her bottom. A few had used all three orifices, and sometimes in an order that had left her mouth tasting of jism, earth and her own juices, a flavour that even the bowl of highly spiced stew she had been served for lunch had done little to dispel.

It was the second day of her confinement. Her whipping had been on the first, and once her hurt and bedraggled body had been released from the frame she had been bathed, washed, chained by the neck and left to rest, face down on a crude bed. Vea had given her an evening meal of stew and rice, also a draught of some heady wine, spiced and drugged to make her sleep.

She had woken to the light of dawn, her body still stiff and her buttocks smarting from her welts. It had made no difference to Madame Hivies, with men already queuing for Iriel's use on their way to their daily tasks. Still too groggy and dazed to resist, she had been dressed in a ridiculous parody of Aeg costume, made of uncured leather and held together with thongs.

Her resolution to fight had lasted until the fourth group of men had been let in to her chamber. In each case they had taken turns to fuck her while the others held her down, yet not one had escaped without bites and scratches. Finally her arousal at being ravished and at the way the men jostled to go first had overcome her resistance. The fifth set of men had found her willing, the sixth and seventh wanton.

By then she had been nude and tired, her nipples aching, her jaw aching, her tuppenny as sore as her welted bottom, her anal ring flaccid and bruised, both holes and her mouth running with sperm, also her nose, her belly and the valley between her breasts. Men had come in her face, her hair, her bottom crease, her belly button. She had been made to adopt obscene poses, to suck her own breasts, to masturbate, to finger her anus, to suck cocks that had been up her bottom.

Still it had not finished, group after group being admitted to her room, each man determined to get his money's worth out of her ravaged body, not one caring in the least for the state she was in. Only an hour before had it stopped, and then because the House of Cunt shut for food and to give the girls a chance to put everything in order. Iriel had eaten, and was praying softly that she would be given the full hour to rest before the lunchtime rush she had been told to expect, yet already she could hear the excited conversation from the queue in the street beneath her window.

For what seemed an age she lay still, her mind barely focused, not even bothering to move her bottom out of the pool of jism and juice beneath her. Vea had given her a perfunctory wash, but no more, commenting that it made little difference with so many men still to serve. Iriel barely heard and cared less, thinking only of the endless procession of cocks she had attended to, and which now seemed to march in columns through her mind.

The bead hanging that blocked off her room rustled and she looked up with a groan. Men were pushing into the room, one squat and as fat as butter, a second beefy with youth and vigour, the third and fourth the brothers, Yoides and Loumank the clerk. None bothered to acknowledge her, merely setting about her body, the fat man in her mouth, Loumank between her thighs, the others masturbating as they watched.

They used her thoroughly, laughing and joking among themselves all the while, but never once addressing her save to order some new position or action. She was made to suck all four cocks, Loumank's after he had come in her tuppenny. She was made to masturbate in the clerk's jism while the fat man fucked her breasts. She was fucked two-in-one, squatting over Yoides while the young man drove his short, thick penis in and out of her bottom ring, entering the aching little hole repeatedly and then milking his jism into her open rectum. Yoides came last, pulling his cock from her tuppenny, poking it briefly up her slimy bottom ring, then finishing off in her mouth to leave her gagging on dirty sperm. They left, joking and complimenting one another on their performance.

Again Iriel collapsed back onto the filthy bed, only for the curtain to rustle once more. She choked back a sob, lifting her head with an effort to see yet another group of men, but ones she recognised, Captain Baltrank and the Navigator, Steithes. Both were grinning and their trousers showed distinct bulges.

'You also?' she croaked.

'Certainly,' Baltrank answered. 'Would I insult you by not paying a visit? Indeed, we would have come earlier, but by first light there was already a queue halfway around the compound. I must remark that you are somewhat soiled.'

'Fifty men have had me, more perhaps,' Iriel managed. 'I . . . I can barely –'

'This is the lot of the whore,' Steithes remarked, 'still, console yourself in that your overwhelming popularity is bound to wane a little once the novelty has worn off and the price returned to normal. By and large, I feel you have made the right choice.'

'Choice?' Iriel answered feebly. 'I have no choice! I am chained by the neck to prevent my escape!'

'The chain is real?' Baltrank queried. 'I thought it part of this "captured barbarian" fancy Madame Hivies has thought up, along with your clothes.'

He had picked up the badly soiled remains of Iriel's leather dress and was inspecting it.

'It is real,' Iriel answered him. 'I have been taken, imprisoned, robbed of my money, made a whore, whipped and chained here for fucking, all because Luides and his friends played a cruel trick on me.'

'I know nothing of this,' Baltrank answered in surprise. 'I had heard you were here, yes, and of your whipping. I thought it a ploy to raise interest. Prior to that I was seeing to the sale of our nymphs at the caravanserai, so have heard little. You did not choose to become a whore, then?'

'No!' Iriel wailed. 'Luides tricked me into fucking. When the guard came I fought. I was arrested, tried, sentenced, brought here, whipped and chained up like this!'

'I shall have Luides whipped himself,' Baltrank assured her. 'Now –'

'Leave Luides alone,' Iriel broke in. 'What of my friends? Do they not know?'

'By no means,' he answered. 'Kaissia, Aeisla and Cianna have been with us, extolling the virtues of Aegmund nymphs. We received five hundred gold Marks for the cargo, a fine price. Yi, I do not know, save that at Oxtan's Yard she was speaking with the stablemen from House Eriedes. Perhaps she has taken employment'

'Get word to Aeisla, please?' Iriel begged.

'To what purpose?' Steithes demanded. 'You are a registered whore, a place many would envy. Do not fret, the worst will soon be over and you will laugh to remember how sore you were. Who knows, one day you may have your own brothel!'

'You do not understand,' Iriel said miserably. 'My ancestors cry out against this, not for the fuckings, but for the shame of having my body sold as if I were a goat or pig, and worse, my coming branding.'

'Branding?'

'I am to be branded, in the Watchhouse yard, when my first week is done. For an Aeg, any Aeg, branding is the final shame, reserved for those whose sins damn them utterly!'

Baltrank shrugged, then spoke. 'The pain will pass, that is the only consolation I can offer, other than to have Luides soundly whipped. As to your other concerns, this is Oretea, you need not worry for things shameful in Aegmund, any more than Kaissia.'

'Say I am here, at the least?' Iriel pleaded.

'Certainly,' he answered, 'but I shall also advise prudence. There is to be no disturbance here. Now, enough talk, we have paid for your body not conversation. Steithes, I wish to see if she sucks as well as Kaissia, you may have her cunt first.'

Steithes nodded and freed his cock, then hauled Iriel's legs high to get at her tuppenny as Baltrank fed his own cock into her mouth. In a state of miserable resignation, she began to suck.

* * *

One day merged with the next, an endless round of men and cocks, Iriel used over and over, in every hole. Only occasionally were there breaks, just long enough to allow her to recover a little. Even when she grew too sore to be used she was put out in a different room for the specialist customers, men, and even women. Unlike the barely furnished fucking cubicles, it contained several curious pieces of apparatus. There was a big pot of heavy glass into which she was obliged to urinate while being watched, a glass-topped table for a similar and yet ruder function, a system of traces into which she could be fastened and made to crawl around the compound with her client drawn behind her in a little cart, even a device like an enormous set of tongs with which the interior of her body cavities could be inspected. All were used more than once.

Her fear grew day by day, yet although she was constantly obedient, her collar and chain were never removed, and three guards invariably accompanied her at those times she was not securely fastened to the wall. Even while towing the cart Hundact walked with her. She had also been forbidden to speak to the other girls, who shied away in fear of Madame Hivies' quirt at her attempts to talk, leaving her feeling more isolated and vulnerable than ever.

At last the day came, Iriel waking from her drugged sleep not to the sound of men queuing for the use of her body, but to Hundact winding a length of tough cord around her wrists. She was bound before she could clear the fog from her head, and her ankles followed her wrists – despite her best attempts to kick him – not bound tight, but hobbled. She was already nude, having been up until the early hours so that all those who wanted to have her before the price went up could be satisfied.

Hundact left her, bound naked on the bed as the rest of the brothel continued as normal. She lay helpless, desperately seeking a way out, or even some means of bringing herself to an honourable death. Nothing came to her, her bound limbs and chained neck making combat impossible, while nothing she had could possibly have served as a weapon.

At last, with the sun already reaching its full heat, Vea came to feed her, no more than a cup of spicy soup, but also the drugged wine. It was an act of sympathy, and one Iriel forced herself to refuse, knowing that at the very least she had to retain what little pride remained to her, and hope. Shortly after, Hundact returned, and with him the same two watchmen who had originally led her to the brothel, Zeidat and Prumes, both of whom had come to fuck her more than once during the week.

She was led from the room in which more men than she could count had used her body, down the stairs and out into the compound, where the girls sat idle, drinking wine or nibbling sweetmeats and fruit to restore themselves after the morning's work. Curious glances were turned to her, some sympathetic, most amused or openly cruel. At the arch Hundact gave her over to the watchmen and she was led out into the street, tottering in tiny steps on her hobbled legs.

Zeidat went in front, with her lead thrown casually over her shoulder, Prumes behind, his trident just inches from her naked bottom, ready to prod her into renewed zeal if she slowed. Faces turned, many following them, to remark with amusement on Iriel's naked body and the way her short, fast steps made her bottom wobble and her breasts jiggle. The blood rose to her face, despite the way she had been exposed and used over the week, Iriel finding it harder to cope with derision than lust.

Yet she kept her chin up, struggling to imitate Kaissia's calm in the face of shaming and fervently wishing that all she had coming was spanking and a little dung in her face, even tattooing, even being put to a troll, anything but the brand. Only when they came in sight of the Watchhouse did the first seeds of panic start to grow, her stomach knotting, and her muscles twitching. The urge to run rose high, reinforced by the voices in her head telling her to fight, to die on Prumes' trident, to choke on her collar, anything but to submit.

She resisted, telling herself she would simply be hurt for no gain, probably put in a net, that her attempts would only draw more laughter from her captors and the crowds around them. Yet still the voices screamed at her, in rising urgency, until at last she could resist no more, and broke.

Her flight lasted five short paces before her collar brought her up short at the same instant she tripped over her hobble. She went down, flat on her face amid a gale of laughter from the crowd, and an instant later the trident was pressed to her neck. Prumes began to speak, then stopped abruptly. Iriel looked up, to find a pair of sandalled feet inches in front of her face. A burly Oretean stood over her, in the watch uniform but with gold sleeves to his green tunic.

'Twelveman Cound,' Prumes stated, saluting.

Cound did not answer, but took hold of Iriel's lead to pull her sharply upright, indifferent to her pain as she struggled to find her feet. For a moment their eyes met, his small and black, showing neither sympathy nor humour, only cold distaste. Then he had turned, jerking on the lead to set her stumbling behind him, under the high arch of Staive Cintes Watchhouse. Stronger fear gripped her as she caught the smell of burning coals, undercut with the sharp tang of heated metal. She began to struggle, unable to help herself, pulling against the lead, merely jerking at the sudden prod of the trident into one fleshy bottom cheek.

Then her arms had been taken, held hard by the two watchmen as Twelveman Cound pulled her hard forwards. The crowd in front of her broke wide, revealing a squat frame of iron and wood, stained with sweat marks, and the brazier, an iron cage filled high with glowing coals, the handle of the brand protruding from among them. She fought back a scream, panic welling up once more at the thought of the horrible thing searing into her flesh, of the agonising pain, the smell of scorched meat, the hideous scar it would leave, marking her forever.

'Hold her!' Cound growled, and as he stepped away two more watchmen replaced him, one on her lead, one behind her.

She began to fight, writhing in their grip, heedless of pain, clutching with her fingers and snapping with her teeth, yet for nothing as she was forced forwards and down, pressed hard to the warm iron of the frame, head down, bottom high. Somebody laughed as her cunt came on show, and for one moment she thought her hobble would be removed to let them spread her legs for fucking, only for it to be fixed straight to the frame. Her wrists followed, locking her in place, bent hard down so that it was all she could do to wiggle her bottom in despairing, urgent protest.

Something pliant touched her waist and she looked back, to find the watchmen with broad leather straps, thick and a handspan wide. Both were put on her, trapping her legs and thighs so that even her wiggling became a useless, pathetic thing, her body held so tight that it merely made the meat of her bottom wobble.

'To ensure we get a clean brand,' Cound remarked. 'I know how you women like to stay pretty.'

He laughed at his own joke, full of contempt as he pulled on a thick leather glove. Iriel met his eyes, using every last part of her willpower to prevent herself from begging, and succeeding only because she knew it would be futile. There was no sympathy in his face, no mercy whatever, only derision and a cold, evil humour. Taking hold of the brand, he pulled it up, the tip yellow with heat, an elaborate E struck through with a double line.

'A little hotter, I think,' he remarked.

Iriel shut her eyes as he thrust the iron back into the coals. She shook her head in raw terror, yet still held back her pleas for mercy, her teeth sunk into her lower lip, the prayer for strength to her father running over and over in her head. Again she heard Cound's voice, cold and level, rich with amusement.

'You're tough, you barbars, I'll grant you that. Usually they grovel and plead. Let us see though, just how tough you are. Beg sweetly and I shall brand your fat behind, otherwise it goes full on your c –'

His voice broke off in a thick, gristly sound. Iriel's eyes sprang open as screams and shouts broke out on every side, to find Cound's head staring at her from among the coals of the brazier. Beyond was Aeisla, bloody axe in hand, her face set in a crazed grin. Prumes sprang into her way, trident lifted, only to go down to Aeisla's backswing, then another watchman came, his sword smashed from his grip by the sheer power of her blow.

Hot blood spattered Iriel's body, but her ankles were free, then her hands as Yi appeared to slice through the bonds. As her body was released she wrenched herself from the frame, snatching at the fallen trident even as she hit the ground. Cianna was above her, sword sunk to the hilt in the body of Zeidat, and Kaissia was there, screaming defiance at a wall of a dozen watchmen, who held back, swords and tridents ready.

Iriel rolled up, her heart hammering, sick with rage and fear, gaining her feet the same instant the watch charged in, to be met by a shower of hot coals as Aeisla kicked the brazier over, then swung her axe. One man fell, headless, a second on the backswing, a third to Cianna and the girls charged, slashing and stabbing as the watchmen gave back in terror. Breaking through, they ran for the open archway, full tilt into the net even as it fell across the opening.

4

Oretes

Looking up into the face of Justice Eriedes Ghaidus, Iriel found none of the easy condescension he had shown before. His face was a mask, absolutely cold. Nor was he alone, nor seated, but standing beside the great chair, on which sat another man, similar of feature but of still richer dress, the Eriedes himself. On the far side of the chair was a younger man, Eriedes Argenus. Others, known and unknown, stood about the room, including Captain Baltrank, Luides and others of the crew.

The girls were chained and yoked, each with a heavy bar of wood across her shoulders, to which her neck collar and hands were fastened. Chains joined the yokes, and also their hobbles. All five were stark naked. All five bore the marks of their desperate struggle beneath the net.

They were also gagged, wads of sour leather thrust into their mouths and tied off behind their heads. Iriel's hurt, and her body ached in every limb, yet she struggled to hold the same pose of haughty contempt maintained by Aeisla beside her, also to concentrate on her pride rather than fear. Beyond Aeisla the other three also held their pose, Cianna defiant, Kaissia cold, Yi sullen. A full twelve of watchmen surrounded them, tridents at the ready. Clerk Loumank cleared his throat.

'So that the five barbarian females accused may answer for the charges brought by Watchmaster Eriedes Voilus, application is made for death by wasting, each murderess to be hung in a cage, at the Citadel, at the Watchhouse, at the Oretes Gate, at the Desert Gate, on the docks. Secondly, that when dead their bodies be buried at the feet of Twelveman Cound in his tomb, as is traditional for the corpses of vanquished enemies.'

Eriedes Ghaidus reacted with a flicker of one eyebrow, the Eriedes himself not at all. Eriedes Argenus spoke.

'Death certainly, but to bury them at Cound's feet is a mockery. Let the House Veides –'

He went silent at a gesture from the Eriedes. Eriedes Ghaidus spoke.

'The demands are just, no question. Yet I have an alternative proposal. Their value as slaves is high, and –'

'Slaves!' a voice objected from among the watchers.

The man stepped out, a solidly built greybeard with an air of authority, plain anger on his face as he continued.

'Slavery is no suitable penalty! Death is the only appropriate choice, and the only one acceptable to the House Veides. Indeed, I consider Watchmaster Voilus' demands insultingly lenient! I make application for torture prior to encagement, to the satisfaction of the relatives of the deceased –'

'It is not your position to make application for justice, Veides Cinctus,' Eriedes Ghaidus interrupted him, 'yet rest assured that your nephew's death will not be put aside lightly, nor those of the other eight watchmen. Pray hear me out as regards the option of selling them.'

'Slavery is unsuitable, an insult to my House,' Veides Cinctus answered.

'Not so,' Eriedes Ghaidus stated. 'They are Aeg. As Captain Baltrank will vouch, to them slavery is a fate worse by far than death.'

Veides Cinctus responded with a contemptuous snort and made to continue, only to be cut off by Eriedes Argenus.

'If this is true, let them choose: slavery or death. Father?'

'A wise decision,' the Eriedes replied. 'Is this satisfactory, Veides Cinctus?'

'Entirely,' Veides Cinctus answered, a touch of cruel humour in his voice. 'Ungag the giantess, I should like to put the question myself.'

'You may,' the Eriedes stated, nodding to the watchmen, one of whom stepped forward, to gingerly remove Aeisla's gag.

Veides Cinctus stepped forward.

'What is it to be, girl, slavery, doubtless as the pampered plaything of some rich House, or death, death by slow wastage as you hang in a cage in the hot sun, without food, without water, jeered at, pelted with dung –'

'My Lord Eriedes!' Loumank objected. 'This is not due procedure!'

'Indeed not, make the choice simple,' the Eriedes instructed.

'My pardon, Lord,' Veides Cinctus answered. 'So, girl, slavery or death?'

'Death,' Aeisla answered.

Veides Cinctus stood back in surprise, then spoke again, to Kaissia.

'And you? Do you prefer to die hung in a cage also?'

Kaissia gave a single stiff nod, Cianna also. Iriel followed suit, and Yi. Aeisla spoke.

'Pit us in combat, as we slew your watchmen, so that we may join in the Feast Hall of Heroines.'

Veides Cinctus paused, then spoke again.

'I see, so it is a matter of superstition. You believe that if you die you go to some afterlife of assured bliss?'

'We do,' Aeisla answered.

Veides Cinctus gave a low chuckle. 'So be it, I accept the verdict.'

'Slavery,' the Eriedes stated. 'Take them –'

'No!' Aeisla cut in. 'We asked for death!'

'Thus I condemn you to slavery,' the Eriedes answered her. 'Gag her again, Twelveman.'

Two watchmen hurried forward to hold Aeisla's yoke as a third forced the leather wadding back into her mouth and tied it off, to leave her glaring at the Eriedes.

'Slavery, yes,' he stated, 'but not here in Staive Cintes. Take them to the caravanserai, for Oretes, where we will without question gain a better price while ridding ourselves of them as well. As compensation, I award one third of their sale price to the House Veides, one third to the Watchhouse, one third to the House Eriedes, the distribution to be calculated after the costs of the civic authority have been deducted. Take them away.'

Iriel winced as the guard's cock was forced into her anal ring. He had barely bothered to lubricate her, merely sucking on a finger, sticking it up her bottom and wiggling it around as he masturbated himself erect.

He filled her slowly, his cock crammed in bit by bit, until at last the hairy mass of his balls met her empty tuppenny. With a grunt of satisfaction he mounted her back, scooped one dangling breast into each hand and set to work buggering her. She was still in her yoke, unable to resist as he and another had positioned her body in a kneeling posture. Her yoke rested on the floor of the wagon, trapping her head and arms, while two sacks of spiced fish beneath her belly kept her bottom lifted and available.

The prison line had become a slave coffle. Beside her, the other four girls were in the same humiliating position, all in a row, their linked yokes helping keep them in place. Each had a cock either in her tuppenny or up her bottom, leaving nearly half the caravan staff immersed to the balls in wet girl-flesh. Only Aeisla had put up more than a token fight, and her buttocks and thighs bore a fresh set of welts in consequence.

The two guards who had chosen Iriel had tossed a coin, the winner fucking her and depositing so much jism up her hole that the second had declared her too sloppy and forced her bottom ring instead. Now, with the pain of the rough entry dying slowly to pleasure and her nipples rubbing in his hands, she was struggling not to show her responses. Not that he seemed to care, enjoying her body simply for the pleasure of what it was, fondling her breasts as her bottom ring pulled in and out on his erection, until at last he came in her rectum.

They had left the caravanserai at dawn, after their third night spent chained in the cells of the citadel. During that time perhaps a dozen watchmen and others had taken advantage of their helplessness to relieve their cocks in one hole or another, but otherwise they had been treated far more easily than she had expected. The wrist and neck holes of their yokes had been padded with rags to prevent chafing, also where their chains touched their skin. They had also been given plenty of water and fed well, not merely lentils, but spiced stew, rice and bread. The good treatment was purely in order to keep thier bodies in prime condition for sale, as a clerk had explained to Iriel shortly after fucking her.

She had accepted it, also Aeisla's argument that it was best to keep their strength up, yet for all the tall girl's efforts to keep their hopes alive, Iriel could find little to be optimistic about. She was stark naked, stripped of her clothes, her possessions and her dignity, in a land over a thousand leagues from Aegerion, and was about to be sold into slavery. The concept of slavery was as shameful as it was incomprehensible. She was not a piece of goods, to be traded, nor an animal, and yet she was being treated as such. It left her numb with an angry misery that had barely faded even when some of the men had rubbed her off to make her penetrated holes tighten on their cocks.

The guard who had been up her pulled out, wiped his cock in the crease of her bottom and gave a long sigh of satisfaction. Iriel stayed down, unable to move until the others did, listening to the gruntings, smacking noises and liquid sounds of her friends being fucked. Only Yi was responding, whimpering gently into the floor in what might equally well have been distress or ecstasy.

The man in Cianna came next, pulling his cock free at the last moment to ejaculate all over her upturned bottom and dipping back into her tuppenny to finish. She blew her breath out as her hole was filled once more, but gave no other reaction. The guard in Kaissia made a joke over the state of Cianna's bottom, grunted and imitated his friend, only with great force, spraying jism over the blonde girl's back and into her hair as well as over her buttocks. Kaissia gave no response beyond a little cluck of disgust. The man in Yi also came, deep up her bottom, holding himself well in until he was finished and using her hair to wipe his cock clean. Last was the one in Aeisla, the caravan's cook, who had been rubbing his well-greased erection between the cheeks of her bottom, but thrust himself inside her at the last instant. As come spurted from around his cock shaft the first man who had fucked Iriel spoke.

'Always the last, Ortac, you should lose some weight.'

'Nonsense,' the cook puffed, 'they enjoy the feel of bellyflesh on their bottoms. It reminds them of the spankings they are given back in Aegmund to arouse them. So my cousin Corbold assures me.'

He finished with a laugh and fetched Aeisla a hearty slap across her bottom before taking hold of her yoke, his hands placed well away from her teeth.

'Ready?'

The girls were hauled up, pulled by their yokes, back into a sitting position. Quickly the guards replaced the sacks, while Ortac began to spoon fish from an open one at the end of the wagon, piling it into a long trough of beaten copper that ran the length of one side. Iriel watched in puzzlement, then outrage as she realised that in order to eat she would have to kneel down once more with her face in the trough, as if she were a farm animal. Kaissia gasped and began to speak, only to stop, her mouth hanging slack in raw outrage as one of the guards emptied a bucket of some sweet-smelling, yeasty pulp into the trough.

'Grape pressings,' the guard stated, 'and you are lucky. The baboons and brush pigs get only fruit peelings and water.'

'Baboons!?' Kaissia demanded. 'Brush pigs!?'

'Just so,' the guard stated casually, and jumped down from the wagon.

'Assanach specialises in the haulage of livestock,' Ortac explained.

Kaissia was left speechless, her mouth wide, Cianna looked angry, Yi sullen, but Iriel was surprised to find a small, ironic smile on Aeisla's face. Before she could speak their yokes had been pushed forwards once more and was she forced to brace herself as her face went into the trough, fouling her nose and the fringe of her hair before she caught her balance.

Ortac laughed as she began to eat, and gave her a swat across her bottom with his spoon. Iriel shut her eyes in shame, thinking of the way the eating position left her bottom spread, with jism still dribbling from both cunt and anus. Ortac gave another chuckle and began to walk down the line of girls, applying random swats to their raised bottoms and at the end sliding the spoon handle into Yi's open tuppenny to leave it sticking up in the air above her buttocks.

'Five hundred leagues to Oretes,' he stated happily. 'At perhaps twenty-five leagues a day that is twenty days or so of abundant cunt, and when your cunts grow sore or sloppy, well, up your arses we go!'

He gave another chuckle, only to break off suddenly and pull the spoon from Yi's hole. A man appeared in the opening of the wagon, his round, red face shaded beneath an elaborate hat. Ortac climbed down and for a moment the two conversed while Iriel struggled to swallow her mouthfuls of the foul-tasting, coarse-textured mash beneath her face. Soon she had taken in as much as she could eat, but she was forced to stay down until the others had also finished. By then the red-faced man had climbed into the wagon. He was directly behind her, eyeing her bottom. Both her holes twitched in anticipation of another fucking, but there was no lust in his voice when he spoke, only amusement.

'Come, girls, snouts out of the trough, I wish to speak with you.'

'Expect nothing from us,' Aeisla answered him. 'Move back as one, girls, when I say. Now.'

Iriel obeyed, taking the weight of the yoke up with difficulty but managing to rock back onto her heels. The man stepped away, then clambered over the linking chains as they shuffled backwards, to leave him facing them.

'Why so brusque?' he asked Aeisla. 'I am merely Assanach the caravaneer, who plies his trade in all innocence and probity. I had no part in the trick played upon you.'

Aeisla held a stony silence, but Kaissia answered.

'Trick? What trick?'

'The trick played by the Eriedes,' Iriel pointed out, 'to make us slaves.'

'Not that, no,' Assanach stated. 'There I had a part, I confess, but purely a commercial one. It was I who suggested to Lord Eriedes Ghaidus that you be sold in

Oretes rather than Staive Cintes. Naturally I take a commission as caravaneer and agent.'

Aeisla spat on the floor. He ignored her, continuing.

'I refer to the death of Twelveman Cound. Surely you realise that you were manoeuvred into this?'

'No,' Aeisla admitted.

He shrugged. 'I am a caravan master, and hardly privy to the councils of the House Eriedes, yet I can guess fairly at their machinations. Twelveman Cound was of the House Veides, the second most powerful of Staive Cintes and the ruling House of Staive Mainides, a city some eighty leagues south along the coast. His influence was rising, and with Watchmaster Eriedes Voilus in his eighty-third year it could not have been long before the position would fall vacant. The watch would have been sure to demand the appointment of Cound, thus seriously weakening the influence of the House Eriedes. Thus and so, when you, Iriel, came before Eriedes Ghaidus in his position as Justice, he seized his chance.'

'How would he have known the outcome?' Aeisla queried.

'He would not,' Assanach replied, 'but all in Staive Cintes had heard the tale of how you fought for Kaissia on the docks in your homeland. If you were prepared to challenge your own people, how would you react in a strange city under similar conditions? Thus the details of your punishment, Iriel.'

'How did the Justice know so much?' Kaissia demanded.

Again Assanach shrugged.

'Doubtless he consulted with Captain Baltrank, whose niece is the wife of his third son, and whose aunt was first wife to Eriedes Voilus.'

'Why then did not Voilus hail us as champions?' Cianna queried.

'As champions?' Assanach demanded.

102

'For slaying his rival,' Kaissia pointed out.

'Absurd!' Assanach scoffed.

'Plain sense,' Kaissia answered him, 'and also the only honourable choice.'

'Not so, not for a moment. All know how the gambit was achieved, but you would hardly expect them to speak of it!'

'In Aegmund he would have a saga sung for his victory,' Kaissia went on, 'but he would also have challenged Twelveman Cound face to face, like a man, or, given his age, appointed a champion. There is no honour in your ways.'

'To us, yours seem barbaric,' Assanach answered. 'Simple also. Secondary to this, but doubtless important, is the matter of finance. As five desiccated corpses you bring not so much as a copper to Staive Cintes; as five exotic slavegirls in Oretes you bring perhaps as much as two thousand gold Marks, an optimistic assessment, but then the Palades is known for his exotic tastes and a marked disregard for thrift. Staive Cintes is a rich city, the House Eriedes a wealthy House, yet not so wealthy that they would cast good money into the sea.'

Aeisla gave a tired nod.

'Always this is the way in Apraya, greed, dishonour, and yet you call us barbarians!'

'You speak as if you had been here before?' Assanach queried.

'In Vendjome,' she answered wearily, 'from where I escaped. I will do the same here, if I am able. Never will I submit to slavery.'

'You may surprise yourself,' Assanach answered. 'And with Vendjome comes another reason for selling you. For a generation now we and the Vendjomois have been at war, and recently the tide has turned against us. Taxes, already high, have risen to alarming levels. You were a slave then, in Vendjome?'

Aeisla made a wry face.

'What did you sell for? Tell me, or I will have you whipped, this is important information!'

'Whip me then,' Aeisla answered him, 'but no, it makes no difference. Slavery is a state of the mind, not of the body. Eleven hundred gold Imperials.'

'Eleven hundred Imperials! And it is a heavy coin, the Imperial, worth three Marks by Dwarven weight of gold. If I achieve a third part of that the five of you would make over five thousand gold Marks. The Eriedes will grant me a House, marry me to their line even! Fortunate day!'

'If we are so valuable,' Kaissia put in, 'perhaps you would spare us our fuckings from your men?'

Assanach frowned, then spoke again.

'Why so? Regular fucking keeps a girl in trim, this is common knowledge. It is not as if you were virgin.'

Kaissia winced. Assanach went on, as much to himself as to them, and pulling gently at his beard where it sprouted from his fat chin as he spoke.

'The Palades is said to enjoy bursting girls' hymens, and cruel tricks in general. I wonder how I might present you to best advantage? As barbarian Princesses perhaps, yes . . .'

Feeling as foolish as ashamed, Iriel stared at her reflection in the mirror. If Madame Hivies' idea of what she should wear as an Aeg had been five hundred years out of date, then Assanach's was simply ludicrous – not only indecent, but wholly impractical.

Her costume was composed mainly of feathers, large, fluffy ones from some huge bird, dyed in brilliant pink and a vivid pale green. These were fixed to a belt of crudely beaten copper, to form what might have been considered a skirt had it not failed to cover all of her tuppenny mound and a good half of her bottom cheeks. The top was as bad, her breasts quite bare, but supported in puffs of smaller and yet fluffier feather, like two melons on a bed of sorrel. She also had fanciful sandals, with crisscrossed laces reaching from just above her ankles to the tops of her thighs, a feather headdress, and a copper collar studded with rough-cut tiger's-eye and blue john. Her nipples and tuppenny had been painted green.

The others had fared no better, each in her own version of the ridiculous outfit. Kaissia in particular had suffered, making the mistake of complaining that her rank should entitle her to special treatment. Assanach had left her breasts on the grounds that they were colourful enough, but had her tuppenny painted blue rather than green, stating that it went well with her hair. He had also painted her bottom, prompting jokes about her resemblance to a baboon from the caravan men. The girls still wore their yokes, never once removed, also their hobbles.

'Thus and so, we are done,' Assanach stated, rubbing his hands together happily. 'Haul down the covers, boys, and we shall enter Oretes in high style!'

He jumped down from the wagon, taking the mirror with him and still chuckling at his own wit for allowing the girls to see their reflections. Iriel drew a heavy sigh, less confident in the idiotic guise than she had been naked, and anything but happy at the idea of being paraded through the streets of a city.

Yet she was helpless as ever, their hobbles fixed to the floor of the wagon, chains leading up to the supporting hoops from the end yokes, preventing them from squatting down. They had been chained that way to be dressed, on what was the morning of the 22nd day out of Staive Cintes.

Over the course of the journey she had been endlessly molested, fondled, fucked, buggered and more. Her bottom crease and cleavage had been used as slides for men's cocks, often greased, often slimy with jism. She had been spanked repeatedly, the first time for losing control of her bladder and peeing on the floor because she had been unable to hold out until the potmen arrived, thereafter because the men had discovered how wet a spanking made her tuppenny. She had had her face pushed in the food trough, a pimento inserted in her anus for an entire night, a cup of urine offered to her as wine, and worse, yet there was no question that the costume represented as deep a humiliation as any.

As the awning was pulled away she was biting her lips in a futile effort to hold back the tears already trickling down both cheeks, yet what showed through her blurred vision still had her gaping in awe. They were on a wide, busy road, outside the gates of a city, gates beneath which the keep in Aegerion would have fitted with ease.

'Oretes,' Assanach remarked with a flourish of his hand.

Iriel let herself stare. To either side of the colossal gates ran a wall of smooth blue-white stone, perhaps thirty manheights high, stretching out to a tower perhaps three times taller at one end, and ending at a broad, palm-fringed river at the other. Beyond the wall other towers rose, some to heights that seemed impossible without the aid of magic, all in the same blue-white stone, flat topped and hung with banners of black, crimson and gold. Here and there other rooftops could be seen, suggesting massive buildings, larger by far than anything in Aegerion, in Staive Cintes, even in the other Oretean cities they had passed on the trail.

'Do you perhaps feel a touch less pride now?' Assanach enquired.

None of the girls answered, not even Aeisla troubling to spit. The wagon jerked forwards at Assanach's signal and Iriel was briefly forced to steady herself, but she went back to watching as they moved slowly towards the city. The gates were open, with a knot of watchmen in what were presumably the royal colours checking traffic as it passed through. Assanach stopped the girls' wagon directly under the gigantic arch, with the peak stones seeming to hang in air an impossible distance over Iriel's head as she craned back to look.

Within the gates the city proved more astonishing still. A street led arrow straight to a great palace that towered above a screen of palms. It was wide and paved with blue-white stone, yet barely visible for the bustling crowds, the street alone holding more people than she had seen gathered in one place before. Curious scents assailed her nose, the spices so beloved of Oreteans, but in a richer, more varied mix than those of Staive Cintes. Noise smote her from every side, the calls of vendors, animal noises, an underlying hum created by a multitude of voices.

Yet for all her astonishment, it was no greater than that of the Oreteans. In Staive Cintes, the populace knew how her people looked, at least by repute. In Oretea this was evidently not true. Every single citizen, each yellow-brown of skin and, if anything, smaller than their northern cousins, turned to stare at the five girls. Iriel caught comments; on their pale skin, on their outlandish garb, but most of all on their hair. Again and again citizens pushed close to ask questions, even to make offers of money, but the caravan guards posted at the corners of the wagons gave the same answer every time, that the five were barbarian Princesses and would be auctioned in the market in three days.

Only when they had travelled some two-thirds of the distance to the palace did Assanach order the caravan off the main street, to another only marginally less grand, then again, into a great yard behind a building of eight storeys topped by fanciful turrets of twisted, multihued glass. Men in black and silver livery stepped forwards to assist with the camels and wagons as Assanach looked up at the building.

'Normally I stay at the terminus, but on this occasion only the best will do, and what better than the House

Alwan. Thank you, yes, a suite of rooms, suitably appointed, a bath, suitably scented, then a meal, the best your kitchen affords.'

He had spoken to one of the servants, and they left together, into the magnificent building that to Iriel's astonishment, seemed to be an inn. Their wagon had been taken along with those containing the baboons and brush pigs, all five being wheeled into covered stalls. Ortac appeared briefly, along with the potmen, to attend to their needs at either end and they were left, in warm gloom, the murmur of the city coming faint from outside.

'And now?' Cianna queried.

'We sleep,' Aeisla stated. 'So long as we wear these yokes we are helpless. Until they are removed we play Assanach's game. Behave as he has instructed, with animal vitality and fear. With luck they will think us too dull to require close confinement.'

'In three days we will be slaves,' Kaissia said miserably.

'No,' Aeisla answered. 'In three days money will change hands for control of our bodies. We become slaves only when we accept slavery, when we grovel at our owners' feet, and not merely in fear, but in gratitude. Now let us lie down. As one, now.'

They sank together, now a practised motion, and lay back, resting their necks in the yokes, a position Iriel had come to accept as bearable if hardly comfortable. Closing her eyes, she began to pray, picturing her father as she sought courage, seated at the table in her old house, grinning through his great red beard as he oiled his axe.

One day passed, and another, until the dim, stuffy warmth of the stall had become Iriel's world, bounded by the walls and roof. Ortac the cook and the potmen came regularly to perform their duties, while two of

Assanach's men and one from the House Alwan were always on guard. Both servants and guards fucked the girls regularly and invariably from the rear, the sight of the line of flaunted bottoms having become a standing joke among the men.

They were told nothing, but picked details up from the men, learning that their arrival in Oretes had caused a stir, and that Assanach was spreading the 'barbarian Princess' story in every quarter. For all the fuckings they were treated carefully, with no spanking or unnecessary humiliations, and twice Assanach appeared to show them off to senior men from the city.

On the morning of the third day Iriel was jerked awake by the bang of the stall door, urgent voices, the clatter of wooden-soled sandals and the clang of pails. She pulled her head up, to see the caravan men already clambering onto the wagon and, as her mouth came open in a yawn, she received a bucket of cold water full in the face. Spitting and spluttering, she struggled to fight the water out of her eyes and mouth, even as her yoke was pulled up, then lifted, bringing her to her feet.

Immediately sponges were applied to her body, rubbing over her belly, breasts and bottom without the slightest concern for where they touched. She squeaked as a rag was pushed firmly up between her buttocks to wipe her anus, then up it as Ortac's voice rang out.

'The pots first, idiots! What is the good of cleaning her arse when she is about to take a shit?'

The man who'd been cleaning her grunted in response, but jumped down from the wagon, leaving the cloth wedged between Iriel's buttocks, one soapy fold still in her bottom hole. A potman climbed up with three of the earthenware vessels held together by their handles.

'Squat,' he ordered Iriel, 'and be quick.'

'What is happening?' she demanded, blushing despite herself but grateful enough to get down on the pot as the yokes were lowered, her bladder and rectum heavy from the night.

'Some greatbeard is coming,' the man answered. 'Stick it out, show me.'

'No!' Iriel protested as her bottom settled onto the hard rim of the pot. 'Do not watch, please.'

The man merely chuckled and stayed firmly where he was, behind her, leaving her blushing furiously as she evacuated, acutely conscious of her open body and the rude noises it was impossible to hold back. Still she did it, too urgent to stop.

The moment she had finished and lifted her bottom he took hold of her, spreading her cheeks to show off her anus. Expecting to be washed, Iriel swallowed her embarrassment and stuck it out, only for a stiff cock to be slid up between her cheeks. She squeaked in surprise, and again as he pushed his penis head to her still-loose anus.

'What are you doing?' Ortac demanded.

'Buggering her,' the man replied simply, then grunted as he pushed, Iriel's sloppy hole spreading to the pressure as she cried out in disgust.

'There is no time for games!' Ortac snapped.

'Calm yourself,' the man grunted, forcing the collar of his foreskin in past Iriel's straining bottom ring. 'It's my last chance, and she's dirty so it's going up easily and I'll soon spunk. Now let me concentrate.'

'Idiot!' Ortac answered, but went on with his own task, fingering the sobbing Kaissia's bottom hole because she was having trouble defecating.

The man in Iriel's bottom grunted once more, wedging the last section of his cock up into her rectum. She stuck her bottom out, resigned to buggery and determined to make it as painless as possible.

'That's my girl,' he sighed, 'show the peach, fat and wide.'

He began to bugger her, grunting and mumbling obscenities as his cock moved in and out to the sound of squelching noises and her involuntary panting. Her breasts began to swing, then to slap together as he got faster, adding to the lewd noises wrung from her body. His fingers dug into the flesh of her hips, his pushes grew faster, his balls began to slap on her empty tuppenny, sending little jolts of pleasure through her until she was sure she would come, only for him to fill her rectum with hot jism and leave her on the brink.

'Pig!' she managed, as he emptied himself into her, cock held deep up her bottom.

His response was a sigh of perfect bliss, then a firm slap to her bottom. She gritted her teeth as he began to pull out, and settled on the pot the moment he was free, jism bubbling and farting from her half-closed bottom ring.

'She is right,' Ortac stated. 'You are a pig. Now clean her up, quickly!'

The man laughed, but immediately took Iriel by the hair, forcing her to lift her bottom once more. He slapped the wet cloth between her buttocks, penetrating her anus, then cupping her tuppenny to wipe away the juice, once more sending a jolt of helpless pleasure through her as he touched her bump.

Iriel stayed down, suffering the indignity of having the most intimate parts of her body probed in shame-filled silence, until she had been washed to the men's satisfaction and lifted once more, to stand shivering in the pale light striking into the stall through the open doors. Only then did she discover that her hasty buggering had been seen not only by the caravan men but by several dozen people in the yard.

She sighed and shook her head, the added indignity a small thing beside all that had been heaped on her. The air was cool, and she realised that it was not long after dawn as the men began to pat her down with handfuls of moss. Around her, the others were receiving much the same treatment. Yi had been fucked and had jism running down the insides of her thighs, but otherwise the men had contented themselves with fondling breasts and bottoms and the occasional intrusion of a finger. Aeisla, with three men attending to her, was already dry, and was being rubbed down, her face set in a mask as scented oil was applied to her heavy breasts.

The pots were removed, the remaining sacks of spiced fish taken away and the floor washed. One man handed out more pots of oil and Iriel found herself struggling not to react as she was anointed, the man taking particular care over her breasts and buttocks, but leaving her nipples and the lips of her tuppenny free. Another man brought in their costumes, which had been removed to save them from damage, and she was dressed in the ludicrous little skirt and top, then the high-laced sandals. Her hair was twisted into a crude knot and stuck with plumes, her nipples painted, then her tuppenny, to leave her exactly as she had been first paraded into Oretes.

With the last girl costumed and painted, and the yokes chained to the wagon frame to force the girls to remain standing, the majority of the men dispersed. Only two guards and a man from the House Alwan remained, this last in elaborate livery and wearing an air of cold self-importance as he went to stand by the open door. The people who had watched Iriel buggered had gone, leaving the yard empty, also clear of straw, camel dung and all the other detritus that usually added to the hot reek of her quarters.

She waited, at first expectant and determined to show her defiance, then curious, then bored. Nothing happened, until at last, with her legs aching and the sun risen to its full scorching heat, she caught Assanach's voice, not commanding as usual, but deferential, almost wheedling.

'. . . yet what of others of the House, Great Prince? I have no wish to create enmity. An auction surely would –'

'Do not be concerned,' another voice answered, calm, deep and with far more authority than Assanach had ever mustered. 'You shall be paid, and well, more certainly than you might expect at auction.'

Assanach appeared, accompanied by several men; some soldiers, a little beetle-like creature who appeared to be a clerk and one other, tall by Oretean standards, slender and straight, his beard pure white and not oiled but encased in gold filigree. Iriel met his gaze as he stopped to look up at her and the others, determined only to show defiant pride, as Aeisla had instructed.

'Release them so that they may kneel!' Assanach ordered urgently. 'Bow your heads, you, you are in the presence of Palades Daken, Royal Prince!'

'Do not trouble yourself,' the man answered. 'Have them brought down.'

'With haste, with haste!' Assanach urged as the guards went to the yoke chains. 'Do not keep the Great Prince waiting!'

The guards obeyed, Aeisla returning Iriel's questioning look with a nod, and the coffle was helped carefully down to the ground and lined up in the yard. Iriel stood blinking in the brilliant sunlight, her chin lifted, trying to show haughty contempt but feeling ridiculous in her costume. Palades Daken walked around them, once, then again before addressing Kaissia.

'Do you profess rationality, girl?'

'I do,' Kaissia answered, 'and furthermore I am a Squireling, and highborn.'

'A Squireling?' he queried.

'The Aeg title for Princess,' Assanach responded quickly.

'I see,' Palades Daken continued. 'And you are Princesses, all five?'

'We are not,' Kaissia answered. 'Aeisla is of the rank of Reeveling, the others are lowborn.'

Palades Daken chuckled and looked up at Aeisla, to whom Kaissia had nodded.

'Not Princesses, then? I had suspected as much, given that you wear feathers from the ostrich, a bird the scholars assure us occurs only south of the Eigora Khum. You are Aeg though, evidently.'

Assanach was wringing his hands frantically together, his face now the colour of a plum, but Palades Daken ignored him, speaking again to Aeisla.

'Are you strong, girl?'

Aeisla spat, catching him full in the face. For one instant anger showed in his eyes, and a gasp of outrage rose from his attendants, then he had mastered himself and extended a hand to hold back the guards. Stepping away a little, he spoke again.

'Strong of purpose, that is for certain. I am told that in Staive Cintes you slew eight watchmen, including a Twelveman of renowned skill.'

'I killed five,' she answered, 'Cianna, by me, two, Yi, at the end, one. Twelveman Cound had his back to me, an easy stroke. My last I took while enmeshed in net, Yi's likewise.'

He nodded and went on.

'Following which events the Eriedes ordered you taken here to be sold, thus getting rid of you while also gaining a handsome sum. In his place, I would have done likewise. Thus and so. Inveides, pay Master Assanach a purse of four thousand gold Marks, after which he is to be taken to the marketplace and whipped. Come.'

He turned on his heel, guards immediately taking hold of the coffle chain to lead the girls after him, leaving Assanach's shrill mixture of thanks and pleas behind.

Despite herself, it was more than Iriel could resist not to relax against the well-filled cushions on which she lay. She was still hobbled and collared, also nude and chained to a ring in the wall, but the awful yoke had been removed and her hands were free. She rubbed her wrists as the last of the guards left with a doubtful look at the five of them.

Leaving the House Alwan, they had been led through the streets of Oretes, not to the great palace she had seen before, but to a lesser one still some five times the size of the High-Prince's keep in Aegerion. There, they had been led through formal gardens and pillared halls of the blue-white marble inlaid with more exotic stones, to the chamber in which she now lay. They had been stripped of their foolish costumes and washed but left naked, then very carefully shifted from the coffle to the wall rings, their hands released at last. Palades Daken had stayed with them, watching over his guards, who had then been dismissed. Now he stood looking down at them, his face set in thought.

'So,' he stated after a while, 'you are my slaves. Are you honoured? To judge from your faces, clearly not, which I confess is a new experience for me. Our philosophers state that slavery is the natural role for women, so why so resentful?'

'Your philosophers know only of your own people,' Aeisla stated.

'An observation philosophical in itself,' he replied. 'I am told you have been in Vendjome, as a slave, yet escaped.'

'You know a great deal,' she answered.

'I do,' he answered. 'For instance, I also know that both on the occasion of the death of the Twelveman in Staive Cintes and one other, you have risked your lives for no obvious return beyond the satisfaction of your honour code. Such loyalty is a rare trait, or did you have some other motive?'

'I . . . it is a difficult matter,' Aeisla responded, 'but yes, essentially it was for honour.'

'Remarkable. I am intrigued to know how such loyalty comes to be bestowed.'

'Not from a slave.'

'Just so. I know little of Aegmund, save that it is a cold and cheerless place inhabited by ferocious and gigantic barbarians. So much you confirm, yet it seems you have hidden depths, perhaps useful traits. Would, I wonder, your loyalty be earned if I gave you your freedom?'

'Our gratitude, certainly,' Aeisla said cautiously, as a wild hope rose up in Iriel's breast.

'I would require rather more than gratitude,' he answered. 'As you may know, I am uncle to the Palades and serve in the role of Vizier, while you may have divined that I am careful to ensure that I remain informed of important events in the Kingdom.'

'So we see. What do you wish of us, to gather information for you? From the Vendjomois even?'

'Hardly an honourable occupation,' Kaissia sniffed. 'An enemy should be faced openly.'

'It is an improvement on slavery,' Aeisla replied, the others quickly nodding agreement. 'Pray continue, Great Prince.'

'Hmm, "Great Prince" is an improvement on spittle,' Palades Daken remarked. 'But no, I do not require you to go to Vendjome, nothing so dangerous. What I require is your full loyalty and perfect obedience, only thus may you have your freedom, and then only once the task is done.'

'Name it,' Aeisla stated.

'First,' he replied, 'be assured that should you betray my trust your death will be slow and lingering, so much so that you will wish you were rotting in the hung cage in Staive Cintes.'

'There is no call for threats,' Aeisla answered. 'You have my word.'

'Mine also,' Kaissia added, 'loyalty in return for free citizenship of Oretes.'

Iriel nodded her agreement, Cianna and Yi also.

'It may well involve being whipped, maybe worse,' he stated. 'Certainly it will involve the use of your bodies, and in unusual ways.'

Aeisla merely shrugged. He nodded.

'So be it, and if I am to accept your word, then you must accept mine. For the time being, I merely need you to follow my instructions without committing undue violence. Initially, you will be given as a gift –'

'A gift!' Kaissia interrupted.

'Be peaceful,' Aeisla soothed. 'This is for our freedom, in body as well as spirit. When you grovel by choice, only then are you a slave. Remember this.'

'A gift to the Palades,' Prince Daken continued, 'and you need not feign submission, as it would be a suspicious change in your known characters, which Assanach has built up to a fine degree. Fight, spit, whatsoever you please, until such time as he has fucked you. Only then do you need to change your ways, or rather, to appear to, feigning devotion for the pleasure he brings you.'

'You wish us merely to pass over the details of his personal machinations?' Aeisla queried.

'No, not that.'

'What then?'

'You will be told when the time is right.'

'This plotting does not sit well with me,' Kaissia objected. 'I prefer a plain objective, and if you tell us so little how do we know that you will not sacrifice us to gain some end you have not revealed?'

'You do not,' he answered. 'It is a risk you must take for your freedom.'

'Let us accept,' Aeisla urged. 'At the least we may gain a chance to die well!'

Cianna immediately struck her fist on the floor, a gesture copied by Yi and Iriel.

'I wish to know more,' Kaissia stated. 'At the least the nature of this King we are to be given to, which others we may trust, which –'

117

'Trust none,' Iriel put in, 'but rather assume we are in a nest of vipers, each one turned against us. This is my understanding of Oretes!'

Prince Daken chuckled, then spoke.

'There is something in what you say. Thus and so, pay close attention. To understand what I require of you it is perhaps advisable to know something of the history of the House Palades. The old King was the twelfth of his line, and as has often been the case when monarchs die at a great age, the succession came into dispute when he died. The two eldest of his sons, my brothers, had predeceased, each leaving a son. The legitimate heir, of undiluted royal blood, was one Thraxus, an imbecile. His cousin Uilus claimed the throne, but the council placed me as a mentor to both Thraxus and his infant sister, Sulden. In time Thraxus died, choking on the bones of a poorly prepared mudfish. Again Uilus sought the crown, but again the council preferred to give the title to Sulden while retaining myself as Regent. A year later, Sulden simply disappeared, and at last Uilus took the throne. Thus the situation has stood for eighteen years.'

'Uilus is the Palades?'

'Just so, the fifteenth Palades. In character, he was always something of a wastrel, but in recent years his excesses have grown more outrageous. He drinks to unconsciousness, takes opium and cares nothing for affairs beyond those which enhance his own pleasure. He –'

'You wish to kill him, to take his place?' Kaissia asked. 'Why did you not simply challenge him when you had your full strength?'

'This is not their way,' Aeisla put in. 'Matters do not run to the same course as in Aegmund, where we ensure that the strongest rule. In Oretes it seems to be those with the most cunning. Prince Daken intends that we should kill the King.'

118

Prince Daken's eyebrows rose a fraction and it was a moment before he answered.

'You barbarians are less dull than I had been led to believe. Yes, to speak plainly, I intend that you should kill him.'

'As his guards will kill us moments later. Then you take the throne for your own!' Kaissia scoffed. 'No, you do not understand us, Prince Daken. I will do that gladly.'

'I assure you that your deaths form no part of the matter,' he answered, now somewhat discomfited. 'I will explain. As I have stated, the Palades is no fit ruler. Each moment he grows more introspective and suspicious, until he sees plots on every side. Just a month ago three of our finest generals were arrested for treason and hanged in the marketplace. Palades Tavian, of the family and Commander here in Oretes, was fortunate to escape. Now our armies reel before the Vendjomois, bereft of leadership and spirit. I must act without delay.'

'General?' Yi queried.

'Men who lead armies,' Aeisla explained. 'What Prince Daken is trying to say is that Uilus murdered Thraxus, Sulden, and these generals, but not openly. He fears that he will be next and wishes to strike first, and in the same manner. We see this as an act too shameful –'

'So it is!' Kaissia exclaimed in outrage.

'– to be considered,' Aeisla went on. 'Here, I suspect that assassination is regarded as normal.'

'What is assassination?' Iriel asked.

'Assassination,' Aeisla replied, 'is the practice of killing by stealth rather than open combat – a foul habit, but not uncommon in these lands. Do not be surprised to learn that in Oretes it is the normal means of succession.'

'Hardly that!' Daken said. 'But yes, this would not be the first occasion on which only one claimant of many

119

has survived. Never is it open, and none speak of such things.'

'I do not understand,' Iriel asked. 'How could Uilus be sure that Thraxus would choke on the fish bone?'

'He would not have been,' Daken explained. 'Doubtless it was one of several attempts, all subtle, all untraceable. Uilus himself put the fish cook to torment but drew no confession.'

'The cook died?'

'Of course. How else would it be?'

Aeisla nodded.

'What of the girl child?' Yi asked. 'She was murdered by her own cousin?'

'Evidently,' Kaissia said. 'These people have no concept of honour whatsoever.'

'Uilus would have murdered Sulden, yes,' Daken replied, 'but he did not. Sulden lives, and I intend to see her restored to her rightful place on the throne.'

'All this is remarkable,' Kaissia stated, 'but I will not kill Uilus save openly, on a challenge.'

'We have agreed to follow the Prince's orders,' Cianna pointed out. 'We should do so.'

'No,' Kaissia objected. 'Would I put a knife in my Earl's back merely because my Baron instructed me to?'

'We have no fealty here,' Cianna objected, 'and besides, when he realises he is attacked he is sure to resist. This is sufficient for me, and requires only a table knife, if that.'

She grinned, displaying her pointed teeth.

'Just so,' Daken admitted, with a fastidious shudder, 'although I would prefer you not to express yourselves in such crude terms. Still, as barbarians, this is to be expected, yet if you do this his guards will certainly kill you before I can intervene. Poison is a better choice, administered cleverly so as to avoid his tasters.'

'Not I, then,' Cianna stated. 'Not poison.'

'Another then,' Daken went on. 'He will be suspicious, naturally, but it may be that you can introduce a ball of poison into his anus with your tongue.'

'I have seen this trick in Makea,' Cianna stated, 'but no.'

Aeisla explained. 'I fear that it is impossible. Our honour code forbids it.'

Kaissia nodded in heartfelt agreement.

'When the alternative is certain death?' Daken answered.

'Indeed,' Aeisla responded, equally calmly. 'Against guards we die with honour and thus reach the Feast Hall of Heroines. To give Uilus poison or even to knife him in his sleep would dishonour us and our ancestors before us.'

'Other possibilities exist,' Daken sighed. 'Here is one that may satisfy you. Uilus is cruel, cruel in the manner of a spiteful boy pulling the appendages from an insect. He takes pleasure in the hurt and humiliation of all, hence my certainty that he will oblige you to lick his anus. Another particular joy of his is to make the girls of the harem fight, generally in some absurd parody of combat and with weapons that, while little more than toys, can still do harm. Undoubtedly he will make you do this, perhaps against a greater number of Vendjomois or Cypraean girls. When this happens, you will be in the traditional garb of your homeland, and armed accordingly, for the sake of dramatic realism. You must turn on him rather than on your opponents. I will ensure –'

'How would he be?' Aeisla queried. 'Armed?'

'Unlikely,' Daken admitted, 'or at least with no more than a wine cup. He drinks a heady mixture of strong red from the Glissade Mountains and opium.'

'Five against one man, unarmed, drunk and drugged?' Aeisla queried. 'This is open assassination.'

'Unthinkable,' Kaissia repeated.

'Why so?' Daken demanded in exasperation. 'It is simple enough, is it not? Can you not swallow your high-flown honour code for one moment, and here, two thousands of leagues from your homeland?'

'What you suggest is undoubtedly assassination and as such untenable,' Kaissia insisted stubbornly.

'It is simple combat!' Daken replied. 'There will be guards also, a full Twelve of the Royal House in all probability. Is this not enough for you?'

'Could we not provoke a challenge?' Cianna suggested. 'In Makea there was a man, Ulourdos, who wished to fight me to mark himself as my superior. His pride was piqued by my refusal to be his slave. Uilus is perhaps as proud and vain as was Ulourdos?'

'No doubt,' Daken responded. 'What happened to this Ulourdos?'

'I bit his throat out,' Cianna replied simply. 'Aeisla can provide the full saga if you wish it?'

'Thank you, no,' Daken replied, turning a little pale. He swallowed, then rallied himself.

'Your plan might work, yes. Uilus has been known to join in his little entertainments, and even to inflict a spanking or minor cuts, perhaps to squat on the face of the beaten girl, depending on his mood. Would that suit? After all, you yourself admitted to striking down the Twelveman from behind.'

'It would suit, yes,' Aeisla admitted. 'And I did challenge Cound – he was half-turned when my axe caught his neck.'

'Daken is old,' Kaissia put in. 'One of us might reasonably take his part as a Champion, in which case the challenge would be formal.'

'Possible,' Aeisla admitted. 'It would be your right, as senior among us.'

'I accept, gladly,' Kaissia replied. 'Prince Daken, appoint me your Champion with whatever ceremony is appropriate. I am prepared to overlook the details of my introduction to the palace for the sake of expediency, also to wait my opportunity. To fight a King as

Champion is a fine thing. Even if I fail it will restore my escutcheon.'

'She was shamed,' Aeisla explained.

'Spanked in public, quite naked,' Cianna added. 'Her breasts tattooed, as you see.'

'Smeared with dung and put in the barrel,' Yi put in.

'She was supposed to be ravished by a troll, too,' Iriel concluded, 'a small one, but –'

'Will you four be quiet!' Kaissia snapped. 'There is no need to discuss the detail.'

Daken's eyebrows had risen. 'This is how girls are punished in Aegmund? Remarkable. What was your crime, Kaissia?'

'I would rather not discuss the matter,' she answered.

'She gave her maidenhead to a bull-nymph,' Yi stated.

'Only that?' Daken queried. 'For a virgin of good birth, yes I suppose there might be objection. A good spanking, certainly, what could be more appropriate for a girl's discipline? But to be tattooed, put in a barrel of dung, covered by a troll, is this not excessive?'

'Trolls are known then, in Oretea?' Aeisla queried.

'Indeed so,' he answered, 'but we do not have them fuck our women.'

Aeisla put her hand to her chin as he finished with a disconcerted laugh.

5

The Palades

Iriel stretched, then reached out to accept a cup of wine
from the curiously soft young man who was offering it
to her. Degrading slavery might be, but there was no
denying that it was a lot easier either than working as a
seamstress or in a galley, let alone being part of the
goods in a caravan. Aeisla's advice and the knowledge
that it was an act in any case made her sense of shame
little more than a background irritation, while in the
three days since the five of them had been taken to the
King's harem she had not been so much as touched.

Daken had timed his gift carefully, waiting two days
until Uilus had thrown an entertainment so excessive
that it had taken a further two to recover. Thus the girls
had had a chance to settle in and to restore their
strength. They had also behaved themselves, and while
initially in chains, these had been removed, along with
their hobbles, thus leaving them in simple and slender
collars of engraved silver. Each was connected to a wall
ring by a chain Iriel was sure she could break simply by
twisting it sufficiently.

The palace was enormous, but composed mainly of
open, pillared halls in which the affairs of government
were conducted, along with two great wings of apart-
ments, for guests and staff. Only the central portion was
given over to the King's living quarters, but of that an

entire floor consisted of the harem chambers and accommodation for the curious, flabby little men who saw to the girls' wants.

The main chamber was divided by walls such as that to which the five girls were chained, also by ranks of pillars and screens carved of exotic woods. These formed alcoves, each liberally provided with cushions, a tabouret on which the servants could sit when a girl needed to be spanked, a cabinet for perfumes, and coloured body paints and accessories for enhancing their beauty. There was also a bell, which she only needed to ring to have a servant bring food, drink or a pot.

Although she had seen only a small proportion of the harem chamber, it clearly housed a hundred or more girls, each in her own alcove. Yet Iriel was effectively alone, able to speak to Cianna and Yi through the screens to either side of her, and to Aeisla and Kaissia with difficulty, but otherwise cut off from her friends. Opposite, across a space of open floor, was another row of alcoves, six in all, three of which she could see fully into. All were occupied, and provided what had initially been a shock but had quickly turned to amusement.

The five Aeg girls had been left carefully alone by the servants, who seemed to have no interest in ravishing their charges in any case, nor even taking advantage of the abundant display of female flesh. They did give spankings, though, administered either by hand or with the little silver-backed hairbrushes with which every girl was provided, and the spankings were given with particular spite. It was rare for an hour to pass without hearing the hapless pleas, pained squeals and meaty slapping noises of one girl or another getting her bottom attended to somewhere in the chamber, and not infrequently in the alcoves Iriel could see.

Of the six girls opposite, five had been spanked since Iriel's arrival. Only the one in the last alcove had escaped, a shy Oretean who seldom spoke and always kept her eyes downcast, the preferred attitude of the King and his servants. The other five were bolder, and after initial trepidation had come to speak to the Aeg girls so long as the servants were not around. Next to the shy Oretean was a coal-black girl who came from southern Cypraea, a continent far to the east. She was sulky and homesick, often refusing to paint her face or take trouble with her hair, so that the servants had to do it for her. On the second day she had been taken to task over this and had obeyed, but not to the servants' satisfaction. Three of them had taken her, one holding her upper body, two sitting on tabourets with their knees interlocked and her across them, broad black bottom stuck high, legs kicking wide as she was spanked hard, one hairbrush to each bouncing buttock. With her heavily furred tuppenny and tight black bottom ring on show, Iriel had watched in shocked fascination, and been left feeling distinctly uncomfortable herself.

The girl at the opposite end of the row was a regular victim, although it was hard for Iriel to see more than a pair of shapely legs kicking up and down and some half of the servant's back as he spanked her. She took it meekly, going over the knee to order, but was invariably in tears after just a few swats. Three times it had been done, never for any obvious reason, leaving Iriel certain that the servants chose the girl more for convenience and lack of fight when they felt like taking out their apparently endless stock of malevolence on a bottom.

Of the three alcoves in which Iriel could see every detail, two were occupied by Vendjomois girls whose very terror of the servants had earned them two spankings apiece. Both spoke seldom, and in urgent, excited whispers full of fear. One had peed on the floor in her hurry to finish on the pot, and had simply been pulled down onto the floor in a kneeling position, piddle still squirting from her tuppenny, for two dozen hard swats with her own hairbrush. The junior servant sent to clean the mess up had then repeated the punishment with the unfortunate girl held squealing across his knee and her face pushed down into the puddle she had made on the floor. The other had been more luckless still, caught masturbating late at night and held upside down by her legs while a hairbrush was applied to the swollen lips of her cunt. She had come while beaten, driving the servants into an unreasoning fury, and they had taken turns with her, over one knee after another, until she was blubbering brokenly on the floor in a pool of tears and juice with her bottom purple with bruising.

The most frequently spanked was directly opposite Cianna, a young Oretean girl, exquisitely pretty. The servants held a particular grudge against her, and it was plain to see why. Her every word and every action seemed calculated to mock, not only the servants but the other girls. Frequently she had commented on the size of the Cypraean girl's bottom, and had teased her mercilessly after the spanking. The Aeg girls also came in for ridicule, for their height, their looks, their embarrassment over being in the nude and a dozen other details.

Again and again she had been upended by the servants, six times in all, yet no matter how often she was punished, she remained constantly insolent and also messy. Time and again she spilled her food or drink, smeared paint on her cushions and, on one occasion when the pot failed to arrived fast enough, simply came out to the limit of her chain and peed on the floor.

Each time she was spanked, and each time she fought, forcing three or even four of the servants to hold her down as she was put across the knee, or even with her bent over her tabouret with one of them sat on her back. She inevitably cried, wailing and cursing and beating her fists on the cushions, all the while with her little yellow-brown bottom cheeks jumping and her tuppenny growing more juicy. The servants referred to her simply as 'the Brat', a name the Aeg girls had quickly adopted.

The latest spanking was under way. The Brat was apparently a favourite with the King, and had been called for to satisfy him after his recovery from the entertainment. Although the girls were usually kept naked, Uilus preferred them brought to him dressed. The Brat had been oiled and perfumed, assisted with her make-up and given a wrap of heavy golden silk, richer than anything Iriel had seen or worked with. It had been worn low on her hips, leaving her apple-like breasts bare and also her navel, in which she had worn a great yellow stone.

No sooner had the servants left than she had taken a peach she had secreted in her cabinet and eaten it without the slightest thought for her appearance. The juice had left long streaks on the oiled skin of her breasts and belly, and also soiled her wrap. Once finished, she had casually dropped the wet stone on a cushion, at the precise moment the servants had returned.

The leader among the servants had responded with a squeal of outrage, then gone into a torrent of recrimination and instruction. The Brat had squealed just as loudly as she was quickly stripped and hauled over a servant's knee, buttocks up and towards Iriel, who was watching with her fingers in her ears. The spanking had started and the Brat's squeals had grown louder still.

'It reminds me of my village,' Cianna remarked from beyond the screen, 'a pig-killing.'

Iriel chuckled, amused by the joke and delighted to have a spectacle to break her boredom, especially as it was the Brat getting another spanking, something she longed to do herself. It was due to be a good one as well, with the leading servant red-faced with anger as he pulled up a tabouret to add his own efforts, then stretched out for her hairbrush.

He gripped the Brat's body, lifted it a little to settle her waist comfortably onto his lap, and set to work,

128

applying the hairbrush to her bottom with all his force. It sent her into a pained frenzy, neat yellow-brown buttocks pumping wildly to the motion of her legs, her fists hammering on the cushions, her little breasts jumping under her chest, her hair flying free as she tossed her head, her squeals rising to an ear-splitting crescendo.

She was hardly contrite though, her piglike squeals interspersed with insults and curses, which only served to stoke the servants' rage. All were shouting, furious demands for her to behave, delivered in high-pitched excitement, and all the time spanking, as hard as they could, hand and hairbrush slapping down on her trim cheeks. She was showing everything, grossly immodest, with her legs repeatedly spread to the full, her tuppenny agape, the pink centre clearly visible and clearly moist.

Her bottom ring showed too, a little pink hole that started to wink as Iriel watched. Her own tuppenny was tingling and she was wishing she had some opportunity to take a cock, even if it meant a spanking first. Not that it seemed likely, but as a particularly hard double swat caused a squirt of white juice to erupt from the Brat's cunt, she was sure that at last there would be a fucking.

Yet the servants continued to spank, apparently as indifferent to the Brat's physical beauty and helpless arousal as they were to her squeals of pain. Even when she broke down, bursting into tears and begging for mercy they never stopped, slowed, nor took advantage of her condition, despite her tuppenny being swollen and so ready that her hole showed as a little black mouth each time her legs kicked wide.

Leaning close to the screen, Iriel spoke to Cianna.

'See how she juices! Why do they not fuck her, or bugger her if that is their preference?'

'They are eunuchs,' Cianna answered. 'They have nothing with which to fuck.'

'Nothing?' Iriel queried.

'Neither cocks to fuck with nor balls to provide the jism,' Cianna assured her.

'They are freaks?' Iriel queried. 'But there are so many, and all so similar.'

'They are eunuchs,' Cianna explained, 'their cocks and balls cut off to prevent them fucking the girls and getting bastards on the Palades' property.'

Iriel turned back to where the spanking continued, as hard as ever, despite the Brat's bottom being purple with bruising and her pleas and apologies taking on a hysterical edge. She stared in horror, suddenly understanding not only the reason for the servants' reticence, but for their malice towards girls. It was a disturbing thought, and she pulled her hand from between her thighs, where she had been massaging herself in the hope of masturbating while the Brat was fucked.

The servants was finishing the tear-streaked Brat off with a few hard swats to her thighs when abruptly all was silent, even the spanked girl's last wail dying and then cutting off abruptly as she looked back across her shoulder. Iriel followed the direction of her gaze, to find a man stood to one side, middle-aged, of typical Oretean build save for a heavy paunch overhanging the sash of a robe patterned black, crimson and gold. A wreath of golden leaves circled his head, and she realised it could only be the King himself even as the servants dropped to their knees.

'Where is the slut I called for?' he demanded.

The girls in the alcoves opposite had put their faces to the ground and extended their arms in front of them, palms flat to the floor, even the Brat, a position that left her rosy bottom cheeks the highest part of her body.

'Here, Great King,' the leading servant answered, his voice a trembling falsetto. 'Chastised for daring to show improper respect to the honour you –'

The King kicked him, to sending him sprawling onto his back. He scuttled away, crawling and babbling so fast his words were unintelligible. The King scratched his ear, his gaze wandering lazily over the scene before fixing on the Brat. His mouth twitched into a smile. He lifted his robe, exposing a dark, ugly penis, the head already showing damp from the mouth of the thick foreskin. Reaching down, he took the Brat by the hair and pulled her up, onto his cock.

She squeaked in protest, but took him in, her eyes setting in disgust, her cheeks bulging briefly, then caving in as she began to suck. He gave a contented sigh and began to twist her hair in his hand, turning her expression to pain. Still she sucked, his cock growing in her mouth, the tears rolling slowly down her face as he twisted and jerked at her hair. At last he came, with his cock jammed into her windpipe so that the jism exploded from her nose. She was left gagging and spitting on the floor, twin ropes of sperm hanging from her nostrils, yellowish drool running out from her lower lip as she grovelled down at his feet. He took no notice whatsoever, picking up the golden silk wrap from the floor to wipe his cock, then looking down at the remaining servant.

He paused, glanced around, then picked up the pot into which the Brat had peed and smashed it down on the servant's head. The servant screamed, knocked sideways to grovel in the mess on the floor as the remains of the pot was brought down on his head again, and again, until he lay sprawled unconscious, blood seeping from gashes in his scalp to mingle with the Brat's spilled urine.

'Is it really suitable that the Palades should fetch his own sluts?' the King enquired, immediately soliciting agreement, condemnation of the injured man and a chorus of weak laughter.

The King gave the servant a final kick and turned to look around, focusing on Iriel. She gave a formal nod, her muscles tense, her throat so tight she could barely breathe, yet determined to obey the voices in her head, each screaming at her not to grovel.

'What are these?' he remarked.

A servant crawled forward, looking at the ground as he answered.

'Aeg girls, Great King, from the barbarian far north, the continent Kora, presented as a gift from the Prince Palades Daken.'

'They are huge,' the King stated. 'Pretty, but huge. What monstrous udders! Do they speak!'

'We do,' Iriel answered.

'Insolence!' a servant hissed, moving forward only to be sent back again with a kick from the King.

'They are barbarian, Great King,' another servant blustered, his head to the floor but well back from the King. 'They have no respect, not even the intelligence to recognise your greatness, little more than animals.'

'Even animals recognise true greatness,' the King stated, sending the servant into babbled apologies and admissions of his own stupidity. 'Do my horses permit others to mount them? No.'

He stretched, gave the servant on the ground another kick and glanced around once more at the girls, before speaking again.

'That was fine. I feel quite refreshed. Some girls, I think. I am in leisurely mood, so no barbar sluts at present. So let me see. Yes, the black one with the fat bottom, another of the same and a pair of Vendjomois, any will do. Put them in their clothes and bring them.'

He turned on his heel, snatching a goblet of wine from the tray of a servant as he went, to drain it and overturn it on the man's head, leaving trickles of red running down from beneath the rim. Immediately he was gone the other servants hurried to carry their injured colleague away and to clean up the mess in front of the Brat's alcove and elsewhere, all the while casting black looks at her and the other girls.

* * *

At the edge of sleep, Iriel lay staring up into the blackness, wondering if she should masturbate. Nobody could see, light never penetrating to the inner parts of the harem chamber no matter how many moons were up, yet the wet noises her fingers made in her tuppenny tended to grow loud when she was coming towards orgasm. Despite the fact that the other girls did it she invariably found herself embarrassed afterwards. It had not stopped her the night before, coming with her legs spread to the darkness as she thought of cocks and spankings and more cocks, wishing she was back in the slave coffle with a hot bottom and an erection in each hole as she came. Afterwards the Brat's giggle had sent the blood rushing to her face.

She lay back, stroking her belly and trying to tell herself that it would soothe her to sleep. Yet it was difficult, the Aprayan night too hot as always, and the soft noises of the harem niggling at the edge of her mind, the gentle susurration of girls breathing, sighs, sometimes sobs, sometimes moans or the sounds of fingers applied to moist cunts. The chains prevented the girls from touching each other, the King too jealous to permit lesbianism save when he ordered it. Yet Iriel knew that sometimes girls came out to the end of their chains to whisper to each other as they masturbated. Even Yi had done it, with the Cypraean girl, to Iriel's surprise, yet with the Brat opposite her it hardly seemed practical.

Thinking of the Brat put new thoughts into her head, of what had happened during the day, both the spanking and the brutal intrusion of the King. An image of the Brat's little yellow-brown bottom dancing to the slaps rose up in her mind and she found her fingers slipping lower, wishing she had been able to dish out the same treatment, even that the eunuchs would do the same to her, anything for some sexual contact.

With a sigh of resignation she began to masturbate, taking one breast in hand and spreading her legs as her fingers moved to the sticky, sensitive groove between her thighs. She was wet, her hole open enough to accommodate two fingers with ease, and she spent a moment pushing them in and out and thinking of how the caravan guards had liked to fuck her until her arousal pushed down the inevitable shame. Her little finger found her bottom hole, teasing the tight ring as she thought of how it felt to have it penetrated by an eager male cock. In memory, even the pain seemed welcome.

Her excitement was rising, and not for the first time she wondered if she dare suggest trading her dirty thoughts with Cianna or even Kaissia. Yet both were asleep, while the Brat was sure to overhear in any case, leading to the announcement of her most intimate thoughts in the morning, a whisper that could be guaranteed to have spread around the entire harem chamber by the following evening.

Determined to be quick, and silent, she put her palm to her tuppenny, pressing to her bump and rubbing as she imagined being fought over and ravished by the victor, always her favourite fantasy. The Oreteans were no good, too small and weak, too devious. An Aeg was better, some huge warrior with a massive cock, his opponent lying defeated on the ground, herself caught, thrown down, her legs forced apart, mounted, his cock driven hard up into her tuppenny, over and over as she was fucked.

Iriel came, tight-lipped, but unable to suppress a gasp of ecstasy as the thought of being ravished without the slightest choice for who did the fucking ran over and over in her mind. The climax held well, the picture of the man standing over her with his huge erection sticking up ready for her hole perfectly clear in her mind, his opponent too, and the scene beyond, a forest glade, lush green grass, woods, flowers, and clouds and gentle rain. Her climax broke in a welter of homesickness and she slumped back onto the cushions even as a voice spoke from the darkness opposite, a whisper soft as velvet and rich with mockery.

'How was that, big slut? Good?'

Iriel sighed as the blood rushed to her face. One of the other girls opposite giggled. Encouraged, the Brat went on.

'What did you think of? A troll? No, too small for that huge cunt. A horse? Barely enough, but don't be sad, think of your giant friend, with her arse up under an elephant, cock in her cunt and still not touching the sides!'

The Brat finished with a long, lewd snigger. Aeisla's voice sounded.

'Enough insults, Brat. Go to sleep.'

'Who are you to call Brat!' the voice came back, now sharp but still mocking. 'You wait. You will get your big arse spanked in time. Then we will see how wide your cunt is, won't we? Easily enough for an elephant, I'm sure.'

'Enough,' Aeisla repeated.

'I shall speak when I wish,' the Brat responded. 'What will you do to prevent me? Yes, Aeisla, you will be spanked, just as I am, if it takes every servant to hold you. Then we shall see how you look, with your big buttocks red and your cunt and arsehole spread for all to see. You will cry. You will howl! Maybe they will even stick the hairbrush handle up your fat arse when they have finished with you! Oh, how funny that will be, and it will come, soon enough.'

'Not so soon as yours.'

'No? Who can say, Aeisla? Soon the King will order you to him, and when you fail to satisfy, as such a crude barbar bitch is sure to do, then you will be spanked, long and hard, maybe whipped, maybe given the bastinado, to teach you to suck and fuck properly, Aeisla, to –'

She broke off at the sound of a metallic snap. Iriel sat up, biting her lip in sudden excitement. There could be no mistaking the noise. Aeisla had broken her chain. The Brat seemed to think otherwise, laughing, then speaking.

'You seek to break your chain, Aeisla? You wish to get at me? To spank my bottom? How you wish it, I am sure! How you would love to, how –'

She broke off with a squeak, abruptly muffled, then followed by soft noises, an odd drumming sound, a meaty smack, another click, then Aeisla's voice in an amused whisper.

'Who is awake? Iriel, yes?'

'I also,' Yi's voice sounded.

'Yes,' Iriel answered. 'You have the Brat?'

'I do,' Aeisla answered from just in front of Iriel's alcove. 'Hold her, and keep the cushion over her face to stifle her squeals.'

'I shall,' Iriel promised as Aeisla passed her something warm and wriggling, the Brat, held with a cushion pushed to her face and both her wrists twisted hard into the small of her back. Iriel took over, ignoring the Brat's squirming body and kicking feet, but holding the cushion just firmly enough to allow breathing. The Brat made no effort to cry out, but seemed more worried about her bottom, wriggling it frantically about so that the firm little cheeks moved against Iriel's thighs and arm.

Another snap sounded from the next alcove, a puzzled grunt, then Kaissia's voice.

'What . . . Aeisla? Why? Is it now?'

'No,' Aeisla hissed back. 'I have the Brat, come and play with her.'

'Gladly.'

There was a world of cruelty in Kaissia's voice, also revenge. Immediately the Brat's squirming grew more urgent. Iriel found herself grinning and tightened her grip, then threw a leg over the Brat's body, seating herself on the little thighs, which pumped madly for an

136

instant and then went still. As Kaissia joined her in the alcove, Iriel felt her friend's hand, on her wrist, then lower, to the Brat's bottom.

'I have longed to spank this,' Kaissia hissed, drawing a muffled squeak and more writhing from the Brat.

'What of the noise?' Iriel questioned.

'No matter the noise,' Cianna's voice sounded from the blackness. 'Spank her well!'

'The eunuchs will come,' another voice came, the Cypraean girl's. 'Their chambers are near.'

'No matter the eunuchs!' Kaissia laughed. 'She'll be well spanked before they can get me off, be sure!'

'No,' Aeisla hissed, 'spank her later. 'For now, we make her lick our tuppennies.'

Yi's distinctive giggle sounded before Kaissia replied.

'A good thought, our bottom rings as well. Then we spank her.'

'Just so. Iriel, turn her over.'

Iriel obeyed, twisting the Brat's body beneath her own with Kaissia's help as Cianna held the cushion. A long, muscular leg touched her arm as Aeisla swung aboard, straddling the Brat's face. Cianna spoke.

'Now listen, Brat. You have seen my teeth, yes? Well, they are filed because we barbar girls eat raw meat. We are also cannibals. Lick well and we might spare you.'

The Brat's writhing became abruptly stronger and she cried out as the cushion was removed, only to be abruptly silenced as Aeisla squatted into her face. It didn't stop her struggling, though, her body squirming beneath Iriel's, more frantically than ever as Aeisla spoke.

'Lick, little Brat, or we will eat you. You do not believe me?'

She broke off with a sigh, liquid noises starting at the same instant. Aeisla spoke again, her voice full of delight.

'There, Brat, you have done it. Is it so bad? Now lick well, there first, yes, deep inside.'

Again she sighed, and Iriel felt the Brat's body shiver. Taking her breasts in hand, she began to massage them, thinking of the few times in Aegerion when other girls had licked her tuppenny and trying to push back memories of being made to do the same by Mistress Loida. Her nipples were quickly stiff, and she made no objection as a hand curved around her waist to settle onto the swell of her hip.

'She licks well,' Aeisla sighed. 'Suckle me, two of you.'

Aeisla had reached for Iriel's breasts, cupping them, then taking hold to pull her gently forwards. Iriel came to the pressure, their lips meeting. Aeisla let go as they began to kiss. Iriel's breasts swung forwards, to touch the hair of whichever two girls were suckling, tickling her nipples. The hand at her waist went lower, to stroke her bottom, following the curve of her cheeks, exploring her, then slipping between to cup her tuppenny.

Still the Brat licked, the wet noises now faster, more urgent as the five girls cuddled together, stroking and kneading. Iriel had no idea who was where, save for Aeisla, and that it was probably Yi who was masturbating her from behind. She responded anyway, releasing the Brat's hands to take a plump breast in each, to discover that it was Kaissia and Cianna on Aeisla's breasts, as she had expected.

Aeisla came with a gasp of pleasure, spent a moment more riding the Brat's face, then dismounted with a pleased giggle. Kaissia replaced her immediately, wriggling her full bottom down over their victim's head until her cheeks were well spread out, bottom ring to mouth, as Iriel realised when she spoke.

'Clean me first, Brat, and think on what you have said to me as you taste my dung. Do it . . . do it!'

She gasped, then spoke again as Yi's finger slid up Iriel's tuppenny.

'She is doing it, girls, she is licking my bottom ring. Yes, Brat, that is right, put your tongue in the hole . . .

taste my dung ... taste it. Who is dirty now, who uncivilised? You may think me a barbarian, Brat, but I do not lick clean other girls' bottom rings! Ah, but that is good. I used to have my maid do this, in Aegmund. How she hated it, how she pouted, how she begged. But always, once spanked, her tongue would go in, just as yours is Brat, deep up my bottom ring ... deep up.'

Yi giggled. Iriel gasped as juice from her tuppenny was wiped on her bottom ring to let a finger in. Both holes full, Yi began to manipulate the soft flesh between. Iriel sighed, allowing her own hands to slip lower, to Yi's own bottom and also Cianna's. Gently, she began to spank Yi, just pats, and to knead Cianna's bottom. Both responded, pushing their cheeks out for more as Kaissia began to gasp in pleasure, first rubbing her tuppenny as her anus was probed, then breaking into babbling, ecstatic speech.

'... lick it ... yes, right in, all the way. Taste me ... feed on me ... in your mouth. Yes, more ... and swallow ... swallow, you dirty little brat!'

She screamed, pure ecstasy as a gulping noise sounded from beneath her. Cianna gave a delighted squeal and wriggled her bottom in Iriel's hand, Yi began to rub harder, all five of them coming together, to stroke and paw Kaissia as she went through climax, all the while squirming her bottom in the Brat's face.

'Quieter,' Aeisla urged as Kaissia at last finished, 'we must all come, Kaissia.'

Kaissia's answer was a satisfied purr. She dismounted and Cianna quickly took her place. The Brat was no longer protesting and began to lick immediately Cianna's tuppenny settled into her face.

'She is enjoying it!' Cianna laughed. 'She has my thighs! Yes, lick well, Brat, and my ring too if that is to your taste. Suckle my breasts, Aeisla, and you too, Iriel.'

Iriel went forwards immediately, to take one firm nipple into her mouth, her bottom lifting to Yi's finger as she did so. She was getting near climax, but in no mood to stop, too high to care if she came under Yi's fingers or the Brat's tongue. Aeisla had closed again, to suckle Cianna's other breast, and Iriel reached out, first to put an arm across her friend's back, then to touch the huge, heavy breasts hanging beneath her. Aeisla gave an encouraging wiggle and Iriel began to fondle, all the while with the noise of the Brat's tongue working on Cianna's cunt directly beneath them.

In moments Cianna had come, writhing her bottom in the Brat's face, tuppenny to mouth, little pert nose pushed up her bottom hole. Iriel was too locked into Aeisla to take her rightful place, and Yi mounted up, backwards, her rounded bottom pushed out. Delighted, Iriel took hold, feeling the meaty little cheeks as the Brat licked between them. Kaissia came close, to take Iriel in hand, fondling her dangling breasts and spanking her gently. Iriel wiggled, wanting to be masturbated, but Kaissia only spanked harder in response, filling Iriel's head with the urge to put her face between Yi's buttocks and join the Brat in licking bottom ring.

She resisted, with difficulty, contenting herself with kissing the rounded cheeks and briefly wiggling her face between them. At that moment Yi pushed herself back to get her tuppenny to the Brat's mouth. Iriel's face was abruptly smothered in bottom, the little wet ring an inch from her mouth. It was too much, and she stuck her tongue up, her head filled with shame but also ecstasy as her own bottom quivered to the slaps of Kaissia's hand. Then Yi had come and it was her own turn.

Yi dismounted, giggling. Iriel rose and swung forwards, imagining the Brat's tiny, pretty face as she sat her bottom on it, ring to mouth, determined to have her own hole licked to compensate for having done it herself. The Brat began immediately, tongue probing the tight hole as the others closed in around Iriel. A mouth fastened to each nipple, sucking firmly. Yi took her head, their mouths meeting in an open, dirty kiss, pleasure and a delicious feeling of naughtiness welling up in Iriel's head as they shared the taste of bottom. Behind her, Kaissia continued to spank, harder now, the slaps ringing out, Iriel's cheeks jumping, jolts of exquisite pain running through her every time. Yi's finger found her tuppenny, to fiddle in the fleshy folds and tickle the little bump between.

Iriel caught the change in light through the lids of her closed eyes as Yi began to masturbate her. Nobody stopped, the Brat unable to see, the others not caring. At the next instant Iriel was coming, her anus tightening on the Brat's tongue even as the high-pitched screams of the eunuchs' outrage reached her. She ignored them, her every sense fixed on the feel of Yi's tongue, the stiffness of her nipples in Aeisla and Cianna's mouths, Kaissia's firm, stinging spanks on her bottom, the Brat's tongue in her anus, and above all the finger on her bump.

She was still coming as fingers took her shoulders. Her balance on the Brat's face went immediately, there was a gasp of pain and the fingers slipped loose, but she was already falling, backwards on top of the Brat, who gave a squeal of surprise and consternation at the sight of the eunuchs. Lantern light surrounded them with flickering orange, sending shadows dancing among the alcoves and showing the faces of the girls in them, most frightened, the Cypraean girl wearing a smug grin.

One eunuch was sprawled on the ground, and as Aeisla rose to her full height the other two quickly gave back. Neither reached her chest, and their expressions turned to raw fear as she stretched the broken chain between her hands. The one on the ground also retreated, scuttling backwards on his hands, heels and buttocks, but speaking as he did, his voice high and piping.

'Obey! Obey! The guard will be called! Obey!'

Kaissia chuckled. 'Call them, and the tub of suet you call a King!'

'You will obey!' the eunuch squealed from beyond the end of the line of alcoves. 'You will! You shall be made to!'

'Be calm,' Aeisla stated, holding her hands out to the girls as she addressed the eunuchs. 'Disturb the guard now, and no doubt at all the Palades will have you soundly punished as well as us. Otherwise, you may return to your rest and we to ours. Is this not wise?'

The eunuch had risen, and for a moment his face worked between fear and spite before he answered.

'No. The broken chains will be found, and we shall be whipped twice as soundly for lying. It must be reported!'

Aeisla shrugged.

'You will be broken!' another of the eunuchs squealed from further back. 'The Great King has met with Palades Daken, who has told him much. A remarkable diversion has been arranged!'

'Then no doubt we shall need our rest,' Aeisla answered.

Iriel drew her breath in. She was back in costume, this time a creation of the King's, with a few hints from Palades Daken. It blended the ideas of Madame Hivies and Assanach the caravaneer, and was as absurd as either. Her high-laced sandals had been retrieved, also the feather skirts and tops, only for the King to quibble about the use of ostrich feathers. In consequence she had the sandals and skirt and top, but of torn leather, the one so short half her bottom showed at the rear, the other with holes cut to allow her nipples to protrude. A copper band confined her hair, into which an eagle feather had been stuck, the result of Cianna admitting it to be the largest bird of Aegmund. She had also been painted, her face, her shoulders, the upper slopes of her breasts and her belly decorated with blue and red patterns approximately similar to those on Kaissia's breasts.

Once ready, they had been brought down to an open court somewhere to the rear of the palace. A stepped cloister surrounded the court, providing shade and seating for a considerable crowd; harem girls and eunuchs, courtiers and dignitaries, nobility and royalty, including Palades Daken and the King himself. Many sipped chilled wine or nibbled at fruit and sweetmeats, the Brat was on her knees between the King's legs, sucking his cock with her bare bottom stuck out towards the gate through which the girls had been marshalled. Cianna spoke quietly as it closed behind them, addressing Aeisla.

'Clearly Daken has made his arrangement, there are but six guards in all. We should strike.'

'Shall I present a challenge?' Kaissia queried.

'No,' Aeisla answered quietly, 'the King's response is unpredictable. Allow him to choose the time.'

Kaissia nodded and at Aeisla's signal the five began to advance together, towards where the King sat, wine cup in hand, his eyes glazed with pleasure as he twisted his hand into the Brat's hair. Aeisla folded her hands across her chest, watching boldly. The Brat's head bobbed up and down, faster and faster, only to stop suddenly, held tight down, his cock wedged in her throat. Her eyes screwed up in disgust, her cheeks bulged, jism exploded from her nose, then sick from mouth, all over the King's balls as he sighed with pleasure. Servants hurried forward with water and sponges as the Brat was kicked to one side.

Aeisla began to whistle and to look around the court, pretending to admire the statues set on the cloister roof. Several courtiers gave gasps of outrage or made offended remarks, but the King ignored everything, waiting until he had been washed and dried before speaking as his robe was rearranged.

'Yes, my friends, they are insolent indeed! They do not kneel. They do not so much as bow. But why? It is

143

because they are untrained, ignorant, with no understanding of their place in the great scheme of things. Should I have them spanked, perhaps, to impress upon them the realities of the world?'

There was immediate laughter and a chorus of agreement mixed with compliments on the King's wisdom and wit. He listened for a moment, his face flushed with both pleasure and drink, then raised one hand for silence.

'No,' he stated, to an immediate murmur of agreement. 'I shall not have them spanked. Only a fool would have them spanked. True, once they have come to appreciate their place, then they may be spanked, and often. Not yet though, anymore than one would cuff away a wild baboon.'

There was a ripple of laughter before he continued.

'Yes,' he stated, 'essentially they are beasts, and must be treated as beasts, broken to the command of man. Yet each beast is different. The dog is easily cowed, the horse less so. The mandrill or baboon will fight and never fully succumb, save to force. The cat is less pliant still. What then of these barbar girls? How shall we treat them? What animal do they most resemble?'

'Dogs, Great King,' a plump young man in a robe of blue and silver silk answered immediately. 'They are like dogs, snarling defiance, yet all the while fearful underneath.'

'Not dogs but baboons, Great King,' another called out. 'When they came into the city, she, the one with the palest hair, she even had her behind painted blue!'

The King laughed, then spoke again.

'No, my friends, not dogs, nor baboons. To all intents and purposes, they are wild nymphs, and their obedience, and indeed devotion, will come only when they learn the pleasure to be derived from the feel of cock in cunt. Yes, I hear you say, this is true of women generally, but here we have a special case. Women of breeding and sense place their foreheads to the ground in my presence, these do not, and nor do nymphs. When I have fucked them, then they shall!'

Clapping and calls of encouragement broke out, along with praise for the King's virility, also a murmur of agreement and comments in praise of his wisdom.

'And so I will teach them, here and now!' the King called out. 'Quaedes, a draught!'

A man hurried to the King's side, offering a tiny bottle of ultramarine glass. Uilus took it and upended it over his mouth, drew a deep breath and stood up, the crowd cheering and clapping all around him. Climbing over the low cloister wall, he stood to face the girls. One pull and his sash had fallen away, a tug and his robe fell around him, to leave him naked, his body a pale, unhealthy yellow in the blazing sunlight, his paunch hanging down to half obscure his penis.

'Five, he will fuck all five!' a voice called out in awe from among the crowd, then others.

'He is man indeed!'

'Just so, and he will leave each begging for more!'

'Then we shall see them kneel!'

'Which first?' the King queried, putting one hand to his gold-encased beard in thought as he began to stroke his cock with the other. 'The giantess, perhaps? But no, a true artist leaves the grandest movement until last. The pale-haired beauty? Again no, her hauteur must be allowed to soften as she watches the others broken and comes to realise her own fate. You, perhaps?'

He had reached Cianna, to take her chin in hand, tilting it up. She met his gaze, looking down her nose into his eyes. As he let go she smiled and for a moment his eyes opened in surprise. He moved on, to Iriel, then to Yi, all the while playing with his slowly expanding penis.

'The answer is clear,' he stated, reaching out to take one of Yi's breasts in hand. 'They are barbars, and so I shall fuck them in that order they doubtless see themselves, from the least to the most ferocious. First, this brown-haired slut, who may be smallest among them, but whose breasts are as full as any but the milk mothers in my harem.'

Yi gave a single glance to Aeisla, who nodded. Uilus appeared not to notice, still fondling one plump breast, his cock growing as he rubbed a thumb over Yi's nipple to make it stiffen. Behind, the crowd watched in delight, drinking, and in a few cases fondling their own girl slaves.

'Also,' Uilus stated, 'to add jest to their lovemaking, I will have any who fail to be entirely pleasing suitably punished, in a fashion which I understand is the way Aeg girls are traditionally treated if they fail to live up to expectations.'

Raucous laughter spread through the crowd, along with more comments on the King's wit and cleverness. He responded with a mock bow, snapped his fingers and, as a gasp went up from the crowd, Iriel turned. From the same entrance through which they had been brought six servants were carrying a cage. In it was a troll, and no youngster, but a huge, grey-black adult male, some twice the height of the tallest of the servants and bulky in proportion. From between its bowed legs hung a cock larger by far than any she had seen save on horses.

Excited chattering rose from the crowd, giggles, speculation as to whether the man-beast would split a girl, bets also on who would be put in with the troll and whether she would survive the experience. Uilus spent a moment admiring the troll, another basking in the adulation of the crowd, all the while playing with Yi's breasts, before she was pulled down by her now stiff nipples, onto his cock. She took it in, eyes closed, cheeks pulled in, sucking gently. His hand tightened in her hair, twisting hard. Yi's body stiffened and she began to suck harder, her breasts swinging out as she adjusted herself, knees wide, her hand going to her tuppenny as she readied herself for cock. Uilus laughed.

'See? Already the slut rubs at her cunt, and she barely has me hard in her mouth. Perhaps there is more of the dog in them after all. A quirt!'

A man in the crowd threw out a dog quirt not unlike the one Iriel had been whipped with in Staive Cintes. Uilus caught it, turned the handle and brought it down across Yi's back and bottom. She flinched but kept sucking. Again he struck, and again twisting his hand harder into her hair to hold her on his erection as she was whipped, cackling with laughter as the long red welts sprang up on her back.

In the crowd, several men had moved their slavegirls down onto their cocks, not ostentatiously, but with their robes over the girls' upper bodies, so that only their bottoms and the soles of their feet showed as they sucked. One, an enormously fat man, even had two girls under his mustard-coloured robe, their heads jostling beneath the silk as they sucked and licked at his genitals.

Uilus pulled out suddenly, still laughing as his now fully erect cock left Yi's mouth. She swallowed, looked up, her eyes wide. He still had her hair, and used his grip to force her around and down, her welted bottom lifting to receive him as he poked his cock at her tuppenny. It went in, pushed cleanly up the juicy hole, and as he began to fuck her he whipped her again, lashing her back, which was held in a tight arc by the grip in her hair, her head pulled back, her bottom rising to accommodate his cock.

The crowd clapped the manoeuvre, and again as Yi began to gasp, apparently overcome by the pleasure of her fucking. Uilus gave a cheer and laid in harder with the lash and with his cock, whipping and pumping, to draw thick red weals across Yi's lifted bottom and her back as she began to grunt and squeal.

147

'A pig!' a voice called from the audience. 'That is what these girls are, brush pigs!'

At that moment Uilus grunted, dropped the whip and jammed himself to the hilt in Yi's cunt. She cried out as jism burst from around his cock shaft to spatter his balls and the sand of the courtyard, and then he was sinking back, his cock sliding from her sopping hole to the frenzied cheers and clapping of the crowd.

Uilus moved his hand in a gesture of appreciation, reached out to take the eagle feather from Yi's hair, inserted it into her anus and gave her a resounding smack across the bottom. She jumped up, her whole body trembling, the feather quivering where it protruded from between her buttocks as she scampered away, to Aeisla's side. For a moment Uilus' face showed astonishment, then anger, then a grimace of malign humour.

'No respect? I have been too gentle! So, in with the troll she goes!'

Laughter spread across the crowd and more bets were called as the six guards closed in on Yi, who gave Aeisla an imploring look. Aeisla gave a single firm nod as two guards took Yi's arms. She began to fight, struggling futilely in their grip, and to whimper, her face working in fear as she was dragged across the court, her fingers clutching in raw terror. Uilus folded his arms on his chest, watching in amusement until she had been pulled as far as the cage.

The troll showed interest immediately, his lump of a nose twitching in appreciation at the scent of cunt. His hand went to his cock, to pull at it as his hideous face began to work with excitement. Two guards with spears came close, to prod at him, forcing him back as the door was opened. Yi was screaming, and clutching at the bars of the cage, her face wild with fear. The guards broke her grip, and hurled her backwards to sprawl on the floor of the cage even as the spearmen stood back. The troll was on her in an instant, lifting her one-handed as if she were a doll, holding her for a moment, her feet well clear of the ground, as he brought his cock to full, monstrous erection with a few last tugs. Ready, he stuck her on, Yi screaming as she was penetrated.

Yells of delight and frenzied betting calls rang out from the crowd as the troll began to fuck Yi. He had encircled her waist with both hands, and was jerking her up and down on his cock. Her legs, arms and hair were flying in every direction, her breasts bouncing wildly on her chest, and still she was screaming. Iriel tightened her fists, praying for her friend, and then Yi's arms had come around the troll's neck, her legs had locked above his massive buttocks and she was riding the huge cock. Still she had no control whatever over her fucking, but she was supporting herself, while her face had gone slack with bliss.

Gasps of astonishment rose up from the crowd, then curses for the troll and yells of encouragement for Yi from those who had lost or won money on the encounter. Iriel thumped her fist into the palm of her hand. Her own tuppenny was twitching despite herself, with the aromas of heated male troll and aroused cunt thick in the air. As the troll grunted and a great splash of jism appeared beneath Yi's buttocks, Iriel had to close her eyes to make the urge to be entered die down.

Satisfied, the troll dropped Yi, leaving her to scramble hastily for the cage door. The spearmen came forward, but the huge man-beast merely hunkered down in a corner and began to investigate the contents of one nostril. Yi crawled from the door, apparently too weak to walk. Aeisla ran across the court to scoop Yi up in her arms. Reaching the others, she quickly hoisted Yi's leg wide, exposing her gaping, sperm-sodden sex. Cianna leaned in quickly, to suck at Yi's tuppenny, then Kaissia after a fastidious grimace. Iriel followed suit, putting her mouth to the fleshy little hole to suck out troll sperm and swallow. Aeisla went last, holding Yi to her mouth, then pushing two fingers into her cunt, then her mouth.

'What do they do?' a voice from the crowd demanded.

'Some revolting barbarian ritual, no doubt,' another suggested as Yi was at last lowered to the ground.

The King stepped forward, grinning as he looked down at her. Yi took a deep breath, then rose, to stand. She was shaking, but firmly upright as she swallowed, sucked her cheeks in and spat a gout of mixed saliva and troll jism full in his face.

For one brief instant there was nothing, the crowd absolutely silent, the King staring as if unable to take in what had happened as the clot of filth rolled slowly down his cheek. Then the crowd was screaming, demanding death for Yi, by hanging in a cage, by impalement, by burning, and a dozen other agonising choices. At last Uilus wiped the mess from his face, now dark with fury. When he spoke, each word was spat from between his teeth.

'Still no respect, you barbar slut? Die then, if that is your wish, on the pyre . . . no, drowned like the rat you are and the pyre also, upside down in a tub of pig filth as you are stoned. There, that is fitting is it not?'

He had turned to the crowd as servants hurried to him with water, towels, wine and more. Laughter and calls of approval answered him and his anger vanished as swiftly as it had come. He stood, took a deep breath, then reached out to take a cup of wine from a proffered tray, downing it in one before speaking again.

'Quaedes, a second draught. I shall show the next what a fucking is. Clearly I was too lenient with the first . . . yes . . .'

The moment he had swallowed his elixir he turned to Iriel, whose stomach was tying itself in knots. She glanced to Aeisla, who responded with a soft nod. She took hold of her foolish leather top, pulling it high to

150

spill her breasts free. Uilus grinned and reached out to take her breasts, squeezing them hard to make her nipples pop as she took a mouthful of the leather and bit hard into it. Then he had taken her by the hair, jerking hard to pull her down to the ground. She went, caught off balance, to sprawl on the grass. Uilus immediately clambered over her, legs straddled, his square and meaty buttocks over her head. He squatted down, and the crowd roared with laughter as first his balls and then his buttocks settled onto Iriel's face.

She began to kick and struggle, unable to stop herself as she was smothered in the reeking crease between his buttocks, and her response drew fresh laughter and jeers from the crowd. He lifted a little, to dangle his balls onto her lips, and as he settled again she forced herself to open wide, thinking of how obedient Yi had been.

Iriel was already gagging as Uilus' scrotum filled her mouth. He tasted foul, of rancid spice and sweat and dirt and unwashed man, of Yi's cunt and of the Brat's sick. Yet she sucked, rolling the fat balls in her mouth, only to have him sit lower, spreading the soft flesh of his anus over the tip of her nose. He began to masturbate, his hand thumping on her chin as he tugged his cock. Her head was filling with angry voices, an insane elation rising within her, yet her tuppenny was tingling and the urge to spread her thighs was rising, even as he began to squirm his buttocks against her face.

Again he settled, pressing her nose deeper up his anus, to set her kicking again, in blind misery and shame and rage as he eased forwards, to drag his balls from her mouth and present her with his bottom. She began to lick, pushing her tongue into his bottom ring even as spasms began to shake her body for her shame and anger, her control slipping, the voices rising to screeching fury even as her thighs came up and wide.

Uilus laughed. His balls stopped slapping on her chin as he rose and she was left gasping on the ground, struggling to control herself, her whole body shaking, her mouth wide with dirty saliva running from the sides, her legs still open, her tuppenny juicy and ready for fucking. His cock was erect again, a column of gnarled flesh sprouting from beneath his heavy belly, the head glossy and purple with blood. Behind him, she saw Aeisla bite into the leather of her costume, then break into a grin.

Uilus stepped between her thighs, brandishing his cock as he sank down, blocking her view. The head was put to her tuppenny and in, filling her as his weight settled on her belly, her chest. His mouth found hers, and as he attempted to kiss her she broke. Raucous screaming exploded in her head. Her body jerked, bucking upwards to hurl Uilus off and send him rolling away. He cried out in anger, then pain as she clutched at his throat, screams breaking out on every side, curses, orders. A body slammed into her, knocking her aside, Kaissia, screeching.

'Mine! He's mine!'

Iriel let go, her head suddenly clear as Kaissia took her place. Guards were rushing towards them, the leader slashing out at Cianna as she tried to block his path, his sword cutting into her arm even as Aeisla's fist took him in the neck. Cianna screamed and went down, the guard also, as Iriel rolled frantically to one side. For a moment she saw Uilus's face, black-purple, the eyes bulging, dribble running from his open mouth, the abandoned dog quirt twisted right into his neck. Then she had bounced up, to fall again immediately as a guard barrelled into her.

They both went down, he struggling to get off Iriel and at Kaissia, she clinging to his sword arm in raw fury, indifferent to the scratching of his mail on her naked flesh. She twisted hard, throwing the guard, who grunted in pain as he hit the ground, and she was on top of him, triumphant screams ringing in her head. Every

152

hurt and indignity she had suffered boiled up inside her as she wrenched at his wrist, twisting viciously even as his fist drove repeatedly into her side. The sword fell loose. She snatched it. For one moment she hesitated, until her father's voice came cold and clear into her head, then she had thrust the point deep into the guard's neck. Blood sprayed her face and chest, the salt tang rich in her mouth and she was screaming in glee, all thoughts of mercy gone.

A leg was near her, male, and she hacked out viciously even as she scrambled up, cutting deep to evoke a scream of agony, abruptly silenced. The man collapsed, his neck cut half through, and Iriel found herself standing in clear space, and silence. Aeisla stood near her, her long legs set wide, a bloody sword in hand, braced in defiance of two guards. Cianna was down, clutching her arm, Yi also, a sword full through the flesh of her leg, both white-faced with pain. Beyond, the cloister was all but empty, those few who remained staring horror-struck at Kaissia, now knelt up on the King's chest, her face set in a feral grin. He was plainly dead, his body limp, his tongue lolling from his mouth, yet still she held the quirt tight around his neck. From somewhere in the distance screams sounded, then the clang of arms.

'Now?' Iriel demanded.

'Now we die,' Aeisla answered, her voice high with hysterical laughter. 'Come, Kaissia.'

She hurled herself forward at the guards, who broke, one running, one hesitating, then leaping into the cloister an inch in front of Aeisla's cut. Fresh guards burst into the court. Aeisla gave way, Iriel and Kaissia moving quickly together, their backs to the two wounded girls. The guards moved closer, warily, a Twelveman shouting commands, each and every one glancing at the body of their dead King. More followed, another twelve and a third, a man in Royal colours and brilliant armour with the last, Palades Tavian. Iriel braced, her throat painfully tight, her stomach churning as she waited for the rush, knowing that with thirty-eight to three there could only be one possible outcome, yet with her rage still singing in her head.

Prince Daken's voice rang out, demanding that they be taken alive. Aeisla answered with a curse, but he spoke again, a demand for allegiance, not to himself, but to the Princess Sulden. Iriel risked a glance back, to find him stood up on the wall of the cloister. Beside him, naked, her breasts and belly still soiled with the dead King's sperm, her features twisted in terror, was the Brat.

6

Erijome Forts

Standing at the window of their chamber high in Prince Daken's palace, Iriel looked down across Oretes. They had been there for nearly a month, unchained, free but confined in practice. Yet it seemed that Prince Daken had kept his word. There was no guard, Cianna and Yi had been tended to with care, and their needs had been attended by female servants.

In the court she had fully expected to die. With the King and four of the Royal Guard dead, it had seemed inevitable, and as she waited for the rush she had heard the clash of cups and yells of encouragement in her head. It had never come. With both Prince Daken and Palades Tavian proclaiming the Brat as Princess Sulden, attention had moved away from them. Order had been restored with a flexibility that would have been impossible in Aegmund, while it was clear that the overwhelming reaction to the death of Uilus was relief.

Palades Tavian had come forward to negotiate with Aeisla, ending with them being spirited away, ostensibly as captives. Only a handful of people now knew where they were, and those old and trusted servants of the Prince. He had visited only twice, and then briefly, with all his time and resource needed to smooth the transition from the rule of Uilus to that of Sulden. The girls had remained cautious, but with Cianna and Yi wounded they had had little choice but to follow Daken's instructions and hope that he acted in good faith.

Iriel turned at a noise, to find him standing in the doorway, smiling quietly. Aeisla, who had been by Cianna's bed, rose quickly, but her hand left the hilt of her sword as Daken raised a calming hand. Cianna pulled herself up, wincing at the pain in her shoulder. Kaissia made a last stroke on the sheet of charta she had been using to set down the events in the court as a saga. Yi remained peacefully asleep.

'It is done,' Daken remarked. 'You are now free citizens of Oretea.'

'We may come and go as we please?' Aeisla queried.

'Hardly that!' he laughed. 'It was no easy matter to justify not having you put to death in some elaborate manner, and as it is I have been only partly successful. Yet you are not slaves, and no man may claim to own you, myself included.'

'I thank you,' she answered him.

'Partly successful?' Kaissia queried.

'Partly,' he answered, 'in that the populace think you dead. I had no choice, as you can no doubt readily imagine. Normally, regicides would be executed at a lengthy and public ceremony, the details of which I shall spare you. In order to calm the mob I have had Sulden declare you animals, and the ceremonial execution therefore no more appropriate than for a troll or bear had Uilus fallen to such during a hunt. I therefore stated that you had been netted and killed by my personal guard. Hardly flattering, perhaps, but it was a question of expediency.'

'It would have clearly been easier to order the guards to finish us in the court,' Kaissia remarked. 'You are a man of high honour, for an Oretean.'

'More likely he has preserved us for some yet deeper scheme,' Cianna put in.

'Do not be ungracious, Cianna,' Kaissia replied. 'Prince Daken has behaved with honour, let that be sufficient. It is a remarkable saga, our part alone being worthy of perhaps thirty stanzas, yet the whole would be a fine thing to record indeed. I would gladly write it for you if I had the details, Great Prince.'

'Again our customs differ,' Daken answered. 'These are not matters for public record, nor record of any form. In Aegmund you would record these events?'

'In so far as they do credit to the participants, certainly. You have shown courage and intelligence, surely it is fitting to have your deeds recorded for your escutcheon?'

'Not so, at least, not for deeds such as these.'

'Tell us then,' Aeisla demanded. 'How, for instance, did the Princess Sulden come to be in her cousin's harem?'

Daken grimaced, then shrugged. 'Strange, that I may speak to Aeg as I never would to my own kin. That part was simple enough, and not to my credit. When Palades Thraxus died, the general expectation was that Uilus would be declared King. However, it was already plain that his character was unsuitable, and therefore Sulden was proclaimed Queen with myself as Regent. As such, a stalemate existed between Uilus and myself, neither able to remove the other, yet there was no question in my mind that he would have Sulden killed, just as soon as it could be made to seem a simple accident. So I took her, allowing him to think I myself had done the deed. Another council decision followed, and on this occasion he secured the Kingship. He was clever, then, before addling his brain with drugged wine, and for some years it was as much as I could do to defend my own position.'

'He attempted assassination?' Aeisla queried.

'Naturally, as did I. Neither of us succeeded, until your intervention. Indeed, for the last ten years or so we have lived in comparative amity, each content to let the other be. Meanwhile, Sulden grew up on my estates, not as a Princess, but as the child of one of my own slavegirls. So matters might have continued, but with Uilus becoming ever more debauched and ever more arrogant, my hand was forced. He began to make gestures designed to humiliate me, and other members of the House Palades – a mistake – also to promote his debauched friends to positions of importance and trust. Palades Tavian, for instance, was entirely loyal to Uilus before the titular command of the army was given to another, and not even of the House.'

'This I understand,' Aeisla remarked.

'It was the same with Sulden. Uilus and his friends visited my estate, and wished to play a cruel game with the slavegirls, making them eat to capacity and then fucking them to see who would be sick first and in what manner, with bets on the outcome. I was foolish, and spared Sulden on the pretext of illness. Uilus realised she was a favourite of mine, although not why. Inevitably he demanded her for his harem and I could not refuse without making an open defiance, which would have been madness, so I made a present of her. That was two months before your arrival, since when he has treated her with endless cruelty, as have his eunuchs. You saw how he made her choke on his cock in the court, a favourite trick of his.'

'We did, and yet, in the harem, it must be said that much of her woe she brought onto herself,' Aeisla put in.

'That I can imagine. I fear I indulged her whims too greatly as a child.'

'No question. Does she know we live?'

'She does. It is not my intention to hold back from her, as was necessary with Uilus. There are difficult times ahead for Oretea, and palace intrigue has taken up too much of my resource.'

'Much of this intrigue is simply too sordid to find a place in the saga,' Kaissia remarked. 'Yet I shall include your tricking of Uilus into bringing the troll, that was a valid use of your cunning.'

'Yes,' Daken replied. 'I felt I seeded his choice well enough. The true art was in making him believe he had conceived the idea himself. Yet troll or no troll, I had fully expected you to die. That is a remarkable trick. Never have I seen such speed, nor ferocity, in women or indeed men.'

'It was taught me by the witch Aurora,' Aeisla explained. 'She gave me a vial of elixir to provide me with the strength and will to bring a girl free from the celibentuary at Kavas-Arion . . .'

'Celibentuary?'

'It is where the Mundics confine those highborn girls who have shamed themselves,' Kaissia explained.

'I will not pretend to understand,' Daken answered. 'Go on.'

'The girl was Sulitea,' Aeisla continued, 'who in the course of time spent in the Glass Coast and the halfling lands in the northeast of Apraya gained that secret, and others. She herself is now a witch.'

'There are none such in Oretea, nor have I ever heard of such an elixir.'

'This is no surprise. An activant is needed, and in any event, what girl, especially one of your tiny Oreteans, would drink the jism from her tuppenny after being ravished by a troll?'

'Just so. It is widely known in Aegmund then?'

'No!' Kaissia laughed. 'Consorting with man-beasts is an unthinkable shame, even for a lowborn girl, even for Yi, who is the daughter of the town dung-gatherer.'

'Yet it is done, by these witches?'

'Witches do as they please,' Aeisla explained, 'yet they are essentially pariahs, set apart from all others, save for certain ceremonies and occasional mediation.'

'Such things must also be used with care,' Cianna added, 'while milking trolls for their jism is no easy task.'

'There are drawbacks, it is true,' Aeisla admitted, grimacing. 'The full elixir calls for a complex array of ingredients, each of significance. For some while I took a raw version, as we did this time, mere troll's sperm activated by a taste of leather. Slowly, and without realising it, I became more masculine in trait, until by the time I returned to Korismund it was too late. Now I seldom use it, and only when I must, yet still there are times I cannot control my rage. At Kaissia's shaming in Aegerion this was so, when I saw she was to be put to a troll.'

'And in Staive Cintes?' Iriel queried.

'I had two vials of true elixir,' Aeisla stated, 'prepared by Sulitea herself.'

'Which she gave us,' Kaissia put in, 'but she did not say the elixir was largely troll's jism.'

'You might have refused to drink it,' Aeisla chuckled. 'So, Prince Daken, what of us now?'

He paused to seat himself on a couch, then went on.

'Cianna is right to say that my motives were not purely altruistic, but there is no great depth to my scheme. I wish to explore the possibility we discussed before, of your going into Vendjome. Firstly, some of you have association with these witches. Could any master an effectuation?'

'My ability is poor,' Aeisla admitted. 'I have no sleight for magic.'

'Four years I served Sulitea and I can achieve only the simplest cantrip,' Cianna added.

'No more will be required,' he answered.

'Are we wanted as agents, to bring out information?' Kaissia queried.

'No, not as spies. Your task –'

He broke off at the sound of bells from somewhere beyond the chamber, then of voices and female laughter.

Two girls appeared, both familiar to Iriel from the harem, but now clad in silk wraps of gold, crimson and black, and clearly handmaidens as they were scattering red and yellow rose petals on the floor. Two more handmaidens appeared, one with a fan, the other with a fly whisk, then the Queen herself, unrecognisable as the naked, impudent slut of the harem whose face Iriel had sat on.

She was dressed in golden silk, but no mere wrap. The main part was a magnificent robe, high-collared, long-sleeved, angled across her chest to leave one breast bare, snug to her neat hips, then flaring to a loose skirt the rear of which formed a train supported by two more handmaidens. Crimson and black embroidery covered the material in elaborate patterns, some curving to enhance the shape of her body, others depicting flowers, birds, cats. Her hair was piled high on her head and trapped within an elaborate cage of golden filigree set with a great ruby at the centre of a starburst of jet, with lesser stones. Her slippers were also golden silk, again sewn with rubies and pieces of jet. Her face was painted in elaborate detail, exaggerating the natural pout of her lips, the height of her cheekbones and the size of her eyes.

'Great Queen,' Daken acknowledged her, rising and bowing his head but immediately sitting back down.

Sulden responded with a nod, then spoke to her handmaidens.

'Away, all of you, run off, or I will have the barbars eat you for their supper.'

She laughed, light and high, a sound full of arrogance. The handmaidens retreated, backwards, bowing as they went. Sulden turned to the girls.

'I will not ask you to kneel, as you should, for the Prince Palades Daken has counselled me to the respect of your barbarian customs. You have served me well, and I thank you for your part in bringing me to my rightful place. To reward you, I now appoint you my personal guard. Livery is to be made in appropriate style and colour, while –'

'Great Queen,' Daken said patiently, 'this cannot be. There is a Royal Guard, whose loyalty is to the Palades, and you must express your faith in them. To set up a group of outlanders as your personal guard is madness, and the more so when these same outlanders have killed four of the guards' number. Besides this, and as I have explained –'

'I am Queen,' Sulden answered, 'and I will have my way, in this, and in all other matters besides the great questions of diplomacy and war, as you shall see.'

'Sulden –' Daken began patiently, only to be cut off by her.

'And I think it would be appropriate if you were to address me formally, Uncle, at least in the presence of others. All should address me as Great Queen, is this not so?'

'Indeed it is,' he answered, 'and yet –'

'Then do so,' she interrupted. 'Come, Uncle, you would not seek to make me seem a puppet, would you? I shall defer to you in matters of state, and always my voice will be as yours in the Council, yet in matters such as these –'

'Sulden . . . Great Queen,' he corrected himself. 'Be assured that in such matters I shall provide no more than the lightest of advice, yet in this instance –'

'No, Uncle. Here I am firm. They are to guard me.'

'Sulden, I –'

'No, Uncle.'

She stamped her foot, showing the same petulance that had earned her so many spankings in the harem. Iriel suppressed a chuckle, thinking of the contrast between the haughty queen and the naked slut who had licked all five of them to orgasm, then wondering what Sulden's true intention was in wanting them to guard her. A desire for revenge seemed likely, that or a hidden desire to be given the same treatment once more in the quiet and privacy of her chamber.

Daken had gone quiet at Sulden's show of temper, and for a long moment gave no response at all, only to suddenly reach out, grab the sleeve of her gorgeous robe and with one even motion haul her across his knee. An instant later, even before the echoes of her horrified squeal had faded, he had twisted her arm high into the small of her back and was disarranging the train of her gown.

She fought crazily, screaming and kicking and clawing with her free hand, but it made no difference whatsoever. Up came her gown, revealing her pert bottom, nude, with the cheeks pumping frantically to the motions of her legs, the split fig of her cunt on plain show, and the spanking began.

Daken showed no mercy, his face set in determination as he slapped at Sulden's bouncing bottom cheeks with the full force of his arm. Her response was no more dignified than it had been in the harem, a rude and ludicrous squirming that served only to show off her cunt and anus, mad, piglike squealing noises punctuated by curses and threats, and screams of pain. In no time her bottom was a rich red, and as Daken lifted his knee to give himself a better angle and so force her to flaunt her bottom more rudely still, she burst into tears.

It didn't stop him. Still he spanked, smack after smack applied to her seat, his hand covering the full width of her little cheeks or brought down under her tuck to slap her bottom meat up and forwards. Her shoes kicked off, her hair came loose, her other tit fell free of her gown and still he spanked and still she writhed and wriggled and bucked, showing everything to the delighted girls.

With her entire bottom a glowing red ball, Daken began on her thighs, and Sulden's howls and screams redoubled in force. Still he spanked, turning the skin of her legs a blotchy red before going back to her bottom for a last few hard swats and then stopping. She lay still, snivelling across his lap, her legs spread in heedless display of her tuppenny, broken and miserable, her beautiful make-up a mess of coloured streaks, her hair a bird's nest, her skin flushed with sweat.

Iriel gave a thump of her fist on the wall in salute of Daken's action as he finally let go of Sulden. She slid from his lap, to sit heavily on the floor, her mouth wide, breathing hard, the tears still trickling down her cheeks. Daken waited, immobile, his hands folded lightly over his stomach, until she looked up at him, to stare in adoration at her uncle's face.

'I was always doubtful of the benefits of spanking you,' he remarked as she settled down to squat on the floor.

'Well, it serves its purpose,' she answered, suddenly sulky, 'but you should not, not now.'

'To the contrary,' he answered, 'I should spank you, and I shall spank you, regularly, as it has always been. It will be private, rest assured of that.'

'Hardly private,' she answered, glancing to the five girls, 'but no matter, and yes, it is as well that you should spank me.'

She gave a wry smile and Daken reached out to tousle her hair as he addressed the girls.

'My apologies, but that necessity has been building since the day of her ascension. Now tidy up, Sulden, and I shall tell you what our barbarian friends will be doing.'

Sulden obeyed, initially attempting to rearrange her own hair, but quickly giving up and calling her handmaidens, who had undoubtedly heard her being spanked in any case. All six trooped in, the faces impassive masks, and they quickly set to work. Prince Daken went on, ignoring the spanked Queen.

'Yes, you are to go to Vendjome, and there kill an individual who has been causing us difficulty.'

'The Panjandrum?' Aeisla queried. 'Unless he has been succeeded by another he is a squat toad of a man, barely able to tell girl from boy he is so dissipated.'

'This I know,' Prince Daken responded. 'The Panjandrum is unimportant. Indeed, it is to our advantage for him to rule. No, the situation is this. In Vendjome there is a new Vizier, one Aurac.'

'Aurac?' Aeisla queried. 'I knew an Aurac, the assistant to the Panjandrum's cousin, a scrawny youth, but learned.'

'Very likely the same man,' Daken concurred. 'In any event, he has a fine grasp of tactics, while through virtue of the depredations of our late and unlamented King, we have barely half the senior men we did five years before. Most of our reverses in recent years have been due to Aurac and I would dearly like to see him dead.'

'You wish us to be taken to Vendjome as slave girls and there kill him?' Aeisla sighed.

'Precisely. You are ideal. He would be suspicious of an Oretean girl, were I able to find one capable of the task. In any case there are plenty of Oretean slaves in Vendjome, a glut indeed, since the sack of Reites. Yet you, with your exotic colouring and extravagant figures, are sure to go to the palace. Nor need you worry for your pride –'

'A moment,' Kaissia began, only to stop as Aeisla raised a hand, then spoke.

'Do not be concerned for our pride. I have a debt to settle in Vendjome.'

As their boat slid out from the channel, the River Phaetes spread before them, broad and placid between the palm-fringed banks, islands dotted here and there, each thick with copses of blade tree and straggling wild vine. Iriel attempted to relax into the cushions of the area set aside for their use beneath an awning, but found it impossible to clear the details of Prince Daken's plan from her mind.

The boat was a supply vessel bound for where the Oretean and Vendjomois armies straddled the River Phaetes some two hundred leagues down river. At their destination, two sets of earthworks faced each other, each built around the ruins of forts themselves constructed from earlier ruins. These were the Erijome forts, built on what had once been a city when the Vendjomois Empire had stretched the full breadth of Apraya.

Prince Daken was mindful of spies and keen to keep the girls' continued existence a secret. The boat was crewed by Palades Tavian's own men and by Dwarven mercenaries, while the awning through a gap in which Iriel watched was to shield them from inquisitive eyes as much as the sun.

Once at the forts, they were to move north into the great Eigora Khum desert, escorted by a band of the Dwarven mercenaries. They would move east, at length meeting the great Ephraxis River as it flowed south through the desert, at Gora-Jome, the northernmost of the Vendjomois cities. There would be nothing to suggest they had come from the east, and all agreed that they were certain to be taken to Vendjome itself. Aeisla was still technically an escaped Imperial slave and, as such, already the Panjandrum's property. Once in the palace at Vendjome, they were to make their own choices, kill Aurac and escape as best they could. Daken had urged the use of poison, pointing out that they might escape detection entirely, but he had been refused.

As Iriel watched the towers of Oretes recede slowly into the heat haze Aeisla, Kaissia and Cianna began to discuss their task, and in particular Prince Daken's true intentions. Kaissia believed him honourable; Aeisla was more doubting.

'He served us well before, why not again?' Kaissia queried.

'No,' Aeisla stated. 'As Uilus disposed of the fish-cook, so Daken seeks to dispose of us, by sending us on a mission from which he is sure there is no chance of our return. Should we kill Vizier Aurac, all the better – he has disposed of the assassins, the most dangerous of his enemies is dead and he alone knows the truth.'

'He gave his word,' Kaissia responded, 'doubtless he simply wishes to give us an opportunity for honour. After all, no Oretean could hope to succeed.'

'No doubt if we succeed we shall have a fine saga sung for us,' Aeisla said, 'or a statue raised among those about the palace. Nevertheless, he will be heartily grateful to see us elsewhere or by preference dead. Recall how he treated Sulden when she suggested we would make a good personal guard.'

'Nonsense,' Kaissia laughed. 'If he wanted us dead, he need simply have given the order when we stood at bay in the courtyard. Surely he took a risk there in demanding loyalty to the Brat . . . Great Queen Sulden the Palades, that is?'

'I do not think loyalty extends beyond death for Oreteans,' Aeisla responded. 'Certainly there was no show of it for Uilus.'

'Uilus deserved only death,' Kaissia went on. 'Even the Oreteans have enough honour to realise this.'

'What of his offer?' Iriel asked. 'Does this not suggest honesty?'

'True,' Kaissia agreed. 'Had he intended to see us dead he would have offered riches, titles and servants, not a mountain hut.'

'If he wished us dead,' Cianna put in, 'why spend two days teaching me a cantrip to report our success? He is not a man to waste his time. Not only this, but Sulden wishes us as her bedmates, I am sure of it.'

'I also,' Aeisla agreed.

'Yes,' Kaissia laughed, 'once we are installed in our hut in the Glissades she will come to indulge her lust for licking bottom rings and being spanked.'

'She will be spanked often enough in Oretes,' Aeisla answered, 'and yes, she would prefer us alive, yet we know just how little Daken respects her opinion. I for one would prefer to take myself elsewhere should we succeed in slaying Aurac and escaping Vendjome.'

'Not I,' Kaissia stated. 'I am for trusting Daken's honour.'

'Where else would we go?' Cianna queried. 'Not Makea for certain, while in the Glass Coast you would be taken on sight.'

'Cypraea?' Iriel suggested. 'The continent the dark-skinned girl came from. She was gentle, and spoke well of her homeland.'

'Naturally, for it is her homeland,' Cianna answered, 'but yes, the Aprina States would make a fine home.'

'From which dangerous barbarians are banned,' Aeisla pointed out. 'No, we must either attempt to make for Mund or –'

'Not Mund,' Kaissia objected instantly.

'– or some city of dwarfs or halflings,' Aeisla finished. 'This is the wise course, yet I would not be separated.'

'I for one prefer to risk Oretea,' Kaissia answered, 'but I make no commands.'

'Aeisla is right,' Cianna put in. 'We should take ourselves elsewhere.'

'What of you, Iriel, Yi?' Kaissia demanded.

'Sulden will assure our lives,' Yi answered. 'I am for returning.'

Iriel paused, uncertain, trying to decide between risks known and unknown. The Eriedes had betrayed her, yet Prince Daken had kept his word and promised a life of simple security. Finally she answered.

'I am for returning.'

'So be it.'

After several days of moving with the slow current of the Phaetes they reached the Erijome Forts, the ruined walls and the great banks of dug earth showing red to the light of the setting sun. The boat's crew dropped anchor, not moving again until long after dark, with two crescent moons high against a field of stars. The boat was unloaded at an ancient jetty of huge stone blocks, some the parts of a statue so that as Iriel stepped ashore she found herself treading on a vast face, half-dog, half-man, eerie in the moonlight.

A tent had already been put up for them and they were hustled inside, a handful of dwarfs remaining on guard as the boat was unloaded. Aeisla advised sleep, but Iriel found it impossible, restless after days of inactivity on the boat and her mind full of thoughts of what was to come. She accepted a cup of wine from one of the dwarfs, sipping it as she lay among the cushions, but it made no difference. Yi came to her, to cuddle sleepily by her side, but the feel of the smaller girl's body against hers provoked more lewd thoughts than comfort.

Both in Daken's palace and on the boat they had taken to sharing the pleasures of each other's bodies, Cianna with Aeisla, Iriel and Yi either together or under Kaissia's instruction. Some of the crew members had come to them too, both full human and dwarf, some successfully. Now, with Yi warm against her as the heat of the day faded rapidly to chill, Iriel found herself keen for a taste of cunt, or of cock. Gently, she shook Yi's shoulder, provoking a sigh and a slight movement, their breasts rubbing together. Again she shook.

'Suckle me, Yi.'

'I'm tired, rub yourself.'

'No, you rub me.'

Yi responded with a sleepy sound but moved lower, to take Iriel's nipple in her mouth, sucking lazily until the bud had stiffened between her lips. Iriel purred and pulled her thighs up, spreading her sex as Yi's hand went down. Long, agile fingers settled into the groove of her tuppenny and Iriel sighed in pleasure.

'Beautiful . . . yes, be firm.'

For a moment Yi rubbed harder, right on Iriel's bump, to make her back tighten and her mouth come wide. She took Yi's head, stroking the soft hair and holding her in. Yi moved, pulling free to mount Iriel's body, head to toe, cunt to face. Iriel put her face in Yi's bottom, licking at the fleshy folds, probing the hole until it began to grow soft and open, and higher, her tongue lapping at her friend's tight, musky bottom ring. Yi returned the favour with a spit-wet finger, penetrating Iriel's anus, then her tuppenny, licking all the while.

Iriel rolled her legs high, trapping Yi's head to her sex. Yi's licking grew more urgent. Iriel stuck fingers into now wet holes and began to lick at Yi's bump, both girls rapt in each other, lapping and probing, ever more urgent, ever ruder. Yi's cunt went tight as she started to come, her anus too. Iriel stuck her fingers in as deep as they would go, her tongue flicking at speed, concentrating on her friend but with her own pleasure rising towards a climax that hit her even as Yi's started to fade.

Clamping Yi's head tight to her cunt, Iriel pulled her fingers out and stuck them in her mouth, sucking her lover's taste down as she squirmed in orgasm, her holes pulsing, her back arched tight. It was long and beautiful, and at the very peak she pushed her tongue up into Yi's bottom ring, as deep as it would go, revelling in the intimacy and impropriety of the act to bring her ecstasy higher still.

They broke, giggling as Cianna's voice sounded from the darkness, calling them both sluts. Iriel made to answer, intent on inviting Cianna to come and sit on her face, only to be told to go to sleep by Aeisla. She lay back, smiling happily as Yi once more cuddled into her shoulder, yet still ripe for mischief.

Briefly she considered leaving the tent and offering to suck the Dwarven guard's cock. They tasted strange, somewhat reminiscent of nymph and the scent of goblin, invariably bringing her to a fine peak of arousal. Yet, while keen enough usually, she also knew that they could be guaranteed not to accept any offers while on duty. Going further afield was also out of the question, with strict orders not to make themselves known to the general Oretean soldiery. The dwarfs would neither fuck her nor let her past.

Her fingers went to her tuppenny, just to stroke her hair and the groove between her sex lips, soothing herself. Before long she was half asleep, her mind drifting in and out of dreams, of Mistress Loida's shop in Aegerion, of being whipped on the roof of the House of Cunt, of kneeling in the slave coffle with a cock up her bottom.

A sharp noise brought her awake, a thud, somewhere far off in the night. Another followed, a crash, screams in the distance. She sat up, the other girls moving around her. Aeisla's voice came, edged with fear.

'Bombards.'

'On the southern shore,' the dwarf on guard answered. 'Too distant to warrant concern. Now if that were dwarven artillery, then . . .'

He broke off with a curse as yells rang out, nearby, from towards the desert, then the clang of steel, the roar of a bombard, another, a horrible whistling noise, a thump, more screams, curses, men's voices calling orders. Iriel leaped up, snatching for her dress even as the dwarf screamed for them to lie down. A roar, a whistle, and the tent was snatched away from above them as if by a giant hand, to leave them in the bright moonlight, flat to the ground in raw fear, snatching at the cushions to cover themselves at Aeisla's order.

Again came the roar of the bombards and the whistle of balls, each ending in a dull thud. Sand showered them, once, then again, closer still, to leave Iriel praying hard to each and every ancestor as she clawed at the desert sand. Another whistle, another thud, more sand pattering down on cushions above her and Iriel wet herself, urine squirting out between her thighs. Another roar, and she was writhing in her growing puddle, screaming as the shot shrieked above them, to thump into the sand ahead of them.

It stopped. She lay, the piddle still trickling from her cunt. Her teeth bit into her lip, waiting for the next. Nothing came, only the more distant clash of metal, yells and screams, but drawing closer. Trembling hard, she lay still under the cushions, indifferent to the damp sand beneath her belly and legs. Finally Aeisla spoke.

'It is done. Now the men come.'

Iriel nodded, weak with fear but struggling to find her courage. All around was chaos. Tents showed black against red fire on the south bank, some burning, knots of men struggling among them. On the Phaetes itself were boats, more fire reflected red on the water. Nearer, pits showed as shadows in the sand among a rubble of tents, bodies and gear, with the survivors already running towards the fortifications. The dwarf was nowhere to be seen, but his axe lay on the ground. Aeisla bent to pick it up and made to speak, only for the roar of bombards to drown her words.

Even before the rumble died away Iriel had thrown herself down into a pit. The shot whistled over, to end with a great splash in the river, then another, and more, roar after roar, whistles and thuds, near and far, to leave her clutching her ears in pain, terror also, her feet kicking, what remained in her bladder erupting from her cunt in little spurts. At last the bombards stopped, and when she opened her eyes it was to find herself alone. She stayed down, sure it would begin again and not knowing where to go or what to do, shaking with fear.

Somewhere off in the night she heard Aeisla's voice, calling out. She forced herself up, struggling to gain strength in prayer, to find a reeking smoke drifting in across the desert, lit red and grey by moonlight and fire.

172

A half-toppled tent stood nearby, one pole broken. She made for it, calling out to Aeisla even as the other girls responded, Cianna and Yi, then Kaissia, and Iriel sighed in relief to know that all five lived. A nest of spears had fallen beside the tent and she snatched one up, clutching the shaft as she padded towards Aeisla, who called again, softly, then in anger.

Iriel saw the line of men advancing from the smoke at the same instant, black figures running softly on the sand. Metal clashed, a man screamed and Iriel braced, too close to run, praying to her father and yelling defiance as the line closed on her. Her spear thrust out, to clang on armour as flame illuminated the man's face, red on brown skin and dull metal. He stabbed in. Iriel parried and darted back as his companions closed to either side, her spear tip clanging on armour as she swept it wide. She thrust again even as she danced clear of a sword stroke, wild, senseless elation rising in her head, screaming in defiance, expecting every moment to die, the clash of cups and yells of encouragement loud in her ears, her heel catching in the folds of the tent.

She went down, backwards, grinning brown faces showing in the flickering light as the men closed on her, her spear knocked aside even as she thrust up, swords falling, hands gripping her legs, her arms, one already between her legs. She was spread, still fighting, kicking one man free only for two more to take her leg. She was mounted, the man between her legs climbing on, the metal strips of his armour scratching her as he rubbed his cock on her tuppenny. She was fucked, his cock driven home the moment it was hard enough, deep up her hole, until his balls met her twitching buttocks, slapping on them as he began to pump.

Iriel cried out as her cunt filled, still fighting, but helpless, two men to each limb, more beyond, pinned and penetrated, her breasts starting to jiggle as the rhythm of the fucking picked up, her fingers clutching

173

in rage and frustration and a burning, all consuming arousal. They pushed her legs up, spreading her further onto the man's cock as others ducked low, to paw her breasts, groping hard, one nipple taken into a mouth and sucked stiff in an instant. At that she broke, with a last faint cry of shame as she let her body go limp, surrendered to her ravishment.

The man in her cunt chuckled, sensing the change in her body. A leg was swung over her head, a large, hairy scrotum was settled onto her mouth, then in it as she opened up, to suck on his balls as her body shook to the cock thrusts. Another called out, a leader, demanding that the man inside her hurry up. The answer was a dozen furious shoves and an explosion of jism deep in Iriel's cunt.

No sooner was he out than the leader was in, pumping deep up her, his cock squelching in his companion's jism, grunting and cursing. The man with his balls in her mouth had begun to masturbate, jerking on his cock and rubbing his anus in her face as she sucked. He came, hot sperm spattering her breasts and immediately rubbed in by the groping hands. Another replaced him, cock in her mouth, her head held by the hair and twisted into his crotch.

She sucked, eager and wanton, her body receptive, and as her cunt filled for the second time and the leader withdrew, she groaned in disappointment. Still they held her, legs rolled high, cunt spread to the night, until once again she was filled with cock. One came over her breasts, grunting in glee as he sprayed her with jism, and then the man in her mouth, pulling it free to soil her face and hair.

More moved in, yet another cock stuffed into her mouth, with men all around her demanding their turn, laughing, complaining of having to fuck in each other's jism, boasting of what they were going to do with her. Another leader arrived, shouting, not for the fucking to stop, but for the use of her anal passage. She was rolled, mounted onto a man beneath, a new cock stuck into her mouth as the leader squatted onto her bottom, his cock already hard as he pressed it to the slimy opening between her cheeks.

She pushed out, letting her ring relax to lessen the pain as she was forced, the leader's fat cockhead jammed in. Her hole was wet with jism and juice and gave easily, her rectum accommodating the thick penis in three hard shoves, each making her swallow hard on the cock she was sucking. A cheer went up to see her with a cock in a very hole and they began to fuck to a rhythm, Iriel's mouth, cunt and anus working together as the man beneath her sucked and licked at her breasts while two others jerked their cocks in her hair.

A man began to whip her, smacking a thick leather belt down across her upturned buttocks as she was buggered, one smack to each thrust of the cock in her hole. The one in her cunt began to bite at her nipples, and to pump faster. One spunked in her hair, the pushing in her bottom hole grew harder, deeper, faster, also the whipping. She was pushed down, the groove of her tuppenny spread over the coarse tangle of pubic hair, rubbing it directly onto her bump.

Instantly her body had begun to rise towards climax, only for it to break as the man in her mouth came down her throat, to hold his cock well in, forcing her to swallow and leaving her gagging with a froth of sperm bubbles at both nostrils. He pulled clear, another replaced him and she was sucking again, still with her clit rubbing, cunt and anus pulling in and out, buttocks burning beneath the whip, nipples painfully hard, all of it going into contraction, her entire body in spasm as she started to come.

Sperm exploded into her rectum, the man's cock jammed to the hilt, her pulsing anus milking him into her bowels. Another came in her hair, the whipping rose to a mad crescendo of agonising strokes to bottom and back, and at the very highest peak of her ecstasy the men in her mouth and cunt came simultaneously, to flood her with sperm even as the man up her bottom pulled free, his jism spurting from her anus as it closed.

Iriel lay sideways on the hard wooden floor of the wagon, her anal ring moving gently in and out on the cock of perhaps the thirtieth man to bugger her. More had been up her tuppenny, in her mouth, between her breasts, along the crease of her bottom, in her armpits, her hair, even against the soles of her feet. There had been foot soldiers, cavalry, bombardiers, wagoners, even cooks, as the victorious Vendjomois had revelled in the sack of the Erijome Forts.

She had seen the sun rise on her knees, with an obese pastry cook in her mouth and a storekeeper up her tuppenny from behind. By then she had been raw with fucking and faint from use, barely conscious, yet still capable of coming as the storeman fiddled with her bump to make her hole close on his penis. She had barely taken in the smoke-hazed ruin of the Oretean encampment, and had passed out as soon as she'd come, only to wake up in the wagon, naked, trussed up like a chicken for market and with yet another cock up her bottom.

The man in her anus came with a sigh, pulled out and went back to his work of harnessing the camels. She lay still, the sperm pulsing and dribbling from her anus to trickle down over her bare bottom cheeks and into the pool of mixed fluids in which she lay. Very slowly her mind cleared to the aches of her body, her sore holes, her stiff jaw, her smarting nipples, the bruises on her breasts, bottom, and elsewhere. A sense of defeat followed, and fear for her friends, vying with the discomfort of her body, until suddenly it was all too much and she was violently sick.

She was still coughing and spitting when the wagoner appeared again. He gave her a single, disgusted glance and vanished, only to return a moment later with a bucket of river water, which he threw over her, leaving her spluttering, but glad of the cool water with the sun's heat already rising. A second bucket followed, and a third, before he climbed into the wagon, calling for a colleague to set up the awning as he rolled Iriel out of his way.

With her body turned she could see the other way, up a long row of wagons around which men worked, tending to the huge double-humped draft camels, putting up awnings, greasing axles and loading the spoils of the battle, including girls. Two wagons away a hank of brilliant red hair hung down from the back, and Iriel's heart jumped at the realisation that it had to be Aeisla or Cianna, unless for some reason the Vendjomois sheared the heads of their victims. Then the hair began to move, rhythmic shivers running through it, suggesting the girl was being fucked and therefore had to be alive.

Relief flooded through her, then more strongly still as she saw a group of Vendjomois infantry approaching. Three of their number had girls slung over their shoulders, bottoms to the fore, but with the pale skin and long legs of Aeg unmistakable on two, while the third was a tiny Oretean girl. As they drew closer to the wagons she made out blonde hair and brown, Kaissia and Yi, both alive and still kicking despite having their wrists and ankles bound. Both were dumped into a wagon five along from Iriel's. The soldiers exchanged what was a clearly a lewd joke with the wagoners and left.

Iriel scanned the scene for Aeisla, full of fear and uncertainty, but there was no sign of her. More girls were brought, mainly Oreteans, with some Vendjomois, these last looking smug and relieved, yet still walking with the odd waddling limp that showed they had been fucked as well as any others. Still Iriel hoped, even when a group of senior Oreteans appeared with a charta manifest, moving slowly down the wagons to list the contents of each. Presently they reached her own wagon, the last before the river's edge, to peer within as the wagoner stepped forward with a salute.

'Another barbarian girl?' one commented, making a mark on the charta. 'Four in total then, which will make for a fine commission.'

Iriel opened her mouth to speak, but shut it hastily at the thought that Aeisla or Cianna might have won free. The man spoke to the wagoner.

'You have too little here. Load into this beside you, and take the girl to that two up, which will serve as a slave wagon. Then take your team to assist in bringing the bombards forward.'

The wagoner assented and went to work, grumbling to himself as soon as his superiors were out of earshot. He attempted to lift Iriel as she was, but failed, forcing him to cut the cord that held her legs up to her chest before heaving her across his shoulder. She was carried across and dumped into the same wagon as the red-haired girl, Cianna, who was unconscious, her face and breasts speckled with fresh come.

'Another for you, Cruisack,' the wagoner said, applying a firm swat to Iriel's bottom, 'you fortunate son of diseased goblin and a dung whore. While you drive your sluts to Vendjome I must haul heavy bombards. So says Overman Broidat, may he be fed to Belime's sacred mandrills.'

Cruisack chuckled and hauled Iriel further in, dragging her with difficulty by her bound ankles as he answered.

'Six Oretean sluts and two of these giant barbarians. I shall be up to my balls every league of the way!'

'You will skin your cock, with luck,' the other replied, 'and besides, they are now Imperial property and not for fucking by the likes of you.'

178

Cruisack merely laughed and the other turned back to his work at an angry signal from a distant overseer. Iriel had been dumped with her head on a sack of some grainy substance with a mealy smell and managed to haul herself into a sitting position by wriggling her arms, legs and buttocks. Briefly her eyes met the gaze of an Oretean girl. She forced a smile, but the girl's expression remained one of abject misery. Cruisack hefted Cianna into a sitting position, threw water into her face, then stood. Cianna started to come round, shaking her head as Cruisack began to speak.

'So girls, we are here, together, and I trust you all have the sense to make the best of our time. I am Cruisack the wagoner, and it is I who will be feeding you, watering you and indeed looking after your every need until we reach Vendjome. Some one third of the distance is Fujome, eight days down the Phaetes, to where we bring our wounded and are likely join other wagons. Beyond, the road is better, so let us assume above twenty days of each others' company. Naturally I shall use you as I like, cunt and arsehole too, but those who show willing and make an effort to please may expect better treatment. Is this clear?'

Only two of the Oretean girls nodded but Cruisack went on regardless.

'I am not a hard master, and when all is said and done I must bring you to Fujome in at least moderately good condition, yet there are certain rules. Break these, and I shall apply my camel whip to your dainty backsides. One, crap and piss only in the pot provided. Two, do not squabble, I detest the noise of female bickering. Three, obey my commands promptly and with zeal.'

'How are we to eat with our hands tied?' Iriel demanded.

'Or to use the pot,' an Oretean girl put in.

'Simple,' Cruisack replied. 'Your hands will not be tied. We have been designated as a slave wagon and presently I will be provided with collars, hobbles, coffle irons and other necessities.'

Iriel nodded. Cruisack jumped down from the wagon and disappeared from view. Cianna shook her head, spat, cursed and managed a weak smile for Iriel.

'What of Aeisla?' Iriel asked.

Cianna shook her head. 'I do not know. And the others?'

'They live,' Iriel answered, 'and like us are taken. Both are in a wagon further down the line. I have not seen Aeisla and already a manifest has been taken.'

'Then she is free,' Cianna answered, 'that or in the Feast Hall.'

She pursed her lips and turned to look out of the back of the wagon, determined, only to suddenly dissolve in tears and hot, choking sobs. Iriel pushed out her feet, pressing them to Cianna's hip, the only contact she could make, even as her own eyes filmed with tears. Suddenly Cianna turned, her mouth curved up into a forced smile.

'She will be highly placed indeed, and as to us, by this means as by the other, we shall reach Vendjome.'

For six days they rode the wagon, as part of an army column bringing the loot of the Erijome Forts and the wounded back into the Vendjomois Empire. Always they were beside the Phaetes, first with bleak desert to the left but gradually giving way to scrub, then to groves of blade tree and another with odd feathery foliage, and at last to olive groves, vineyards and fields of melons and wheat.

Cruisack was as good as his word, punishing only those who made his life difficult and rewarding those in whose mouths he could safely put his cock with a ration of meat in the tasteless gruel he drew from the sacks. He fucked both Iriel and Cianna, but made no effort to make them suck. Both behaved, unable to fight or to

180

escape with their legs hobbled and their broad iron collars on a coffle chain linked to the main frame of the wagon.

On the evening of the seventh day Fujome appeared as a smoky blotch on the horizon, visible from the rear of the wagon as Cruisack tended his camels. They were in a broad, dusty area beside a village, and as they waited for the beasts to be attended to the inhabitants came out, to stare curiously into the rear of the wagon, ignored by the guards. Iriel stared back, annoyed by the quality of their attention, as if she were some curious beast rather than a girl.

Presently Cruisack appeared, climbing into the back of the wagon to arrange the girls' feeding bowls and split a new meal sack, part of which he poured into a squat cauldron. Adding water, he began to stir, all the while grinning at the girls, then speaking as he produced a handful of dried meat pieces from a pocket in his robe.

They ate, two Oretean girls being given extra meat for sucking Cruisack, one on his cock and the other with his balls in her mouth, in full view of the villagers, who watched in dumb envy. Amused by his audience, Cruisack turned the girls, buggered one, and had the other lick his come from her dribbling anus. It left the villagers gaping and whispering among themselves, and Iriel with a tingling tuppenny and a shameful desire to do the same.

As the girls ate the villagers began to lose interest, drifting off in ones and twos until as the light began to fade they were alone again. Iriel finished her meal slowly, wishing for the spices the Oreteans had included even in the food they had eaten from the trough in Assanach's caravan. Finished, she used the pot and settled down against the meal sacks, drifting to sleep as she watched the flicker of firelight in distant Fujome.

She came awake what seemed moments later, starting at the feel of a hand on her shoulder. Cruisack's voice sounded by her ear, an urgent hiss.

'Quiet! Do you care to earn a double ration of meat tomorrow?'

'I . . .' Iriel managed. 'How . . . for what?'

'Spiced sausage also, and a cup of wine,' he urged, 'if you will only do as I say and hold your tongue afterwards. Otherwise, I swear I will find a pretext to take a camel whip to your backside, strung from a frame, and –'

'There is no call for threats,' Iriel answered him. 'You have fucked me, have you not? So yes, I will suck without biting.'

'Not I,' he answered, 'a man from the village, one Builard, a retired functionary.'

'He was among those who watched us earlier?'

'No, but his servants were. He dined with our Captain also and knows you are for the Imperial seraglio.'

'We are?'

'Where else? Such exotics are rare. No matter that. Come with me to Builard's villa, please him as he demands and be assured of my goodwill.'

'Just so, but answer me one question, which in turn you must keep to yourself or I shall reveal your doings and doubtless whatever sum this man is paying you will be confiscated.'

'You wish a portion of the money? What would you do with it? You are a slave.'

'I have no wish for money. I wish to know if a fifth Aeg girl was taken at Erijome . . . a barbarian like me, also red-haired, but taller by a head. Taken – or found among the dead.'

'Taller than you by a head? No, if any such girl had been taken alive I would know. I know nothing of those who died, but few escaped.'

'I thank you then, and will keep faith.'

'A wise choice. Now come, and quietly!'

He quickly unlocked the end of the chain and slipped it from her collar. She climbed down, Cruisack helping, and together they slipped into the night. All five moons were up, the largest at full, bathing the fields in silver radiance so bright that they were obliged to keep low as they skirted a vineyard before ducking in among an orchard of lemon trees. Beyond was a track, and across it a low villa concealed within a grove of feather trees. Cruisack went to the door, knocked and hastily pulled Iriel inside.

A Cypraean had opened the door, a man of Iriel's own height, bulky with flesh and darker skinned than anyone she had seen before, naked and with an impressive cock hanging between his legs. He bowed to Cruisack but gave Iriel a knowing wink. She smiled in return as two others appeared, an elderly man, small and dumpy beneath a loose robe and a plump, pretty woman. Others could be heard elsewhere in the house.

'The barbarian, Iriel, Honoured Builard,' Cruisack announced with a polite bow to the old man.

'Excellent,' the man replied. 'Oklin, take it into the ablutions and bugger it.'

'I am not a nymph!' Iriel answered, insulted and surprised. 'I am a girl . . .'

Oklin, the Cypraean, answered her with another wink as he took her arm, to lead her from the hallway through one room and into another, bare but for a number of china troughs, a pipe set with spigots and two padded stools. Builard and the small woman had followed, and sat down as Oklin began to paw Iriel's bottom. Cruisack stood in the doorway.

'It feeds well?' Builard demanded.

'Well indeed,' Cruisack answered.

'Excellent!' he stated happily and sat back, leaning against the wall.

He pulled up his robe, revealing a dark, heavily hooded penis and a bulbous scrotum. Oklin had taken Iriel's breasts in hand from behind and was fondling them as he rubbed his cock in the crease of her bottom.

It was making her tuppenny tingle, and she swallowed her chagrin, realising that it would be the big Cypraean slave who she performed with, at least at first. Builard was playing with his cock and balls, while the plump woman had pulled off her tunic to expose dumpling breasts, a belly soft with rings of fat, chubby thighs and a well-furred tuppenny mound. She too began to stroke herself as Oklin hardened between Iriel's buttocks.

'Down now,' Oklin stated, hoarse with passion. 'Hold your cheeks wide for me, and make sure the Master sees.'

Iriel nodded, embarrassed but good to her word, getting down on all fours before reaching back to spread her bottom. As her tuppenny and bottom ring came on show Builard's masturbation immediately became more urgent, while the woman gave a pleased moan and stuck a finger into her cunt. Oklin got down, to settle his rigid cock between Iriel's cheeks, rubbing gently with his balls tickling her skin. She pushed out, thinking of how big his cock felt and trying to let her arousal rise. It was coming, but slowly, while he seemed more than ready.

Oklin spat into the crease of Iriel's bottom, pushed his cockhead into the piece of mucus and put it to Iriel's anus. She found herself grimacing at the slimy feeling, but forced herself to relax as he rubbed it into her, gradually opening her hole with his cock. His spare hand curled under her belly, to rub at her tuppenny. She sighed in pleasure, then gasped as the head of his cock was pushed firmly into her bottom, spreading the ring on hard meat. Builard gave a little high-pitched giggle of delight, then spoke.

'Good Oklin, that is right. Now push it up.'

Immediately Oklin began to force himself up into Iriel's rectum, making her gasp again as her ring pushed in, then cry out at sudden, bruising pain. Oklin pulled back. His cockhead left her hole. Again he spat, full on her anus, the little ring still slightly open. She felt the mucus go in, then his cock found her hole and she was stretched open again, the now slimy head popping in, and some shaft, until once more he met dry flesh as her ring pushed in.

'Faster!' the woman demanded. 'And tell me if she is packed.'

Oklin answered with a grunt and pushed again. Iriel bit her lip to the pain but held her buttocks as wide as they would go as another couple of inches of thick penis was forced into her rectum. Even the biggest of Oreteans had been easier to take in her passage, and she already felt bloated, as if with a few more pushes the huge thing would come out of her mouth.

'She is packed, well packed,' Oklin groaned as he jammed yet more cock up into Iriel's bottom.

The woman sighed and began to rub at her bump. Iriel glanced back, to find Builard jerking frantically an enlarged but still flaccid penis, the wet head pulled clear of the foreskin. Oklin had stopped pushing, and was working his cock gently back and forth in her bottom ring. She let go of her cheeks and relaxed, enjoying the buggery now the painful part was over, only for him to give a sudden, hard shove, to make her eyes pop and set her panting as the last few inches of his erection were jammed hard up her bottom. His balls met her empty tuppenny and he started to bugger her in earnest. Her breasts began to swing to the motion and the pleasure quickly returned.

'Do it!' the woman demanded. 'Do it now, I am ready!'

Builard gave a little squeal of joy as the woman scrambled down onto her knees beside Iriel and Oklin. Puzzled, Iriel twisted back, wondering if she was to be made to lick. Yet the woman was by her hip, kneeling as she rubbed herself. Then Oklin had begun to push harder and faster and everything but the feel of the cock up her bottom was knocked from her mind. Her mouth came wide in ecstasy, her hand went back to her tuppenny and she was masturbating, helpless in her passion, determined to come with the huge cock still up her bottom.

She didn't make it, her orgasm just rising as Oklin jammed himself deep one last time and filled her rectum with jism. Immediately she was begging him to stay inside her, and rubbing frantically, only to have him pull out as fast as he could and stick his still-rigid erection into the woman's mouth. Iriel was going to come anyway, still rubbing herself as she watched the woman sucking on Oklin's cock, eyes tight in ecstasy, swallowing over and over, then pulling off, to push her face between Iriel's bottom cheeks.

Iriel gasped as the woman's tongue pushed up into her already pulsing anus, to lick and suck at Oklin's jism as it bubbled and squirted from the twitching hole, full into her mouth. The sensation sent Iriel over the edge, into a screaming, gasping orgasm that finished only as the woman pulled back, also spent. Iriel collapsed with a sigh, face down on the floor, bottom still lifted, knees sliding gradually apart on the smooth flagstones. As she opened her eyes again Builard came with a grunt, jism bubbling up over his hand from his still-limp penis. For a long moment nobody spoke, Cruisack finally breaking the silence with a cough. Builard responded.

'Yes, your pay. The two Imperials you may collect from my steward. My nympharium is yours for the night also, should you wish it. Seldom have I known such pleasure, nor, I imagine, has my good lady.'

The plump woman nodded, smiled, then spoke.

'Fine indeed. So now, Oklin, wash yourself and your barbar girl. You may bed her for the night if you wish.'

Oklin responded with a deferential inclination of his head and crossed to the spigot. Iriel stayed where she was, allowing herself to be washed, then led to Oklin's chamber, a mere niche among others in a low, crude

186

extension of the villa in which the slaves were housed. For the remainder of the night she talked, slept and fucked, until at last Cruisack came to fetch her.

Dawn had begun to brighten the sky as they left, and the sun was already rising behind Fujome city as they reached the encampment, to find Overman Broidat stood beside the wagon. Cruisack quickly took hold of Iriel's arm as the overseer turned to them.

'What is this?' Broidat demanded. 'An escape, or –'

'An escape,' Cruisack answered hastily. 'Somehow she forced the lock on the coffle chain. They are strong, these barbars, and perhaps not so stupid as they appear.'

'Not stupid? To run? Looking as she does? Where did you think to go, slut?'

'Nowhere,' Iriel answered sulkily, determined to keep her word.

'What is to be done with her?' Cruisack queried.

'She must be punished, and severely!'

'How so? Mark her with worse than a few welts and you will have the Imperials to answer to.'

'Oh, it is easy enough to punish a slavegirl properly without marking her,' Broidat stated.'I will teach you to run, slut. Kneel, on all fours.'

Iriel glanced at him, and at Cruisack beyond, who was making frantic facial expressions while holding a spiced sausage half out of his pocket. Iriel sighed but got down, determined to keep her word, against which a spanking and probably another fucking seemed a small thing.

'Push up your bottom,' Broidat ordered, reaching down to take Iriel by the hair.

He took a firm grip, making her wince in pain even as she stuck her up into spanking position, her cheeks raised and spread. Broidat reached down to touch her, exploring between her cheeks, one finger loitering briefly on her anus before pushing into her cunt.

'She is slimy,' he remarked. 'Have you fucked her?'

'Not I,' Cruisack said quickly. 'Perhaps she was caught by an ape?'

Broidat gave a sceptical grunt but made no further objection, fingering Iriel briefly, cupping the lips of her tuppenny and once more inspecting her anus before he spoke again.

'Bring down the pot from the wagon'

'The piss pot?'

'The piss pot. What other pot is there?'

Cruisack shrugged and went to the rear of the wagon. Taking the heavy pot, he hefted it in his arms and placed it carefully on the ground. Broidat pulled on Iriel's hair, forcing her to crawl forwards.

'What . . . what do you intend?' she asked.

'Silence, slut,' he answered. 'You are to be pot spanked, a punishment I find seldom needs repeating. Get your head over it!'

Realising what was to be done to her she had begun to pull back, heedless of the pain. Broidat merely tightened his grip and moved the pot towards her, using his full strength to bring her head over the wide mouth.

'No!' Iriel babbled. 'Not this! Not my face! No –'

Her voice broke off in a sticky splash as her face was pushed down hard, right into the pot, her open mouth filling, her eyes closing only just in time. He held her in, bubbles escaping her mouth and nose as she struggled against the grip in her hair, kicking her feet, her hands slapping the ground in useless protest, squirming in his grip. The spanking began, hard swats full across the seat of her bottom, making her cheeks bounce and setting her breasts swinging, to slap in time against the side of the piss pot. Agonising shame and humiliation filled her head, pain too, hot in her lungs as the need to breathe grew sharper. His weight was on her neck, trapping her, until she had grown frantic, writhing in desperation, and all the time with her breasts jumping and her bottom bouncing to the slaps.

For a moment her head was pulled up, only to be reimmersed the instant she had caught her breath, so that her mouth filled once more with the contents of the pot. Again the spanking started, harder than ever, setting her kicking and wiggling her bottom about in a futile effort to escape the pain, and breaking her fight to hold her breath. Broidat laughed as she began to blow bubbles in the piss, and forced her head deeper into the pot, right down, pressing her face to the slimy bottom, still spanking, harder and harder.

Her head was jerked up, urine dripping from her nose and the fringe of her hair, bubbling from around her mouth as she fought for breath, her bottom still jiggling to smacks, but lighter. Again he laughed, and at last the spanking stopped, but only so that he could pull his tunic up to expose his cock, already stiff in erection.

'There, slut, how does that feel? Will you run again?'

'No! I swear it!' Iriel babbled.

'I thought not,' he answered, and pushed her head under again, deep into the pot. 'Cruisack, hold her head under while I fuck her, deep in, and bring her up only when I say. I like to feel them writhe.'

Cruisack ducked down to take Iriel's head, Broidat got behind her and she was dunked once more, even as her cunt filled with cock. Broidat began to fuck her, his upturned tunic rubbing on her warm bottom, his hands on her cheeks, splaying them to stretch her anus. Cruisack began to splash her face in the urine, then abruptly pushed it deep, laughing as her face went into the night soil.

Iriel broke, the betrayal too much to bear. Hurling herself sideways, her cunt slipped from Broidat's cock even as he came, hot jism spraying her bottom as she rolled. Cruisack leaped back with a curse as the contents of the pot washed over his feet, slipped and went backwards. Broidat rose, his cock still spurting jism as he snatched for his whip, only to fall to Iriel's driven fist as it struck his throat.

She stood, gasping for air, dripping piddle, her head a whirl of emotion, rage and humiliation and self-pity and a desperate desire to be elsewhere. The voices in her head were screaming at her to run, but at her first step she went down, tripped by her hobble, across Cruisack's body. He was limp, his head resting against the iron-bound wheel of the wagon, a thin trickle of blood escaping from his scalp. Broidat was down also, clutching at his throat and retching air.

Without further thought Iriel dug her hand into Cruisack's pocket, pulling to spill out the contents, bits of dried meat, sausages, a leather bag and, tied to it, his keys. An instant later her hobble was open, but even as she turned to the wagon angry shouts sounded from across the encampment. For an instant she hesitated, staring at the sleeping Cianna, still chained and helpless, then jerked around as Broidat's hand clasped on her ankle.

'I'll whip you ragged, you vicious she-dog!' he hissed. 'Make you eat camel dung until we reach Vendjome, have you buggered by horses, stuff your cunt with –'

He screamed as her foot hit his face and rolled back. Then she was running, everything but flight forgotten, across the road and into the vineyard. Yells of anger and demands to stop broke out behind her, soldiers pursuing, across an olive grove, a field of scrub, thorns pricking her bare feet, slowing her, the soldiers gaining, two of them, crying out in triumph as she turned at bay in the mouth of a gorge, to see one, then the other cut down by Aeisla.

7

Vendjome

'They are not by nature violent,' Aeisla explained, 'save when threatened, their territory invaded or taken from their natural places. This is difficult, as for best effect the troll must be angry, as was he in Oretes who took Yi.'

Iriel nodded, grimacing as she looked down at the huge lowland troll in the shallow valley beneath them. He was browsing on a feather tree, unaware of their scent with the wind blowing towards them, although she could sense his musk. He was full grown, at least as large as the one in Oretes, and if he seemed passive enough she knew just what he was capable of.

For over a week they had moved down the broad Phaetes valley, keeping to the concealment of the northern escarpment, feeding on grapes, melon and whatever else could be stolen from the fields. At first they had moved due east, eluding pursuit by walking a full league in an irrigation channel and hoping the soldiers would assume they had headed west towards Oretea. It had worked, and beyond Fujome they had turned south once more, shadowing the column of wagons on the Vendjome road, as Aeisla had been since the battle at the Erijome Forts. Now, with Vendjome itself marked by a smoky haze on the eastern horizon, Aeisla had declared the need for a supply of troll's jism to see them through what lay ahead.

Iriel had been half-hoping that it would prove impossible to find one of the lumbering man-beasts as they walked up into the low, wooded hills that now bordered the Phaetes. They had been lucky, from Aeisla's perspective, finding spore, then catching scent to discover the fine adult male, ideal for their purposes.

'The art,' Aeisla explained, 'is to coax, coming to the edge of his territory. He must see you first, creating anger at the intrusion of a human into his domain, then smell you as female to create arousal. They scent tuppenny well, and care little if the tuppenny in question belongs to another troll or a human girl. As you would expect, there is no art to their fucking, the cock goes in, they pump, they come. Having come, they lose all interest and their aggression wanes markedly. Yet it is crucial to be ready first, or you risk being split. Thus and so, lick me for a while, then we move somewhat upwind. He sees me, scents me, fucks me. You catch the jism in your jar.'

Iriel nodded, taking the jar from Cruisack's leather bag, which she still carried. It had been stolen from a farmhouse at the dead of night, as had the loose robes they wore. Aeisla lay back, casually spreading her thighs to show off the pink centre of her tuppenny with a large, glossy bump pushing out from among the folds. Iriel giggled nervously as she got down, pressing her face in to lap at Aeisla's sex. Aeisla sighed and began to stroke her breasts, cupping the heavy globes and rubbing her nipples through the material of her robe.

It was not the first time, as they had taken comfort in each other's arms each night since Iriel's escape, for warmth and friendship as well as pleasure. Iriel's own tuppenny was quickly in need of attention, but as her licking began to grow urgent Aeisla pulled away.

'Later, for now I need my juices for the troll. Come.'

She rose carefully, ducking low as they moved along the ridge and down into the valley, all the while keeping careful watch on the troll. He was busy browsing and paid no attention until they had reached the far side of the valley, Iriel now with her stomach fluttering and a heavy lump in her throat, Aeisla tense. The troll looked up, to sniff the breeze, and Iriel's trepidation became abruptly stronger as Aeisla pulled her quickly down.

'He must not scent us,' Aeisla whispered.

'I scent him,' Iriel replied, wrinkling her nose at the thick troll musk.

'Strange,' Aeisla commented, 'so strong and us across the wind, unless –'

She broke off at a bellow from the valley. The troll turned, his face creasing in anger, then the great mouth coming open in a bellow louder even than the other.

'Two!' Iriel exclaimed. 'Let us leave, quickly.'

'No,' Aeisla answered, extending a hand to Iriel's arm. 'I could not have hoped for more. The elixir is stronger by far when the troll is truly enraged.'

'But they will tear us to pieces!'

'Why so? When we fought the guard did you pause to attack the eunuchs?'

'No, yet –'

'So it is with trolls. They will fight and the victor will fuck me, providing prime jism.'

She moved forwards slowly through the bushes, Iriel following with her heart in her mouth. A narrow stream cut down from the slope of the valley, forming what seemed to be a boundary, as the two trolls stopped at either side, bellowing at each other. They were much of a size, but the newcomer's skin was darker and coarser, shading to near black across his shoulders and on the heavy cranial ridge.

'Had I money, we might wager,' Aeisla joked in a soft whisper.

Iriel didn't answer, but moved close, pressing herself to Aeisla's side. Quickly Aeisla unfastened her sash, setting her axe to one side, then pulling her robe up over her head. Taking Iriel's hand, she put it to her sex.

'Keep me warm, no more.'

Iriel began to rub, gently, moving her fingers in the wet flesh of Aeisla's tuppenny. The trolls were still bellowing, neither keen to make a definite move. Her own tuppenny was more in need of attention than ever, and she was trying to tell herself that there was a difference between being ravished by the victor of a fair combat between men and fucked by a troll which just chanced to have fought another. Yet their musk was strong in her nose, pungent, compelling and very male.

'Slower,' Aeisla gasped suddenly, 'or you'll make me come.'

'Sorry,' Iriel whispered, embarrassed at the realisation of just how urgently she had been rubbing.

She slowed, just teasing Aeisla's sex lips but wishing she could do it properly, also that the trolls would get on with their fight. Her spare hand went to her own tuppenny, sure that it didn't matter if she came when she was not the one due to be fucked, only to be jerked away at a crackle of foliage from behind her. She realised it was a third troll at the same instant it snatched her, lifting her by her robe, screaming, her legs kicking frantically, and screaming louder still as her cunt was unceremoniously stuffed full of troll cock.

Then she was being fucked, held by her robe and by her hair as she was jerked up and down on the huge erection, each stroke jamming painfully deep, to knock the breath from her body and set her breasts bouncing wildly on her chest. Her arms and legs were flailing in empty air, her screams ringing out across the valley, her bottom cheeks slapping firmly to his belly. Shock, pain, terror flooded her mind, then sudden ecstasy as she came, her body tipped over into orgasm from the sheer friction of cock in cunt and the strain on her bump as her entire belly bulged out to a massive explosion of jism inside her.

She was dropped, the huge cock pulling from her hole, to land face down in the soft grass, bottom stuck up in the air, cunt bubbling sperm. As the troll lumbered off, Aeisla quickly clamped the jar in place over Iriel's hole, and was whispering soothing words to her as it filled, only to break off with a curse. Iriel looked up, to find one of the other trolls almost on top of her, a creature half as big again as the one who had fucked her. She scrambled back in terror, but it already had Aeisla, dragged backwards, her bottom put to his crotch and her cunt filled.

The troll began to fuck, Aeisla to grunt and squeal and curse, eyes tight shut, mouth wide and running drool, clutching at the grass with her hands, legs spread wide across the man-beast's huge hips. He came in moments, deep up her, but still pumping as he pulled free, to soil her bottom and back and hair with thick, cream-coloured jism as she collapsed to the ground.

Iriel glanced around, half-expecting to see the dark troll, but it had disappeared, crashes from up the valley suggesting that it was in pursuit of the smaller one who had caught her unawares. Quickly she took the jar, putting it to Aeisla's tuppenny just as a thick clot of troll sperm squeezed from the hole and keeping it in place as she scraped up the remainder from her friend's back and buttocks.

'You see,' Aeisla remarked with a sigh, 'simple.'

Vendjome lay below them, an enormous city straddling the huge Ephraxis and spreading out across the plain beyond, with many buildings lying outside the walls. Much of it was a vast sprawl of two and three-storey box-shaped buildings, huts and lean-tos, yet the centre alone had to be close to the size of Oretes. There were also fewer towers, and yellow or white stone in place of blue-white, but several buildings were as large or larger than the Palades' palace. One stood out, a vast structure of pinkish stone topped with roofs of turquoise blue and domes of verdigris-covered copper. A great plaza fronted it, with broad steps running up to a colonnade.

Elsewhere in the city's heart magnificent arches and colonnades marked many of the grander streets, and most houses were tiled in turquoise or viridian, while other buildings, perhaps temples, showed domes of gold and silver inlay on vermilion tiles. Awnings of bright silk showed in front of many houses, scarlet, lemon yellow, emerald and a dozen rarer colours.

Returning from the valley in which they had been fucked by the trolls, they discovered they had missed the column in which the others were held. The land had been growing richer and more populous, making travel risky, so rather than follow the river road they had moved cautiously east among low hills, at first wooded but growing slowly more barren and inhabited only by herdsmen.

On the third day Aeisla had killed a brush pig, its dying squeals alerting the owner, who had fled at the sight of them. Iriel had taken a crude machete from the house, also leather harness straps to make belts and crude necklaces to allow them to activate the troll jism, and sewing materials. Using the bladder from the brush pig, she had made twin purses, into each of which they had poured a measure of the precious sperm before sealing them and inserting each into their tuppennies. That night they had risked a fire in a secluded niche among the rocks and gorged on pork, moving on the next day across ever more broken country.

As they had mounted one ridge no different from any other they had come out over the flood plain of the vast Ephraxis, a river greater by far than the Phaetes. A spur of the hills to the south had allowed them to approach Vendjome itself without venturing down into the rich farmland of the valley, leaving them no more than a league from the bank of the Ephraxis and directly above one of the poorer quarters of the city.

For a long while Aeisla gazed out at the scene without speaking, then raised her arm, pointing.

'The great pink building somewhat towards the river from the centre is the Imperial Palace. Nearer, roofed in glass, is the Pelucidome, where livestock and slaves are kept prior to auction. There is a great square to the front where the market is held. It is there that the Princess Talithea Mund, Baroness Elethrine Korismund and I were sold. No doubt Kaissia, Cianna and Yi will be also.'

'Matters may have changed,' Iriel put in. 'The wagoners stated that we were already Imperial property.'

'Perhaps this is true of girls taken in war?' Aeisla suggested. 'We were picked up at a border post as we sought to make our way north. No matter, in any event they are likely to end up at the palace, and it is there we must go.'

'We cannot hope to pass unseen in the city,' Iriel answered. 'Do we surrender ourselves and trust that we are taken into the seraglio?'

'No,' Aeisla answered. 'I have had my fill of feigning submission to these honourless pygmies, or any others. No army has approached Vendjome in some two thousand years. Thus the defences are slack and designed more to deter thievery and for the collection of taxes than serious purpose. There are tithing points on the docks and at each gate, or I assume each gate. We passed out before hidden in honey jars. To get in we wait for nightfall, cross the river, approach the palace, scale the walls, find the others, slay Aurac and depart.'

'Now, tonight?'

'No, it is possible the column has not yet arrived. Kaissia would think me rude if she were to arrive and find Aurac already dead.'

'No,' Iriel answered, shading her eyes. 'They are here. Note, on the southern road, a line of wagons leaving the city. The third is Cruisack's. I recognise the awning.'

'You are certain?'

'Certain.'

'Then they are already there. Let it be tonight. Why wait?'

Iriel pulled herself from the boat, a flat punt they had stolen. A single, mid-sized moon hung overhead, gibbous, and providing only enough light to glaze the river with dull pewter. Ahead of her, the narrow streets of Vendjome were sunk in absolute blackness, but the distant light of a cresset cast red gleams on the jetty they had reached.

Aeisla joined her, leaving the punt to drift off into the gentle current of the Ephraxis. Together they slipped into the shadows, robes drawn tight around their bodies. Some way off across the city a mandrill called, answered by another, then silence. Moving with their arms extended to touch the rough stonework of the houses, they followed the twisting streets, judging direction by the moon and glimpses of higher buildings at the city's heart. At length they crossed one thoroughfare, then another, broader, at last reaching a jumble of small streets and alleys behind the palace.

'I have been here before,' Aeisla whispered. 'Across from us are the palace kitchens.'

'I can smell.'

'If we climb to the roof, it is possible to go higher and enter by a window. We escaped from one high up, somewhat to the right, but I am uncertain which. Not that it matters. We enter as we may. Within are corridors, stairs, chambers beyond counting. First we must find the seraglio. I was never taken there, as we escaped first, but it needs must be large and convenient for the Imperial chambers. With the girls free, we seek Aurac's chamber.'

'What of guards, eunuchs, the other girls? Do we take sperm?'

'Take a sip, but do not bite into your necklace unless the need arises. It would make you too headstrong for this task.'

Iriel nodded, trying not to show her fear as she glanced up at the palace. Taking the jar from Cruisack's bag, she took a swallow of the troll sperm, wincing at the foul taste as she passed it to Aeisla. As they crossed the darkness of one last alleyway she quickly took a lick of her leather necklace, and felt her courage rise as they moved into the shadows of the kitchen yard.

They began to climb, first to one low roof, then a ledge and a second roof, from which a colonnaded passage looked out. Slipping between the pillars, they entered a narrow corridor which quickly turned into the heart of the building. It was pitch black and set with doors, forcing them to feel their way slowly along, but when it turned again they found themselves in a broad hall lit dull silver by the moon striking in down a light well. Rows of tables and benches showed as flat grey surfaces in black shadow.

'A feasting hall?' Iriel suggested in a whisper.

'Where the servants eat, I would suppose,' Aeisla replied, 'but perhaps above us.'

She moved to the light well, peering up, then sniffing. Iriel caught the tang of perfume immediately as her eyes settled on another colonnade two storeys up. Above was the roof, edged by pillars, with plants hanging down into the light well. Aeisla nodded and pulled herself out of the window. Iriel followed, stretching up to one ledge, then the next and hauling herself between two pillars and into a warm, perfumed darkness, from which a voice spoke as light flooded over them from every side.

'Welcome, as expected, although I confess not by the light well window, nor two of you.'

Aeisla was already throwing herself forwards, her axe striking out to hurl one guard aside as she snatched a thrown net from the air. Female screams rang out, then a male cry of pain as Iriel drove her fist into the face of the nearest man, snatching for her machete, trying to bite on her necklace as two netman threw at once, enveloping her. The machete came free and she struck out under the net, knocking one man back as her teeth sank into her necklace. A third net came down on her as she jerked back to avoid the stab of a spear, tripped and went sprawling backwards. The netmen were on her immediately, grappling her limbs, pulling at the net cords, the spearmen too, one pressing to her neck, another to her belly.

She rolled hard away, her rage already building, and her strength. Indifferent to spear pricks, blows and clutching hands, she fought, biting, kicking, clawing, jerking at the machete where the net trapped it. All her struggles earned her were harder blows, and harder still as her rage grew, bringing her to a mindless crescendo of strength and fury that only ended when her senses went to the blow of a club.

Pain returned first, red light and an all-encompassing ache that slowly came to focus on her head, her wrists, her ankles. Fear and despair hit her as she realised she was chained, her front to hard, smooth stone, her wrists high and fastened to a ring, her ankles fixed tight at either side, spreading her knees and buttocks, her waist and neck encircled. It grew worse as her vision slowly cleared, to reveal daylight, a pillared chamber and all four of her companions, also chained, naked and helpless.

Aeisla was closest to her, back to the pillar, her lean powerful body blotched with bruises. On the pillar beyond was Kaissia, bottom out like Iriel, but with both full cheeks red with whip welts and a broad puddle of urine around her feet. Cianna was next, face forwards like Aeisla, her mouth wadded and gagged, blood showing on her chin and one breast. Last was Yi, face front, grimacing in pain and misery as a solidly built guard worked his cock in and out between her buttocks, the bulk of it clearly up her anus.

She closed her eyes, trying to find courage in prayer. Nothing came, only a hotter pain at her bruised temple and she slumped against the pillar once more. For what seemed an age there were only whimpers and the soft squashy sounds of Yi's buggery, at last finishing with a grunt as the man came. Silence followed, broken by the hiss of piddle as one of the other girls let go her bladder, then voices, harsh and commanding, the clash of metal and another voice – soft, amused but heavy with authority.

'A bucket might have been in order, do you not think?'

'Apologies, Serenity Aurac,' the guard answered. 'I shall fetch one immediately.'

'A mop also,' Aurac replied, 'and if you must bugger them, pray wipe up once you are done.'

'Yes, Serenity Aurac, apologies Serenity Aurac,' the guard babbled, drawing a derisive snort from Aeisla.

Iriel opened her eyes and forced her head around. Several men had entered the room, four of them armed and armoured guards with long purple cloaks hanging from their shoulders. The fifth was younger, dressed in a simple robe of rich purple silk bordered with gold and held with a gold clasp, his face calm, intelligent and strong. In his hand he carried a stiff quirt with a handbreadth of lash at the tip. Aeisla made an attempt to spit, but Aurac merely smiled as he stepped back out of range.

'Five in all, then,' he stated calmly, 'remarkable. And your intention?'

As he finished he lashed the quirt across Aeisla's breasts, leaving a long red welt and drawing a hiss of anger from her. She spat again, catching his robe, and once more he hit her with the quirt, and again, drawing

201

twin scarlet lines across the flesh of her breasts to add to the first. Again she spat, but he stopped and walked to the window, scraping the spittle from his robe with two quick, fastidious motions.

'You need not answer,' he went on, 'evidently you sought to kill me. Do you really think me so foolish? Four Aeg girls are taken at Erijome Forts and I am not supposed to guess they are assassins? Why would the House Palades send such rare beauties to a dangerous outpost? To be fucked by their military? Hardly! No, it was obvious what Prince Daken intended from the first. I had thought more highly of him.'

Iriel found her voice, determined to show courage and to defend the Prince.

'His scheme was not so simple. We were to come in down the Ephraxis, as if from the north.'

'Better,' Aurac admitted, turning to her, 'but hardly likely to have succeeded. Koran barbarians are hardly common in Vendjome, and so yes, you were sure to be brought to the Imperial seraglio, but as slaves, naked and collared. How did you think to kill me? You would never so much have seen me, save if you were giving service in the audience chamber, and rest assured you would have been well chained.'

'Chains may be broken,' Aeisla answered, 'or employed to slay. Besides, Iriel and I had won free, as you know. Had we come on you in your chamber things would have gone differently.'

'Two men of the Imperial guard stand at my chamber door.'

'We would have killed them, and given you a weapon to make a fair combat.'

'Of you, I believe that,' he answered her. 'Strange creatures, you Korans, as wild and fierce as mandrills, yet constrained by elaborate protocol. Protocol or none, I am glad I have met only the females. And you, tall girl, have your ancestors crossed with trolls or ogres, to be so huge? Are you human at all? Certainly dwarfs are no less strange, either in appearance or manner.'

'We are fully human,' Aeisla answered, 'and you know me. I am Aeisla, who was with two others, highborn girls with blonde hair.'

'You are she? Yes, you are, I remember you, only you were not quite so tall. Old Astripod fucked you, didn't he?'

'Yes, and the Princess Talithea Mund struck you down. I am sorry she did not kill you.'

'No doubt. Yet I am glad of that blow. Each and every experience may be used to provide knowledge, without that one I might have been less wary on this occasion. As it is, I intend to take no further risks. However, first you will be paraded before the Panjandrum, who has demanded it.'

'Better you had killed us in combat,' Aeisla answered him.

'Had I my choice it would have been so,' Aurac answered.

He turned on his heel, nodding to a senior man among the guards as he left. The guard bowed, then turned to his men as the door closed with a thud.

'Audience is within an hour. Wash them, apply coffle chains to their wrists, collars, waist-chains and ankles. Hold blades to their throats as you release them. Take no chances, it is best not to think of them as women, but as wild beasts.'

'It is hard not to think of them as women, Captain,' one guard answered, reaching out to take a handful of Kaissia's bottom flesh.

Kaissia spat and cursed, wriggling also, but only succeeding in jiggling her buttocks against the man's hand.

'Fuck them if you must,' the Captain stated, 'but be brief, and leave the giantess.'

Iriel closed her eyes in shame and bitter misery as a guard immediately stepped close, to lift his tunic, press his limp penis between her bottom cheeks and take her breasts in his hands, fondling them as he rubbed in her crease. Another had gone to Yi, and the one behind Kaissia already had his cock free, stroking it as he pawed the heavy globes of her buttocks. The one who had buggered Yi stood back to watch, while the Captain stepped forward to explore Cianna's breasts, drawing a look of pure fury from her even as he brought her nipples to erection under his thumbs.

Thinking of the bladder bag of troll sperm in her tuppenny, Iriel pressed herself close to the pillar, determined to deny the man entry. He took no notice, continuing to grope her breasts and rub, his cock stiffening rapidly in the sweaty groove between her buttocks. Only when his erection was a rigid pole pushed hard in between her cheeks did he speak.

'She doesn't want her cunt fucked, this one, so I suppose I shall be forced to go up her arse!'

His companions laughed and Iriel closed her eyes in burning shame, yet relaxed her bottom ring, determined not to risk a fucking. His cock moved down, finding her hole, the head pressing to her muscle. Eyes tight shut, she pushed out, doing her best to accommodate him in her ring and hoping she was slimy enough to let it go in. He pushed, grunted, there was a moment of pain and her hole had popped. The guard sighed as he began to force himself fully into her rectum.

She was buggered, his cock pumping rapidly in her anal passage, her ring pulling in and out. Halfway through her bladder gave, urine exploding against the pillar and back over his balls to splash on the floor beneath her. As her pee came, so did her tears, and she was sobbing and gasping as the buggery went on, only to have him force a hand around between the pillar and her belly, to rub her off. She came quickly, helpless to prevent the responses of her body, and making her anus contract on his cock, which brought him to orgasm up her bottom.

He pulled out immediately, leaving her shivering against the pillar as her bottom ring dribbled sperm down between her legs. Beside her, both Kaissia and Yi were still being fucked, bottoms and breasts quivering to the men's pushes as erections were worked in cunts. The Captain had come, masturbating over Cianna's belly and tuppenny mound as he fondled her breasts.

One man spunked, then the second, leaving Kaissia and Yi limp against their pillars. The guards dispersed, to return with water and the long coffle chains. Two middle-aged women accompanied them. The girls were washed, their hair brushed, their welts and bruises attended to, their bottoms and faces smacked to a warm pink. The coffle chains were applied and each released, one by one, with swords held to their throats.

Two guards took hold of the ring linking the front of the coffle chains, another two at the rear. The Captain took the lead, the two women still fussing around the girls as they descended stairs and ramps, walked broad corridors and at last came out in a hall walled in a marble of delicate pink veined with gold. At the end was a door as high as the gates of the keep in Aegerion, with a guardsman at either side. Both saluted the Captain, who called a halt to address the girls as the doors swung wide without apparent aid.

'Say nothing. Under no circumstances address the Presence.'

The girls were marched through in their coffle, Iriel entering last, to a vast chamber. Pillars supported a high ceiling, with a dome rising higher still, to perhaps thirty times her own height. Dome, ceiling, walls and floor were of pink marble inlaid with turquoise, malachite and cinnabar in intricate patterns. Marble fountains stood to either side, clear water rising from the mouths of entwined fish and water nymphs, with couches beyond and silk cushions littered on the floor for the courtiers and slaves, all bright with silks of viridian, copper-gold, fuchsia and vermilion.

Most of those present were girls, save for ten guards and a few effeminate youths. The girls were clearly slaves from the seraglio, collared at their necks and either naked or dressed in loose pyjamas of brightly coloured gauze, their limbs oiled and their jet-black hair set with jewels and flowers. Three men stood out from the others. Aurac stood patiently beside a colossal throne apparently made of solid gold in which lolled an enormously fat man, his cloth of gold robe bulging with ream upon ream of flesh. His head was a blob, his eyes barely visible among the folds of flesh, his tiny mouth open around the erect cock of a black-skinned Cypraean boy who stood to his side.

'This is the Panjandrum of Vendjome,' Aeisla remarked-ed, 'beside whom even Uilus is a model of restraint and manliness.'

'Silence!' Aurac snapped, just as the boy came, the Panjandrum swallowing greedily before turning to face the chamber, come and spittle dribbling from the corners of his mouth.

A eunuch stepped quickly forward with a cloth to wipe the Panjandrum's face as the girls were hustled into a line at the centre of the floor, facing the throne. Aurac spoke.

'As you see, Resplendence, five barbar girls, nothing more, crude and ugly. I suggest they be put to death without delay.'

For a long moment the Panjandrum said nothing, apparently having trouble focusing his eyes. When he did speak his voice was high-pitched and petulant.

'I had some of these, did I not?'

'Indeed, Resplendence,' Aurac answered, 'how remarkable your memory to recall each tiny detail.'

'What became of them?'

'They died, Resplendence. The climate was too warm for them.'

'We escaped,' Aeisla laughed suddenly, 'as Aurac well

knows! I am Aeisla, a Reeveling in Korismund and daughter of Uroth. I was among those here before.'

The third noteworthy man in the chamber stirred as she spoke. He was pale-skinned and brown-haired, clearly not Vendjomois but clearly no slave, a huge man, Aeisla's height but far outweighing her. He was slumped on a couch, a goblet of wine in one hand, the other occupied with the bottom of a Vendjomois slavegirl kneeling beside him.

'Aisla?' he queried. 'Who claims to have slain the Hero Kroth when with the army of the rebel Prince Ythor?'

'Lord Mailor,' Aurac interrupted, but broke off as the Panjandrum raised a hand.

'Just so,' Aeisla answered. 'Kroth died to an axe cut, from a Dwarven weapon of cunning form, made to lift on air. It was a chance blow but a fair one. You are from the Glass Coast yourself, as I judge?'

'I am Mailor,' he answered.

'I have heard the name. Are you not what is called a Hero in your country?'

'I am, as was Kroth, and thus you, at least technically.'

Aeisla gave a nervous shrug.

'In Aegmund,' Kaissia said haughtily, 'only those who fall in combat earn the title of Hero. Still, doubtless it will be valid enough in due time.'

Mailor's eyebrows raised, but he chuckled.

'Ah, Mundic girls, so hard to tame, but so satisfying when it is done.'

'I am Aeg.'

'The wildest of all, better still. I see you are shamed too. Is that not the meaning of your tattooed breasts?'

'It counts for nothing here,' Kaissia answered. 'If you wish to tame me, he who calls himself Hero, merely have me unchained and you are welcome to make the attempt.'

'Do not listen, Lord Mailor,' Aurac advised. 'It is best –'

'I know the Aeg, and what they are capable of,' Mailor interrupted. 'I have fought raiders along my own coast and in the Merim Islands. The women respect only those who will take them by main force, the highborn especially. Thus they breed for strength and size. What is your name, blonde girl?'

'I am Kaissia, a Squireling.'

'No, you are a Vendjomois slave and unworthy of my attention. Yet, should you be inclined to grant me a courtesy, Resplendence, I ask to be allowed to slay Aeisla and thus retrieve Kroth's honour.'

'Like this, in chains?' Aeisla laughed. 'A fine saga that will make in Zihai, how you cut down an unarmed and bound girl!'

'No,' Mailor answered, 'in combat, to any style you care to chose so long as I have my sword.'

'Lord Mailor,' Aurac spoke quickly, 'this is unwise. Let us make an end to them quickly, the giantess first of all. There is nothing to be gained in heroic posturing!'

'No,' the Panjandrum broke in as Mailor began to reply. 'It is a fine idea indeed. You are overcautious, Aurac, and besides, it is too long since I had a triumph. Let it be done.'

'Resplendence,' Aurac objected, 'only last week –'

'I want my triumph,' the Panjandrum snapped.

Aurac responded with a low bow.

'A triumph, Resplendence, a fine thought, and an appropriate end for these barbarian trulls. I shall order the duelling ground prepared, and when Lord Mailor is done we may hang the others for your amusement.'

'No,' the Panjandrum answered, 'there is no sport in hanging them. Let them be raped by baboons, man-apes, trolls and stallions, until –'

'Impossible, Resplendence,' Aurac objected. 'We would need a month to train the baboons, and –'

'I will have my way!' the Panjandrum snapped.

'Just so, your Resplendence,' Kaissia broke in, to snarls of outrage from the Vendjomois. 'In Oretes the late King, Palades Uilus, made sport by pitting warriors of different nations against one another. Would this not be fitting?'

'By all means pit us against trolls if it would amuse your Resplendence,' Aeisla suggested.

'Unwise, Resplendence,' Aurac objected. 'Our spies in Oretes state that at the death of Uilus these same girls drank troll's jism first, in some way enhancing their strength and speed.'

'This was also done in Zihai,' Mailor agreed. 'Yet it is a fine idea for your triumph, Resplendence. Perhaps it should also be done in the open plaza, for the delight of the populace.'

'The populace?' the Panjandrum queried. 'Why so?'

'Such spectacles amuse them, Resplendence,' Mailor responded.

'It is hardly fitting that the Panjandrum's amusements be conducted in front of a vulgar mob,' Aurac stated.

'We will require space,' Aeisla stated. 'I wish to fight on horseback, with lance and axe.'

'And what else?' Aurac laughed. 'A dozen elephants in full battle gear? Perhaps a park of bombards would suit you?'

'I accept,' Mailor stated.

'Resplendence, truly,' Aurac objected in exasperation. 'Can you not see that they seek to twist this matter to their advantage? Let us simply –'

'I seek only to die with honour,' Kaissia broke in.

'It will be done,' the Panjandrum stated with finality. 'All of it, a grand triumph. We will have buffoons, I like buffoons, and man-apes if baboons are impractical, and then the combats. How fine! Take them away, Captain, feed them meat and do not abuse them unduly. Eunuchs, bring me another boy!'

209

8

The Hall

Her prayer done, Iriel opened her eyes to look out across the Plain of Vendjome. The city was behind her and to the right, the walls and nearer roofs thronged with people. Others stood on top of a gentle swell of ground to the west, but only lines of pikemen surrounded the actual field, double around the shaded podium on which a group of workmen were arranging cushions and chairs, also a throne for the Panjandrum.

Aurac had taken no chances. Iriel was naked but for a steel collar and chained to a post. Beside her were Kaissia, Cianna and Yi, also naked, also chained by their necks to the post. Nearby were four horses, each saddled and ready, held by grooms. Beyond was a fifth horse, on which Aeisla sat motionless in the saddle, her face a mask, her long red hair fluttering in the gentle breeze. All she wore were sandals and an ill-fitting tunic that barely covered her buttocks and was stretched taut across her breasts, with as much meat spilling from the sides as covered. She still had her collar, which was chained to her saddle and to a post like those the others stood beside. Her horse was also chained.

Across the field other elements of the coming entertainment were visible. Nearest were the buffoons, a group of men selected for the peculiar appearance of their bodies. Some were exceptionally tall and thin, others the reverse, short and as fat as butter. One had a wooden leg, another huge buttocks on an otherwise spindly body – a third's skin was mottled an unhealthy purple. All were bald, and all wore masks painted in a grotesque parody of human features, staring eyes, huge, leering mouths, and noses a good two handspans long, brilliant scarlet in colour and carved to resemble gnarled and obscenely turgid cocks. They also carried an assortment of apparatus, dog quirts, unpleasant-looking brown balls, and thick tubes of brass equipped with plungers and ending in nozzles that looked suspiciously as if they might be designed for insertion into the orifices of girls' bodies. Beyond the buffoons a group of man-beasts huddled in a stockade, too far away to be seen at all clearly, principally man-apes, but also goblins. Iriel's tuppenny twitched as their scent carried down the breeze.

The boom of a gong sounded from the city. Iriel turned, to see a procession emerging from one of the gates; Imperial guard on horseback splendid in purple and gold, a palanquin draped in the same gaudy colours, Mailor riding behind on a black stallion, a line of less ornate palanquins and another six guards. It was clearly the Panjandrum, and there was no question in her mind that before too long either a cock or some other object would be inserted into her tuppenny.

She squatted down, as if to pee, allowing herself to extract the sewn bladder of troll sperm from her hole. Breaking the thread with her teeth, she quickly swallowed a measure, the taste yet fouler than before, and handed it to Yi. Quickly, with the attention of their guards on the approaching procession, each girl drank, Cianna grinding the empty bladder down into the coarse grass at their feet.

The procession approached at a slow walking pace, Iriel's trepidation rising with every footstep, until she was whispering prayers under her breath and struggling to keep her emotions from her face. Yi gave her a sympathetic look and a smile that did more to weaken Iriel's resolve than bolster it. As the Panjandrum's palanquin was set down Aeisla called out, her voice loud in the hush as the Vendjomois bowed to their ruler.

'Now is our hour. Yield nothing. Accept their buffoons, accept their man-apes and goblins, saving your strength for when it matters. Show no horror, only pleasure. Show no weakness, only strength. Show no fear, only pride. We are watched.'

She turned back, once more sat impassive as the Panjandrum was helped to his throne. Mailor had ridden on, along with five of the guardsmen, who stopped in a group at the far end of the field. Aurac mounted the podium, to stand beside the throne.

'So we do not resist the man-beasts?' Yi asked. 'What of the buffoons?'

'Who can resist goblin musk?' Cianna queried.

'Let them play their foolish games,' Kaissia advised. 'Be passive unless some action risks injury.'

Iriel nodded, glancing once more at the buffoons, who had formed a long line, all bowing to the Panjandrum as he accepted a goblet of wine from one of his Cypraean boys. Most were now settled, the guards in position to either end of the podium. Aurac spoke a word to the Panjandrum, who raised one podgy arm in response. Guards stepped towards the girls to unlock their collars, the pikemen came to present. The buffoons began to move, darting here and there in a curious crouching run, cock noses thrust out before them as if seeking the scent of cunt.

The girls stepped forward as the buffoons spread out, Iriel resigned to her fucking yet disturbed by the bizarre behaviour of the buffoons. They had now strung out into a line, running in the same strange posture as they began to circle the girls. The Panjandrum made a remark to Aurac, pointed and laughed. Iriel moved closer to the others, then realised that she was only playing the buffoons' game, allowing herself to be herded. She strode out, boldly interrupting their line.

They broke, leaping up with arms spread and mouths open in feigned shock. Iriel was surrounded in an instant, five of them around her, capering grotesquely and thrusting out their hips in a crazed, lewd dance. The others moved off, once more running in line, but in groups, four or five to each girl. Iriel shrugged and spread her hands, not knowing what she could possibly say in response to their antics.

Immediately they swarmed in, all five leaping on her to bear her down to the ground. One mounted her back, as if he was riding her, clutching her hair to force her head back as another squatted down in front of her. Something soft, wet and smelly was pushed to her face, a dung ball. It was rubbed well in to the sound of hooting laughter that carried a world of derision, the brown filth smeared across her features as the man on her back began to spank her, urging her to crawl.

She resisted, leading to harder spanks and cries of mock outrage. Her legs were gripped and hauled wide and clear of the ground, forcing her open bottom high in the air. A dung ball was squashed between her cheeks, to her anus, the buffoon's fingers slipping in behind. He was cackling in glee as he fingered her bottom, while the one on her back was rubbing his cock and balls on her skin.

A nose cock was inserted in her cunt and she gasped as she filled, kicking her thighs in their grip as the fucking started. Another filled her mouth, with his real cock, and she was spitted on both ends, still held, still ridden and spanked. Jism erupted down the back of her neck as her rider came, immediately leaping off to perform a mad, high-kicking dance, running around her in circles and still jerking at his erection.

The cock nose left her, her cunt closing with a soft fart only to be filled again immediately as a dung ball was pushed up. Something hard touched her anus, a nozzle, pushing deep into the dirty hole and held there, letting the realisation of what was about to be done to her sink in. They began to whip her buttocks and back, making her bottom squirm on the inserted nozzle, wriggling in desperation at the stinging lashes. The man in her mouth took her breasts, smearing a dung ball to each and squeezing them hard. He came, ejaculating sperm down her throat with an ecstatic cry and instantly throwing himself back, to turn three reverse somersaults and leap high, flourishing his still-spurting cock to all and sundry.

Iriel had given in, her body jerking to the whips, her filthy breasts bouncing, her mouth wide, her hands batting futilely on the ground, all dignity forgotten. The blows got harder, the buffoons crying out to every stroke, her pumping legs still gripped hard, the tube pressed deep to strain her anus wide, the plunger driven home, and its entire contents were forced into her rectal chamber with a single violent push. She screamed as her rectum bloated, hammering her fists on the ground. A buffoon spoke a single word, a mocking apology, and the nozzle pulled free of her bottom ring. The buffoons danced back, laughing and pointing, squealing in lewd joy as she felt her anal flesh bulge, and give.

Her enema exploded from her bottom in a huge gush of dirty water and bits of dung, arching high in the air above her upturned rump to splash down on the ground as the laughter of the buffoons rose in a delighted crescendo. Again they began to run around her, alternately crouched low and capering as spurt after spurt of filthy water burst from her bottom ring, each smaller than the last, ending with a dribble running down over her well-soiled tuppenny.

The buffoons darted in again, three to fill her holes, real cocks and nose cocks thrust hard into her every orifice, filled and refilled, her bottom spanked, her breasts groped. The other two took up a new dance, hands on hips, chests and buttocks thrust out, strutting in an absurd parody of female gait, faster and faster as Iriel was fucked. A dung ball was pushed into her mouth, a cock following, a second poked up her bottom with a nose cock, a third put inside her cunt. Her anus was entered, the buffoon riding high on her bottom to make sure the penetration showed. The third slid under her, to bury his face between her filthy breasts as he pushed up into her cunt.

She was being fucked, every hole filled with cock and dung, the buffoons pumping frantically, the squelching noises of her penetration loud in her ears, soiled and broken, her body jerking to the thrusts. A hand found her tuppenny, rubbing and, even as she realised she was to be given the final indignity and made to come in her filthy, degraded state, it began. Her cunt and anus went into contraction, the buffoons were hooting in glee and calling to let the audience know she was in orgasm and she was snatching wildly at cocks and balls, pulling the man in her mouth, pushing her bottom up for more. They came, their delight in her response breaking to ecstatic grunts as they climaxed simultaneously, jism exploding in mouth, anus and cunt all at once.

For a long while they held themselves in, the dancers giving weird, ululating calls as Iriel's body filled, and then she was left, all three holes bubbling sperm, slumped on the ground, panting and clutching slowly at the coarse grass. The buffoons began to sing, some absurd piece of lewd doggerel that barely reached her senses.

Slowly she recovered, to spit out what was in her mouth, wipe herself as best she could with her hands, and at last stand up, weak, dizzy, but determined. The other girls had fared no better. Yi was in much the same position as she had been, face down on the ground, bottom lifted, both cheeks rubbed brown with dung, a broken-off cock nose still protruding from her anus. Cianna was standing, picking bits of dung from her dirty breasts. Kaissia was still sitting, staring ruefully out from a mask of brown, while a number of the dung balls had been broken on her head and shaped into an absurd parody of a crown. Iriel stepped towards the others as Yi rolled over and sat up.

'A truly vile race, these Vendjomois,' Kaissia remarked.

'The man-apes will come as a relief,' Cianna agreed.

'They are huge,' Yi said nervously. 'How can we accommodate so many such monsters?'

'You have taken trolls,' Kaissia answered. 'At least you know you won't split.'

'Accept them from the rear,' Cianna advised. 'In Makea one had me.'

'What if they bugger us?' Yi questioned.

'Better buggered than crushed,' Cianna answered. 'They are heavy, but gentle. Do not resist and you will get nothing worse than a hard fucking.'

Iriel nodded. Already the stockade had been opened, the man-beasts spilling out. Servants came forwards, to sprinkle the girls with some sweet-sharp perfume. Iriel recognised the tang of female nymph musk. Kaissia laughed as she was anointed.

'You think they will notice, after we have suffered your foul buffoons?'

'They will,' the servant answered her. 'The dung for you was chosen from female man-apes, mixed with camel for the texture.'

Kaissia made a face and quickly got down on all fours as the man-beasts approached. Iriel followed suit, making a line with the others, bottoms presented for fucking, looking back between her dangling breasts. The man-apes were at the front, great shaggy beasts, further from the human even than trolls, their entire bodies covered in coarse red hair, and with big yellow tusks showing as they peeled back protuberant lips in what might have been a gesture of anger or simple curiosity. Big cocks hung from their lower bellies, a handspan or so of leathery brown flesh sticking out from among the hair. Behind, staying well back, came the goblins, big green cocks in hand, already fully erect, hideous little faces set in scowls of jealousy and frustration.

The man-apes were sniffing the air, giving little calls of excitement to each other, and touching themselves, their cocks emerging a little further from the thick foreskins with each tug until they stood proud and hard from the creatures' bellies. One, clearly a dominant male from his great size, had come to the front. He reached Yi, who gave out one faint, frightened whimper, then gasped as her tuppenny filled with a single hard shove, his erection driven home with a loud squelch.

Others were clustering in around Iriel, pawing her body and hooting, soft, leathery hands on her bottom, her back, in her hair, reaching under her to stroke at her breasts in puzzlement. Two were by her head, their erect cocks in easy reach of her mouth. Forcing down her revulsion, she took one in, sucking it deep and quickly swallowing in an effort to clear the thick, earthy taste. He gave a long hoot of pleasure in response and began to fuck her mouth.

Her cunt was entered, and as the others quickly gave back she realised another senior male was in her. Only the one in her mouth stayed, growling defiantly before suddenly filling her mouth with hot, salty sperm. She let his cock free as the one in her cunt began to pump, leaving her immediately breathless, her breasts swinging free, her bottom wobbling to the shoves, jism drooling from her slack mouth.

Only when the troll had ravished her had she felt so full, and the man-ape was both gentler and slower, pumping on and on, building up her need to come until it was irresistible. Giving in, she reached back and took the fat, heavy sack of his scrotum. She began to rub it on her cunt, the matted hair tickling her flesh and the big balls within jostling on her bump. He gave one long hoot in response and he had come, jism exploding from her hole, all over her hand and his balls.

No sooner was her hole vacant than the others moved in, four in all. One filled her mouth, another her cunt, and again she began to rub herself, masturbating with her body rocking to the motion of her fucking. The one in her mouth came first, hooting in glee as she struggled to swallow his load, her orgasm already rising in her head, and breaking as yet another huge cock was pushed into her gaping mouth. She rode her orgasm, sucking hard as the pumping against her bottom grew faster and harder, bringing her up to peak after peak, and to one final explosion as her cunt filled with jism once more.

She began to slump down the moment he was done, a mistake as the fourth caught her by the hips and jabbed his erection in, not to her cunt, but her anus. She screamed as her hole was forced, about half the monstrous cock thrust hard into her rectum in one go. She was giving thanks that she had already been so slimy as the rest was rammed home, to leave her gut bulging and her mouth wide in pained reaction.

Iriel was grunting helplessly as the buggering began, each push spraying jism from her nose and mouth. The pace picked up, until her whole body was quivering, the hairy belly slapping on her buttocks, her breasts bouncing wildly, her fingers locked in the grass. He came, clutching her by the hips with his erection jammed to the hilt in her gut, pumping her full of jism until she felt as bloated as with the enema.

As he pulled out the result was much the same. She sprayed, a fountain of sperm erupting from her buggered ring, over the man-ape and the ground behind her. Six had come in her, but it was done, and she sat up, her anus and cunt burning and sore, but unbroken,

218

her head spinning, feeling sick, ashamed of giving in to the pleasure and having rubbed herself, but also proud.

The big male had come towards her again, holding his cock as the last of the jism dribbled from the end. Iriel rocked back on her haunches, dizzy with shamefilled pleasure, wondering if she was going to get one last fucking before the goblins took her, her mouth open in the hope of being filled. It was. The sudden spurt of urine caught her completely by surprise, full in her face, her mouth filling before she could close it and then only succeeding in getting it splashed in her eyes and hair, while it was already running down her breasts. She realised she was being marked as his mate even she ducked her head down to save her face, what had been done in her mouth spewing from her lips and into her lap.

It stank, a thick, musky reek, the taste worse still, too strong to bear. Her stomach lurched, her mouth filled and the Panjandrum was slapping his fat thighs in delighted mirth as she threw up her bellyful of ape sperm down her breasts and stomach. The man-ape took no notice whatever. His hot urine continued to splash out over her, into her hair, to run down at every side, making wet rats' tails from which trickles ran down her back, her shoulders and onto her breasts, to drip from the erect nipples.

Finally the stream stopped, the man-ape shaking his cock over her in a manlike gesture as she peeped cautiously from one stinging eye. He moved off, to where a servant was splitting melons, other apes already eating nearby. Slowly Iriel's vision cleared as she blinked away the stinging ape piddle, to find that all four girls had been given the same treatment by other ranking males. They now knelt, sodden and filthy, each in her private pool of urine and sperm, their bodies steaming gently in the hot sun. Kaissia was still on all fours the way she had been fucked, her beautiful blonde hair a sodden mess, a thick beard of jism hanging from the hair of her tuppenny mound, a golden drop hanging from each nipple. Cianna was sat splay-legged in her puddle, head back and eyes closed, a clot of ape jism rolling slowly down her belly. Yi had been particularly badly fouled, her pretty face barely recognisable beneath thick wads of jism, while like Iriel she had been sick down her breasts.

The state of the girls made no difference to the goblins, who moved in cautiously, then fast as the last of the apes shambled off to the feeding area. Iriel braced herself for fucking as they crowded in around her, fat green cocks erect and ready for cunt, jism already dribbling and spurting from the tips, waiting for their musk to take effect.

Iriel could already smell it, the rich, compelling scent penetrating even through the reek of ape. Before she even knew she was doing it she had reached forwards once more, gaping wide for a mouthful even as one leaped onto her back. A cock was plunged to the hilt in her sopping tuppenny as her mouth filled, and she was being fucked fore and aft, her lust far too strong to control. One slid beneath her, grabbing her breasts and squeezing them together to make a cock slide, which he fucked with urgent pumping motions, all the while pawing and rubbing at her nipples. Others began to rut on her, against her hips and legs and belly and feet, in her hair, her armpits, anywhere they could find flesh.

In moments they'd started to come. Her cunt filled with jism, the goblin pulled out and she was re-entered immediately by one who had been rubbing himself on her stomach. With her slimy bottom ring on show it was moments before a long, muscular tongue was thrust up into her rectum, licking to open her before it was replaced by a cock. There was pain as two handspans of thick green erection were jammed to the balls in her guts, but it registered only as a vague, distant thing, her

220

mind swimming with musk, her body already rising towards orgasm.

The belly of the one in her cunt was slapping on her bump, each touch sending a new shock of ecstasy through her. As the one between her breasts came she reached the edge, his cock still rubbing in the slimy valley of her cleavage as spurt after spurt erupted into it. As more jism exploded down her throat from the cock in her mouth she was tipped over, writhing on the cocks as she came, her every muscle in spasm, totally out of control. Then her pulsing bottom ring was milking sperm into her rectum, more and more, until she felt herself start to bloat again.

Jism erupted from her bottom as the cock was pulled free. Her anus was still pulsing, to squeeze out a second spurt, and a third, before being filled again, the goblin coming even as his cockhead filled her hole. Iriel's orgasm tailed off with yet more sperm pumping into her rectum, only to rise again as she began to masturbate, rubbing at herself in shameless, abandoned ecstasy, coming again and again as she was used, heedless to everything but having her holes filled.

Again and again she was entered, fucked and spermed in. Most came two or three times, many sticking their cocks in her mouth moments after withdrawing from her cunt or her bottom hole. Even with her entire body plastered in filth, with her holes on fire, with her skin bruised and scratched, still she rubbed at herself, coming and coming. She was snatching at the goblins, to make them fuck her, mounting them, feeding cocks into her own holes, crawling on the grass to get at one even as another squatted on her bottom, erection deep up her ring. The goblin she was trying to catch fled. The one up her bottom came, filling her with jism one last time, to leave her spurting muck as it withdrew.

She collapsed, to lie still on the grass, fluid dribbling from every orifice, mouth and anus equally slack and gaping, her cunt a deep pond of sperm, still stuck high for fucking. Dimly the sound of the Pandjandrum clapping his fat hands in pleasure penetrated her addled senses, but she stayed down, her mind hazy, vaguely hoping that someone, man or man-beast, would come and fuck her.

None did. The goblins were chivvied away by men with spears, the man-apes too, across the field and back into the stockade. As the musk slowly cleared from Iriel's head the overwhelming lust began to die, to be replaced by fear and uncertainty. She sat up, glancing to the other girls, all of whom were in the same sorry state, sodden with sperm, skin red with scratches. Cianna was on her feet, but Yi was still down, her eyes half-focused even as she pulled herself up. She and Iriel shared a worried look, but Kaissia seemed to have no such doubts, rising to wipe at her soiled face and breasts and meeting Iriel's glance with a hard grin. Determined not to betray weakness, Iriel smiled back as she forced herself to rise.

The grooms were already approaching, leading the horses, also servants with buckets of water, the leather tunics worn by Vendjomois soldiers, lances and swords. Kaissia stepped towards them, to take a bucket before it could be thrown over her. Iriel did the same, washing slowly despite the demands for speed from the men, and allow the shaking of her body to die slowly away. When as clean as was practical she accepted the tunic, pulling it on with a sense of relief but resisting the temptation to bite into it. It fitted badly, ridiculously short and uncomfortably tight over her breasts, which she ignored, pulling herself up onto a horse and taking lance and sword belt from the men, who moved hastily away.

Her fingers were trembling as she buckled the sword into place, her need to feel the kick of the troll sperm rising as she wondered if it mattered that she'd been sick. Closing her eyes, she forced herself to calm, mumbling a prayer to her father. His voice came back clear, thick with pride and passion, urging her on, others fainter, demanding revenge, the heads of her victims as trophies, cooked hearts to take their strength into her body and honour each and every one of them.

She opened her eyes and sat straight, determined, looking out in front of her, to where the Vendjomois lancers were already gathered at the end of the field, five men of the Imperial guard, one a Captain, each with a long, pennon-tipped lance held at ease. They had been watching the fucking, and were not in formation, but randomly spaced, talking and laughing among themselves. Iriel called out to them and ringed her fingers in insult.

Kaissia urged her horse forward to point position. Iriel fell in behind, Yi to the left, Cianna to the right, exchanging looks as Kaissia turned, nodded, and with a final salute to Aeisla, began to walk her horse forwards. Pulling her tunic up to her mouth, Iriel bit hard into the leather as her horse started into motion. Across the field the guardsmen moved into formation, spread wide to contain the charge. Iriel dug her heels into her horse's flanks, keeping pace with Kaissia, a trot, a canter as she dipped her lance, a full gallop, tearing across the grass at the oncoming guards, hooves thudding on packed soil, her hair streaming out behind her.

As Kaissia yelled the command Iriel pulled hard on one rein, turning her horse at the last possible moment, at the podium, to crash full against the line of pikes. Kaissia was screaming as she was stuck through, but in pure rage, her own lance plunging into the chest of a soldier as she and her horse went down together, crushing both lines of pikemen to create a gap through which Iriel tore. Her horse hit the podium, rising to the boards, men scattering, others going down beneath the flailing hooves, Aurac screaming commands, then silent as Iriel's lance took him full in the open mouth.

The lance tore from her hand as Aurac's body was slammed down, pinned by the head to the wood beneath, Iriel screaming in triumph as she snatched her sword free. A man went down to her first cut and she was clear, her horse carried clean over the podium, the open plain beyond. Screams of rage and fear and pain rang out behind her as she wheeled, to find the podium half-fallen, people and blood spilling from the boards, Cianna's horse half on it, Yi in the thick of the pikemen, slashing wildly to either side.

She rode in, cutting right and left, the men seeming slow, their every movement laboured. Three strokes and Yi was clear, both laughing as the entire formation of pikemen swung in towards them, guards too, others fleeing, the man-apes hooting with fury as the stockade collapsed, everything seen through a haze of red as the elixir took full hold. Images blurred, mouths screaming at her in hate and pain, flying red hair, the guard Captain spitted on Cianna's lance, the Panjandrum on his back with fat legs kicking in the air, the head of a pikeman cut free as blood sprayed her face, Mailor screaming for the press of men to make way only to be torn from his horse by the biggest of the man-apes, and Aeisla riding full-tilt towards them, screaming that they should break.

Iriel pulled herself into the top branches of the feather tree. From her vantage point the great plain stretched away in every direction, broken only in the south by what might either have been clouds or the peaks of mountains, and the haze above a single city. To the east nothing showed whatever save mile upon mile of dusty plain broken only by rare copses of blade and feather trees, euphorbias and acacia. For a moment her spirits rose, only to drop as she made out rising dust in the extreme distance, then the glitter of sunlight on metal.

'They are still coming!' she called down.

For over a week they had fled west, hiding, running, twice fighting. Once in the hills they had managed to replenish their supply of elixir, but on the plain there had been nothing. Again and again they had attempted to elude pursuit, but with the grasses tall and dry it had proved impossible to conceal their trail. She felt tired, thirsty, hungry, close to exhaustion. With their horses desperately in need of rest and water, they had stopped where a muddy creek crossed the plain.

She climbed down, to find the others grouped at the base of the tree, Aeisla with her back to the trunk, Cianna and Yi sprawled on the ground. All three showed the ravages of the days spent fleeing, their fair skin burned, their muscles tight and lean, their eyes bright and restless.

'How far?' Aeisla queried.

'An hour at most,' Iriel replied. 'They are in a skirmish line, perhaps a hundred.'

Aeisla nodded. 'They will come up with us before sunset, even if we ride on now.'

'We should stand,' Cianna stated. 'Better to do so while we have at least some strength.'

'Sulden will have sent troops, she must have done,' Yi objected. 'Let us ride on.'

'I have recited the cantrip a hundred times,' Cianna objected, 'and we are above half the distance from Vendjome to Oretes. Daken knows, but he has not sent help.'

'As you say,' Yi urged, 'we are over half the way!'

'With another two hundred leagues of featureless plain to cover,' Cianna responded.

'We must be close on the lines,' Aeisla admitted. 'The city to the south is Reites, I think, which is under dispute.'

'If the Oreteans have not been pushed back,' Iriel added.

Aeisla shrugged. 'We are caught. Cianna is right, and here among the trees their numbers will be less of an advantage.'

Iriel nodded. Pulling the jar of troll's sperm from the purse she had taken from Cruisack seemingly an age before, she pulled the cork free. Checking the level, she drank one quarter and passed it to Aeisla, who also drank, and Cianna. Yi took it last, stood and walked to the edge of the copse, draining the contents. She stayed put, biting her lip as she stared west, only to suddenly tense.

'They come, Oreteans, look!'

She was pointing, and as Iriel joined her she too saw the distant plume of dust, right on the western horizon.

'They could as well be Vendjomois,' Cianna objected.

'No matter,' Aeisla answered her. 'We are caught for certain if we stay. Saddle up.'

They hastened to obey, clambering onto their horses and urging the exhausted beasts west. Already the plume of dust seemed nearer, but as Iriel gathered speed she glanced back, to where a similar plume showed in the east, nearer still. Setting her teeth in grim determination, she urged her horse on, the thudding of hooves loud in her ears, their own dust kicking up behind.

Leagues passed, her eyes tightened to slits as she struggled to make out the colours of the approaching horsemen, at first uncertain, her hope rising, then certain. They were Oretean cavalry, the black, crimson and gold banner of the House Palades fluttering above them, maybe six twelves strong, riding hard towards them.

Yi screamed in joy, urging her horse forwards. Iriel glanced back, to find the Vendjomois already well clear of the copses at the creek, Mailor's huge figure clear at their head. Snatching her tunic neck, she bit hard into the leather, then set her teeth as she dug her heels in. Shouts sounded from far behind them, an order to dip lances, Mailor yelling that Aeisla was his alone. An answering shout went up from ahead, the Oretean lance points came down, both lines of cavalry now at full gallop, the gap closing fast.

'Close up!' Aeisla screamed. 'Wheel as they break for us!'

Iriel pulled on her rein, forcing her horse in behind Yi and in front of Aeisla, the line just a hundred paces away, fifty, not breaking, but closing in, to take Cianna from her saddle, a lance driven clean through her body. Yi screamed as her horse crashed into Cianna's, the lance meant for her heart raking her side, the lancer's head struck clean off to Iriel's sword cut.

All consuming rage hit her with the elixir, even as the Vendjomois cavalry thundered in behind them, the two lines crashing together, men and horses screaming, metal clashing, and she was among them, cutting about herself, her head full of angry shouting. One man went down under her blade, a second, and she was set against Palades Tavian, smashing his sword aside to drive her own hilt-deep into his chest by sheer force, as something slammed into her side. She cut back, taking the head off her attacker's shoulders even as she realised his lance was through her body. Once more she cut, a wild sweep meeting empty air, and again, her stroke cutting deep into a man's neck as visions rose up around her, of girls like herself, red-haired or blonde, screaming their joy, striking fists and cups on a great oak table, Kaissia, naked breasts clear and proud, hand extended, Yi laughing, Cianna clutching at a mead horn.

As the feast hall grew solid around her she turned, to find herself looking down on the battlefield, every detail stark and clear, her own body sprawled across the bloody corpse of Palades Tavian, men and horses tangled together, Aeisla stood tall on a pile of her dead, screaming defiance at a dozen Imperial guards, the huge figure of Mailor striding towards her.

Sweet mead hit Iriel's lips as Aeisla and Mailor closed, blades blurring grey around them, bright with sparks, a guard falling headless as he tried to cut in. Horns blared, the combatants broke apart, but not the two, trading cuts, neither one giving an inch, wild, furious, Aeisla's sword shattering, Mailor's driving deep into her body at the next stroke, her head locked to his neck, his blood spurting high, his eyes glazing in death as they sank down together, every one of thousands in the Feast Hall of Heroines pounding the table as Aeisla's soul coalesced among them.

Author's Note

Princess is the fourth and final book of the *Maiden Saga*. The others are *Maiden*, *Captive* and *Innocent*, all of which are set in the same world and feature related characters, with Aeisla in all four books. The world of *Maiden* is not ours, neither in terms of physical characteristics nor of culture. Iriel, Aeisla, their friends and antagonists know nothing of commuting, office politics or supermarkets. They inhabit a world of beautiful girls, stalwart men and strange half-men. This is fantasy, a genre that has long been developing from the romantic myths and which many readers will instantly recognise. Such tales have always had an underlying erotic power, yet in the *Maiden Saga* this is given full, uninhibited rein.

The stories are also pastiche, as should be obvious to anyone with experience of the fantasy genre, principally of Robert E. Howard's *Conan* series, but also of many well-known fantasy authors who had better remain nameless. Hopefully those who have recognised these moments will have been amused by them, while the rest of you won't have noticed at all.

In erotic terms, the stories pull no punches. Why should they, when not set in the real world? Reality is one thing, fantasy quite another. Nobody, after all, can realistically accuse me of promoting goblin sex.

Finally, I trust you have enjoyed reading the *Maiden Saga* as much as I have enjoyed its creation.

Aishling Morgan

NEXUS NEW BOOKS

To be published in March

THE ANIMAL HOUSE
Cat Scarlett

The glamorous and self-possessed Violetta receives a chance invitation to stay at a dream French chateau. Following a casual, train-board encounter with a mysterious and self-assured man, it becomes apparent that her holiday opportunity is not as random as it seemed, and Violetta finds herself drawn into a community whose members take their pleasures disguised beneath animal masks. Behind the licentiousness of her holiday destination, however, she finds a dark tradition of Gallic libertinage and medieval torture she had not imagined, as the Sadean trappings of the chateau are revealed and used upon her in turn.

£6.99   ISBN 0 352 33877 6

HOT PURSUIT
Lisette Ashton

Lucy is Master Donald's second favourite. When she tries to ask him a favour, however, not only does he not hear her out but, in pique, he asks his favourite, Ginger, to discipline Lucy. When poor Lucy runs away, Donald and Ginger wonder if they've gone too far. But as they give chase, they realise that in their bizarre SM society it's really little Lucy who holds all the cards ...

£6.99   ISBN 0 352 33878 4

EMMA'S SECRET WORLD
Hilary James

Becoming Ursula's slave was the most exciting thing that had ever happened to Emma. She is whisked away to the confines of an English country residence, where beautiful but cruel mistresses preside over a bevy of young and wayward girls. Their corrective regime demands ultimate sacrifice in return for absolute fulfilment, and Emma surrenders every dignity of adulthood to learn the discipline necessary for her training. A Nexus Classic.

£6.99   ISBN 0 352 33879 2

To be published in April

THE INDISCRETIONS OF ISABELLE
Penny Birch writing as Cruella

Isabelle is a young student at Oxford, well versed in the giving of flagellation and in the Sapphic pleasures the city affords. When her ageing scout, Stan Tierney, lets slip that he knows about a long-established society of lesbian dominas, Isabelle is drawn in. As Isabelle investigates, together with her girlfriends Jasmine and Caroline, it becomes clear that she will have to endure a comprehensive round of sexual humiliations if she is to get close to the mysterious society.

£6.99   ISBN 0 352 33882 2

STRIPING KAYLA
Yvonne Marshall

Now in their mid-thirties and settled into married lives, former debutantes Charlotte, Imogen and Seona continue to enjoy each others' company as playmates, an arrangement of which their husbands are only too happy to approve. But the ghost of 'Kayla' – the mysterious and cruel courtesan whose identity Charlotte herself once adopted – continues to haunt them. Imogen is convinced that the girl who is no doubt being currently trained as Kayla should be made aware of the dark nature of the project she is involved in. Charlotte is secretly thrilled, having sorely missed the dominance she enjoyed for so long. Can she resist returning to this world of bizarre flagellant delights?

£6.99   ISBN 0 352 33881 4

EMMA ENSLAVED
Hilary James

Emma, having been denied every dignity by her mistress Ursula, is now required to sacrifice something even more precious; access to her own pleasure. Introduced to a world where the bizarre has become the everyday, confined under her skirts and desperate for the unique attentions of her beautiful, strict guardian, Emma learns what it's like to be denied release from her torment.

£6.99   ISBN 0 352 33883 0

If you would like more information about Nexus titles, please visit our website at www.nexus-books.co.uk, or send a stamped addressed envelope to:

Nexus, Thames Wharf Studios,
Rainville Road, London W6 9HA